THE SEA HORSE TRADE

A Nikki Latrelle Racing Mystery

Sasscer Hill

"A page turner."– Sandra McKee, *Baltimore Sun*

PRAISE FOR THE NIKKI LATRELLE TRILOGY

"Sasscer, the honor comes in your accomplishments and talent, and you should take great pride in such a magnificent trifecta. Congratulations!!! Well done. Dick Francis lives!"
– Steve Haskin, Senior Correspondent, *Blood-Horse*. Former National Correspondent, *Daily Racing Form*, winner of eighteen awards for excellence in turf writing.

"If you love Dick Francis, you'll love Sasscer Hill. If you don't love Dick Francis, you'll still love Sasscer Hill! This twisty and fast-paced page turner is cleverly plotted and genuinely entertaining—Hill's insider knowledge and love of the horse-racing world shines through on every page. Sasscer knows her stuff!"
- Hank Phillippi Ryan. Agatha, Anthony, Mary Higgins Clark, and Macavity Award–winning author

"If you miss the late Dick Francis's racetrack thrillers, you'll be intrigued by Sasscer Hill's Racing From Death"
– *The Washington Post*, August 29, 2012

"Hill herself a Maryland horse breeder, is a genuine find, writing smooth and vivid descriptive prose about racetrac characters and backstretch ambeince that reeks authenticity."
– John L. Breen, *Ellery Queen's Mystery Magazine*

"Sasscer Hill brings us another exciting racehorse mystery . . . an utterly unique take on racetrack thrillers." - Betty Webb, *Mystery Scene Magazine*, Summer Issue, 2012

"New novel about a Laurel Park jockey is a wild ride. While compared to Dick Francis and Sue Grafton, Hill's work reflects her respect for horse racing and the influence of the late Walter Farley. A page-turner, the book's sentences are short and crisp. The action comes off as authentic."
- Sandra McKee, *Baltimore Sun*, April, 2012

"If you like the work of Dick Francis or Sue Grafton, you will like Sasscer Hill. With a true insider's knowledge of horse

racing, Hill brings us Nikki Latrelle, a young jockey placed in harm's way who finds the courage to fight the odds and the heart to race for her dreams."
–Mike Batttaglia, NBC racing analyst and TV host.

"This is a major new talent and the comparisons to Dick Francis are not hyperbole."
--Margaret Maron, New York Times Best selling author and winner of the Edgar, Agatha, Anthony, and Macavity awards.

"Facing potential death and long hidden secrets in her family, 'Racing from Death' is an exciting thriller set in the world of horse racing, very much recommended."
– Carl Logan, *Midwest Book Review*, February 8, 2013

"Nikki is one of the most appealing fictional characters I've ever met. You are rooting for her every inch of the way. The descriptions of backstretch life are enchanting."
– Lucy Acton, Editor of *Mid-Atlantic Thoroughbred*

"I thoroughly enjoyed *Full Mortality*–the pages fly by, the characters are vivid, and Hill captures life on the backstretch perfectly."
–Charlsie Cantey, racing analyst for ESPN, ABC, CBS and NBC.

"Sasscer Hill has hit her stride with her second, and hopefully one of many more, race track mysteries, 'Racing from Death'. A page turner that does not disappoint."
- Martha Barbone, *Horse of the Delaware Valley*, April, 2012

"Anyone reading The Sea Horse Trade, needs to be sure to have plenty of time because it's impossible to put it down."
– Martha Barbone, *Horse of Delaware Valley*, June 2013

The Sea Horse Trade
A Nikki Latrelle Racing Mystery

ISBN-13: 978-1515265795

ISBN-10: 151526579X

Cover art by R. L. Hayden

Dedication

For my husband, Daniel Filippelli, and my family– Lillian, Alidia, and Bartholt Clagget.

The Sea Horse Trade

Chapter 1

I heard the SUV before I saw it. The deep thump of subwoofers rumbled in the deserted street as I headed away from the sea, moving west on the sidewalk. Pausing, I glanced back. The vehicle cruised slowly toward me, chrome and glossy black beneath the bright streetlights. At four a.m., it was the only car on Hallandale Beach Boulevard.

I quickened my pace, stepping around a pile of crushed beer cans and dirty party streamers, probably left over from New Year's Eve. Overhead, the palm trees shimmered, and their stiff fronds rattled in the humid breeze blowing along the boulevard from the Atlantic Ocean. I didn't need to be at Gulfstream Park racetrack this early, but sleep had evaded me, nervous energy driving me into these predawn hours. Again, I glanced behind me. The pounding music grew louder as the black SUV loomed closer, its chrome grill gleaming like shark's teeth.

Ahead, an abandoned shopping cart lay against a small bus-stop shelter. Instinct drove me to step behind the shelter's solid rear wall, and from there, I peered around the edge, my senses heightened. Inside the vehicle the music seemed to crescendo into a scream as the glistening metal drew even with the bus stop.

The rear door that faced me jerked open. A girl, her dark hair streaming, pushed herself away from the door frame, flinging herself into space. Her feet hit the pavement, she lost her balance, and went down. Tumbling across the concrete, she landed on her side near the curb. She was almost naked, dressed in a tiny sequined outfit.

The vehicle's transmission slammed into reverse as the girl struggled to get to her feet. She cried out as one leg gave way and she fell back to the pavement. The SUV stopped, and I waited for someone to get out, to *help* her. The passenger window lowered, and loud Spanish rap poured into the street. I glimpsed a stubbled face behind dark-glasses.

"You stupid bitch," his Latino accented voice yelled over the music. "You break your leg? What good are you now?"

The girl tried to crawl away and I almost rushed to her, but a glint of metal shone from the car's window. *A gun.*

"No!" I screamed. "God, no!"

Two hot flames. Gunfire shattered my ears. The girl screamed, jerked twice. A geyser sprang from her chest, spilling blood over little strips of sparkling cloth. The SUV sped away.

Frantically, I searched the boulevard for help. We were on our own.

I ran into the street and squatted next to the girl. I thrust a hand out to steady myself, my palm skidding on her blood. Ripping off my hoodie, I wadded it and tried to compress her chest wound. A second hole darkened the skin above her collar bone.

The girl's eyes were open, fixed on me as her heart pumped a well of blood beneath my hand.

"They're gone." My voice cracked. *Did they hear me scream? God, don't let them come back.*

Carefully, I removed my cell phone from my blood-soaked hoodie. "I'm getting an ambulance." I thumbed 911. "You're gonna be fine," I nodded like I believed it, my left hand pushing harder against the makeshift compress.

She coughed horribly. Blood dribbled from her mouth.

"No," I whispered. *Don't die.*

"A girl's been shot," I said, when the 911 dispatcher

came on the line. "Hallandale Beach Boulevard at –" I looked around wildly. "There's something called a Publix, next to a Walgreens. What? Nikki Latrelle, my name is Nikki Latrelle."

Beneath me, the girl shuddered. Her eyes became fixed and unseeing.

I slumped to the pavement, the girl's blood soaking into my jeans. I stared at her. Beneath the blood, the tops of her small breasts were pushed up by a tight glittering bra. Lower down, a G-string hid almost nothing. God, she didn't look more than *thirteen*. I could hear the dispatcher's voice calling me from the phone. I set it on the curb, turned back to the girl.

Then I saw the dark turquoise sea horse on the flawless skin of her forearm.

Chapter 2

Tattooed on the delicate area between her palm and elbow, the two-inch sea horse was almost lace like. Designed by an artistic hand, the creature's one green eye seemed to stare and glimmer with energy, as if it had stolen the girl's spirit.

In the distance a siren wailed. Blue-and-red lights flashed up the boulevard. These Hallandale Beach cops sure hit the scene fast. The patrol car slowed as it approached, and a spotlight played across us from the passenger window. A police radio squawked as the cruiser rolled to a stop.

Two uniformed officers climbed out, a small man and a blond woman. They wore dark clothes and thick-soled boots. Radios and other equipment were clipped onto their wide belts. Their guns, holstered like muzzled dogs, made me shudder.

Look at their faces. Not at their guns.

The woman officer grimaced. Stepping around the pool of blood, she squatted next to the dead girl and checked for a pulse. "She's gone."

The man pulled his radio and spoke. Behind them, a siren's shriek quieted to a moan as an ambulance pulled up and stopped. Two EMTs rushed toward us with medical kits. The male cop made a slow-down movement with his hand. "You guys are a little late. I already radioed the ME."

"Not your call," said a grim-faced medic. "And we still have to examine her."

Were they going to get into a turf fight?

"Sure," said the male cop. "I was just saying."

The medic pushed past the officer, glanced at me. "Miss, are you all right?"

"Yes." I barely recognized my voice. "This –" I stared at the blood everywhere. "It's – it's her blood."

The medic crouched next to the dead girl, while the woman officer bent one knee to the pavement next to me. A lot of miles on her face, but her eyes were kind.

"I'm officer Hayes, Hallandale Beach Police Department. Are you Nikki Latrelle, the one who called this in?"

"Yes. I -- was walking from my motel, the Sand Castle."

"Did you see what happened when this woman was shot?" Hayes studied my face.

"She's just a *girl!*"

"Yes, Ma'am, I can see she's young. Can you tell me what happened?"

"Yes," I whispered.

"Do you know who she is?"

"No. She – she jumped out of a car, a black SUV, like she was trying to escape. But they wouldn't let her. They *shot* her!"

A sympathetic light warmed Hayes's eyes, but she was all business. Probably afraid I was about to lose it.

"Can I see some ID, please?"

I started. Where was my tote?

"That your bag on the sidewalk, Miss?" She gestured to where it lay next to the bus stop.

"Yes."

When I didn't move, she retrieved and handed it to me. I wiped a bloody hand on my thigh before digging out my Maryland driving and racing commission licenses.

"I'll be working at Gulfstream Park racetrack. Haven't had time to get a Florida trainer's license yet."

She nodded, studying the plastic cards.

A van labeled "Broward County Medical Examiner" eased up next to the patrol cruiser. An unmarked car, bristling with antennas, sped up from the direction of my by-the-week motel, sliding to a halt at a haphazard angle that blocked the

—

center of the street. Another vehicle pulled up behind it.

Strangers closed in after that, with their dark boots, instruments, cameras, and yellow tape. A woman in a skirt and pumps approached. Her jacket was black, her hair short and spiky like mine, only red.

"Detective Bailey, HBPD homicide." She flipped a badge, then crowded me. "I need you to step away from here. Answer a few more questions."

I turned from Bailey and gazed at the lifeless girl next to me. The unseeing eyes were no longer pretty. Blood matted her hair. Her legs were long and athletic. A decade-old memory surfaced. Alone, at night, in Baltimore. A runaway at thirteen. *I could have been this girl.*

"No. I can't leave her."

Bailey leaned over, clamped a hand on my shoulder. "There's nothing you can do here."

A short bark of laughter drew my attention. Beyond Hayes and an officer holding a camera case, a female cop made a shame-on-you wag with her finger and grinned at a male officer. Of its own volition, my hand stretched to the girl. I touched the sea horse.

"Don't do that, Miss," Bailey said.

Officer Hayes crouched next to me again. "Nikki, right?"

I nodded.

She pointed at my cell phone where I'd left it on the curb. "This yours?"

"Yes."

"I'll take that." Bailey motioned to a uniform, who whisked the phone into a baggie.

What was I supposed to do without a phone?

With an almost imperceptible eye roll at Bailey, Hayes sighed. She grasped my hand. "Come on, sweetheart, you better come with me."

I stood and followed her onto the sidewalk.

Detective Bailey stepped past the dead girl, then

—

scraped blood off her pumps onto the cement curb. The air grew heavier, the scent of gasoline-engines, rubber, and blood stifling.

My stomach flipped and I clamped a hand over my mouth. Officer Hayes moved away from me as Bailey approached.

"You're not going to be sick are you?" Bailey asked. When I shook my head, she said, "You need to come to the station." She latched onto my elbow and steered me toward her unmarked car.

I took a last look at the girl. On her arm, the green eye glittered. The sea horse still watched me.

Chapter 3

I wasn't happy when Detective Bailey put me in her unmarked. At least she hadn't stuffed me in the backseat cage of a cruiser. She didn't talk as the car rolled up the boulevard toward the Hallandale Beach Police Department. Didn't introduce me to the squat, powerfully built guy who drove, either. Probably a detective, and a junior one at that, since he was driving.

Way to go, Nikki. You haven't been here a day and you're already being taken in for questioning.

As we passed an entrance to the racetrack, I tried to peer through the dark, but the car moved too quickly to see anything. Some first trip to Florida. I had horses shipping in, a million details to take care of. People were *depending* on me.

I thought I saw the outline of a grandstand silhouetted by the first glimmer of dawn over the sea, to the east. To our left, Gulfstream Park stretched along a seemingly endless tract of ground. Bailey's partner drove several more blocks, then turned left.

I wanted to squirm right out of the cruiser. Instead, I studied the back of Bailey's red hair with its precisely scissored layers. Her eyes met mine in the rearview mirror.

"When we get you to the station, you can clean up in the ladies room. It's got soap and paper towels."

I stared at her reflection, confused.

Bailey shifted around in the passenger seat. "You've got blood all over you, Ms. Latrelle. You don't need to leave our department looking like that."

#

—

Bailey took me to a small room with a metal table and two chairs. She turned on a digital recorder and talked me through what had happened several times, probably hoping to trip me up. Then she stood and left the room without shutting off the recorder. Did she think I'd confess to myself?

I glanced in the one-way mirror on the opposite wall. Bailey was right, I looked like hell, like I'd been using cosmetics and hair products for vampires. Was someone watching me through the glass? I resisted an urge to fidget, forced myself to sit quietly in the metal chair.

They'd taken my hoodie back on Hallandale Boulevard, leaving me in my black sleeveless tee. I felt chilled by the air-conditioning. After an eternity, a guy came in to test me for gunshot residue. He had a humorless expression and a shaved head.

Shaved Head removed some sticky-backed papers from a test kit and after peeling off the smooth covers, he worked the tacky material over my hands. I'd done this before and felt like a pro.

"I still have to get your fingerprints. You're going to have to wash your hands first. You should do something about your face, too."

He should do something about his head stubble.

We walked down the hall to a ladies room. He gave me a hard look. "I'll be right outside."

I got the warm water going and soaped up my hands and face, rinsed. My black tee shirt camouflaged the red bloodstains and didn't look too bad. Further inspection in the mirror revealed red-brown smears on my neck. I'd obviously run those sticky fingers through my hair, too.

"Screw it." I filled the sink and dunked my head. When I straightened and looked at my reflection, I started giggling. If only my friend, the always perfect Carla Ruben, could see me now. The one who'd dragged me kicking and screaming into the world of makeup and fashionable hair. She should have been there. We could have had a good laugh.

—

"Are you all right in there Ms. Latrelle?" Shaved Head, speaking from the hall.

"I'll be right out," I said.

Grabbing paper towels, I dried off as much as I could, fluffed my short hair and returned to the hallway. Shaved Head stared at me a moment too long, before leading me to a different room where he used a machine resembling a copier to get a digital record of my prints. He ushered me back to the interrogation room, then left.

Sometime later, Bailey showed up with a typed statement, which I signed.

"Thank you for your cooperation, Ms. Latrelle."

"Sure." Like I'd had a choice.

"Would you like a ride to your motel." she asked. You said it was the Sand Castle?"

"No, thanks," I said. "It's not like I don't want a shower, but I have to get to the track. Did I see an entrance to Gulfstream across the street outside?"

"Yes," she said. "You can walk over if you want." She pulled a card from her suit pocket and handed it to me. "Anything comes to mind, call me."

I said I would and she told me I was free to go, pointing to the elevator, which I rode to the lobby. I stepped outside the building's chilly air-conditioning into a warm, sunny morning. I paused on the sidewalk, letting the heat sink into my skin. Could it really be January?

Just after eight a.m., rush-hour traffic streamed up and down South Federal Highway. Less than a block away, Hallandale ran perpendicular to South Federal. No wonder the cops had gotten there so fast. Had it been only four hours since the girl died?

I stared across the street. Construction cranes, a bulldozer and other equipment crowded Gulfstream's parking lot, blocking my view of the racetrack. The meet would open January fourth, still two days away.

Waiting for a light at the crosswalk, I noticed where

leftover goop from the residue test was stuck on my jeans. I picked it off, and rolling the stuff into a little gum ball, I smeared it onto the back of Detective Bailey's business card. When the light turned green, I crossed Federal, following Gulfstream's drive through the construction mess until the grandstand came into view.

The words *Colosseum* and *Mediterranean* popped into my head. A terra cotta roof covered a large building the color of desert sand. Two ornamental towers rose near either end. Between them a concave half-moon of columned arches drew my eyes to one of the prettiest paddocks I'd ever seen. A fountain sprayed in its center and stately palm trees lined its edges. Tropical plants and flowers added to my sense of stumbling upon an oasis.

No time for gawking. In the distance, a building rose just beyond the backstretch fence. The location indicated housing for stable help, the appearance suggested upscale condominium. I wasn't sure what to make of that, but I could see the stable gate nearby and that was the place I needed to reach.

After a long march through parked vans, trucks and cars, I reached the gate, where I saw a gray-haired, paunchy man in a security uniform. Good, I could ask him about getting a license and admission to the backstretch.

A shorter, long-haired guy with a lot of moustache spoke to the guard. As I got closer, I heard them arguing.

"I tell you, I have a job working for Mr. Ravinsee. " From the side view I had, the smaller guy looked younger than thirty. He flipped his dark hair back to reveal two gold earrings in one ear. "I supposed to meet some woman here today."

"If you mean Mr. Ravinsky's gal, she ain't showed up yet. You wanna use the phone?"

The handles of the long black moustache twitched up and down in irritation. "I don' wan' call nobody. Her phone turned off. I need to go to barn *tres*!"

Ravinsky? That was my boss. Barn three was my barn. Oh my God. I'd forgotten Ramon's cousin, Orlando. I was supposed to meet him at 7:00 a.m., see if he'd work out as an exercise rider and groom. His bling might be a bit over the top, but our Maryland groom, Ramon, had said Orlando was okay.

I stepped forward, glancing at the guard's badge. It read "Binecourt." I smiled at him.

"Excuse me. I'm Nikki Latrelle, Jim Ravinsky's assistant."

Binecourt's eyes widened and his body straightened into a defensive, military-like posture. "I'll need to see some ID, Miss."

I followed Binecourt's downward gaze. I might have washed from the neck up, but my black jeans were stiff with dried blood. The white laces on my Nikes looked like they'd been injured and tried to scab over.

"I was involved in a . . . car accident earlier." I fished out my Maryland racing license and handed it to him.

He compared my face to the picture and relaxed slightly. "You get hurt?"

"I'm fine." I glanced at the younger man. "Are you Orlando Castellano?"

When he turned to face me, a second set of double earrings flashed into view. He looked me up and down, then he folded his arms across his chest.

"I work for Mr. Ravinsee. Where is Mr. Ravinsee?"

Forcing a smile, I put out my hand. "He's put me in charge for the meet. It's nice to meet you, Orlando."

He ignored my hand. "In *mi familia,* the *men,* they don' work for girls."

Great, just what I needed. I'd be twenty-four in March. How old did I need to be for this jerk?

"No problem, I can hire somebody else."

He pasted on a quick smile, white teeth gleaming beneath the moustache. "Is okay. I ride for you."

"That's big of you, Orlando."

The guard cleared his throat. "I got a call a few minutes ago. There's a van on the way with Ravinsky's horses."

He must be mistaken. "They weren't supposed to ship from Maryland until tomorrow." I wasn't ready for horses. I hadn't even seen our barn yet.

"It's not Ravinsky's van. This was a Mr. . . . " He picked up a clip board. "A Mr. Mal . . . never can pronounce these names."

"Maldonista?" I asked.

"Yeah, that's it."

The Colombian. Niggling doubts about this new owner had kept me awake the night before.

I stared at a black-and silver horse van entering the parking lot. "But they're two days *early.*" I tried not to whine.

"Something going on at the local quarantine facility," the guard said. "Guess the place is overloaded. Anyways, your horses did their time and the authorities wanted them out of there."

A heavy rumble grew audible as the eighteen-wheeler approached the stable gate. When had I started this habit of twisting my horseshoe ring? My finger felt raw.

"That's probably it," the guard said.

It couldn't be. I had to unload supplies, locate a feed and hay man, get the blood off my clothes.

With a loud hiss of air-brakes, the van crawled to a stop. A deep, demonic whinny erupted from inside. Hooves crashed against an interior stall partition, and someone screamed in terror or pain.

Chapter 4

Another agonized scream came from inside the eighteen-wheeler. Orlando and I raced to the last of three doors in the side of the huge trailer. The crashing and screaming seemed to come from back there. Orlando bumped my shoulder with his, pushing me to the side just before he leapt to the small platform beneath the door.

To my left the guard rushed into the security booth. I hoped he was calling for help.

"You get hurt. I do this." Orlando grabbed the handle, and turned it. He swung the door outward.

Macho man. No time for an eye roll as I fastened the door to the latch on the outside of the trailer.

Orlando took one step inside and froze. *"Santa Madre de Dios!"*

I jumped to the platform and stared.

A huge black horse gripped a man's upper arm in his teeth. The man's feet dangled in the air outside the horse's stall. His shirt was ripped and blood stained.

"Get this fucker off me!" The man's words became an unintelligible scream as the horse shook the guy like a rag doll.

The animal, free to move about in a box stall, must have grabbed the guy by snaking his head over the metal partition. Damn, the monster's neck looked seven feet long! I spotted a push broom mounted on the wall and grabbed it.

"Hit him!" the man yelled.

"I don't want him dragging you in there." I kept my voice low, hoping not to make the horse more wild.

Orlando stood rooted to the floor next to me. Useless.

Slowly, I lifted the pole-end of the broom toward the horse. The beast ceased pinning his ears long enough to flick them at the broom.

"Hey big stuff," I cooed, moving the handle closer to his mouth. The long, narrow shaft came at the horse so slowly he never drew back, even as the handle touched the corner of his mouth. I wiggled it slightly, working it into the crease of his lips. The handle inched onto the smooth bar of gum, between the front teeth and rear molars. I pushed and the horse opened his mouth, just like he was taking the bit.

The man fell to the floor, moaning. The horse got his teeth on the broom handle and jerked it out of my hands.

"Have at it, you son of a bitch!" I backed away.

Orlando stared at me with new respect. "You the man!"

I shook my head. "We still have to get him out of here and into our barn."

Dropping the broom handle, the beast glared at the open doorway. The van's driver, a wiry little man with wispy graying hair, had climbed onto the platform and was helping his injured groom to the ground.

"Are we having fun yet?"

I knew that voice! I glanced down from the van into a familiar pair of green eyes. *Will Marshall.*

"Not really" I said.

Will had told me he'd be riding at Gulfstream. I'd all but forgotten. I'd known Will for a few years, ridden races against him, and knew him to be a straight shooter. I was absurdly glad to see him.

The security guard peered into the van. "Is anyone else hurt in there?" When I told him no, he said, "We got to move this rig from here. Traffic's backing up."

Outside, the racetrack ambulance was taking the injured groom away. The van driver walked towards us, wiggling a toothpick in the side of his mouth.

"Are you sure this devil really belongs to Maldonista?" I asked him. Never hurts to hope.

"Sure does," the driver answered with a gleam in his eye. "Him and those two fillies up front." He pointed beyond the solid partitions that separated the black horse from the rest of the trailer.

"Anyways, I got to drive them to your barn." He frowned. "You got some help to unload them?"

"*Sí, por su puesto*, she have me!" Orlando's white teeth flashed.

"I'll help, too," Will said. "Might as well catch a ride." He hopped onto the platform and stepped inside. "Hey, Orlando."

They exchanged some sort of handshake. Everybody knows everybody at the track.

The driver left the door open, probably as an escape hatch. In a moment the rig rolled forward and two minutes later pulled up outside a barn with the numeral three painted on the end.

#

A groom Orlando knew provided the name of his feed man and lent me bedding and hay. In short order, we had three stalls knee deep in straw, water buckets hung and filled to the rims. The two Maldonista fillies were in their stalls. The loading ramp was down, and just outside the van, the driver fidgeted with his toothpick. He couldn't get the horse from hell off that van fast enough.

Orlando, Will, and I stood inside, studying the beast. His baleful expression kept us at a respectful distance. How would we get him out? We might as well have been the Three Stooges.

I held a clipboard with three sets of Argentinian Jockey Club papers. "What do you know about this horse," I asked the driver below us.

He shifted his toothpick. "I know he fits his name, 'Diablo Valiente.'

"Means 'Bold Devil,'" whispered Orlando.

I examined the horse's papers. "Three-year-old colt by Dynaformer, out of a Ribot line mare." Nice pedigree.

"See, what it is, is you got too much Ribot." The driver gestured at the colt with his toothpick. "His sire, Dynaformer, he's from that Ribot family, too. I knew Ribot. He was a mean son of a gun. He'd hurt people."

"How'd you get him on here?" I asked.

"Loaded the fillies first. That wall wasn't up." He waved at the solid metal panels dividing the colt's section from the rest of the trailer. "He could see 'em and came right on. Then he wants to . . . get romantic. We got that partition up right quick. He about climbed out of that stall trying to get at 'em."

I'd have to separate the colt by turning the stall in between his and the fillies into a storage area. Wouldn't do to have him climbing the wall to get at his neighbor.

"How you people plan to get a shank on that horse? Go in there with him, he'll be all over ya."

This driver was enjoying our predicament entirely too much.

"He's a horse, isn't he?" I was losing my temper. "Orlando, get a bucket of feed."

Orlando started to say something, caught my expression, and hurried off the van.

Earlier, I'd noticed a long, thick crop lying on the floor outside the horse's stall. "Why is this crop here?" I asked the driver.

"I wouldn't know." The driver's glance drifted to the ground.

"Your man like to show a horse who's boss?" Will asked.

"I wasn't back here," the driver said.

Will and I exchanged a look. If the savaged groom had been smacking the colt with a crop . . . .

"Nikki, if we can get hold of his head, maybe we can get that chain over his gum." Will gestured at the lead shank I held in my other hand.

I nodded and set the clipboard down. Maybe we could

slide the chain section under Diablo's lip, let it rest against his gum, tighten it in place. The sudden pressure would get the horse's attention. If we were lucky.

Orlando trotted up the ramp with a bucket of grain. He looked at the colt, handed me the bucket and stepped back. I moved closer to the stall gate and held out the bucket. The colt pinned his ears and shook his head, but his eyes were on the feed. I took one step forward, fending off visions of my arms as bloody stumps.

The colt shoved his head into the bucket and ate the grain. I grabbed one side of his halter and Will grabbed the other. Orlando snatched the bucket away. Will's fingers were so nimble and swift, he had the chain over the gum and tightened down while I was still thinking about it.

I'd been told the discomfort caused by the chain makes the equine brain release endorphins, natural painkillers that also act as a sedative. Since it hurts to fight the chain, Diablo didn't. He quieted down.

Will held Diablo's head, while Orlando and I opened the stall gate. Will double-timed the horse down the ramp, leading him into his stall before Diablo had time to come up with a plan of his own. Orlando and I followed at a sensible distance.

"Safe in the barn." I slumped against the wood rail that enclosed the aisle beneath the overhanging roof.

Will and Orlando stood nearby, staring at Diablo.

"Thanks, guys," I said.

"*No problema.*" Orlando shrugged as if he dealt with man-eating horses every day.

"You have to ride this Godzilla tomorrow morning?" Will seemed to have serious doubts.

As I nodded, Diablo rammed his chest into the stall gate with a loud bang. When the gate didn't give, he backed up and kicked the wall. Then he trumpeted in the direction of the fillies. Fortunately, they had better sense than to answer.

What the hell was I going to do with this beast?

Chapter 5

By the time Will left, the Florida sun was high and strong in a cloudless sky, and my watch confirmed that the morning was all but shot.

"Orlando," I said, "can you be here at four o'clock to feed?"

"*Sí, no problema.*" Then he frowned. "How I feed him?" He gestured at Diablo.

We stared at each other. We'd put Diablo's hay and water in before Will had led him off the trailer.

"Good question," I said.

Normally, I'd dump the feed into a tub, then clip the tub to the screw eyes in the corner of the stall. But no one was going in there with Diablo until I'd gotten a handle on the beast. *Too bad he didn't come with a ring in his nose, like a bull.*

I went to our feed room and rummaged through a stack of supplies, pulling out a rubber pan from beneath a pile of rolled horse bandages. I placed the round container in the dirt outside Diablo's stall, and caught Orlando's eye.

"Use this. Once you've poured feed in this pan, shove it in under the gate." I gestured at the almost two foot high space under the wire gate.

"Ah." Orlando's white teeth gleamed as he smiled. "I do very fast. Then he not bite."

I nodded. "Good idea."

Only I didn't know anything about Maldonista's three horses – what kind of feed they were used to, the training regime they'd been under, if they suffered from any old injuries or respiratory conditions. As soon as I got my hands on a phone, I'd call Jim. I had questions about this new owner.

What *kind* of man wanted to own a horse like Diablo?

#

The backstretch guard had sent me beyond the grandstand to a series of gray double-wide trailers hooked together like toy trains. One of them housed a temporary office for Florida's Division of Pari-Mutuel Wagering, the state agency empowered to issue racing permits. Air-conditioning units jutted from the trailers' windows. Their vents radiated waves of heat as their metal frames vibrated and dripped water.

I ducked inside the wagering office where I spent the rest of the morning trying to stay awake while filling out paperwork and posing for mug shots. When I got curious looks, I used the car accident story. When the clerk finally handed me my licenses with the newly laminated photo IDs, I shuddered. I needed sleep desperately. I needed a shower even more.

Back outside, I noticed the racing secretary's office in the trailer next door. This was where I'd enter Diablo for a race. Only first, he'd have to pass a starting gate test and earn his Gulfstream gate card. I wasn't looking forward to being inside the tight quarters of this metal contraption on Diablo. But he'd run before. He couldn't be too violent in the gate or they would have ruled him off in South America.

But what if they had ruled him off? This horse could have killed somebody down there. Crushed his jockey, for all I knew. *Step at a time, Nikki, don't think about it.*

I left the track and discovered almost anything I might need lay within walking distance on Hallandale Beach Boulevard. I passed a public library, a branch of my bank – and just about everyone else's – fast food eateries, grocery stores, pharmacies, doctor's offices, and several upscale looking restaurants. Best of all, I made out a Verizon sign a couple of blocks further down.

First, I had to eat. Before stepping into a Boston

Market, I glanced down at my jeans. They looked stiff and dirty, but were black and didn't really show the blood.

Inside, I had a guy behind the counter load a plate with baked chicken, creamed spinach and cornbread. I'd worry about the calories later.

An old man with liver spots on his bald head stared at me from the next table while I wolfed down everything to the last dollop of cream sauce. Did he have to stare at my chest? I should go over, let him inspect my blood-soaked sneakers with the scabby shoelaces.

I sketched a little wave when I was finished, said, "Have a nice day," and hurried outside.

I reached the Verizon store, bought a new phone, and finally dragged myself back to the Sand Castle, grateful my room was on the first floor.

I'd left in the dark that morning, and as I neared my room, I took a moment to study my surroundings. My room was on the backside of the motel. Outside my door, a concrete walk ran alongside the row of rooms, and a railing separated it from a strip of driveway.

Beyond that, a chainlink fence protected the unwary who might drive or fall into what must be an inlet of the Intracoastal. The salt waterway flowed past the motel, then dead ended against a concrete seawall at the base of an empty lot. Large signs in the lot's broken soil proclaimed a new luxury condominium would be "coming soon."

I fitted the key into the lock, entered my room, and shut the door. In my absence the cleaning crew had blasted through and set the air conditioning to arctic. I shut the unit off and yanked the door open again. Warm, moist air drifted in, and a shaft of sunlight warmed the gray tile floor.

I heard a door chain rattle, and stuck my head out. The door to my left clicked shut. A quick glance at the remaining rooms flanking mine assured me no one was about.

Had I really left the motel only early this morning? It felt more like a week.

21

Closing the door, I stripped off my clothes, threw them into the tub and climbed in after them. I turned the shower on full blast and tried to ignore the blood flowing past my feet and spiraling down the drain.

A lot of soap and two towels later, I hung my clothes on the curtain rod and stretched out on the bed, trying not to think about any of it. Later, I'd make sure Orlando had fed the horses.

Hell, I still had to call Jim.

Rolling to the edge of the bed, I pulled the Verizon bag from my tote. Checking my new phone's call log I saw half a dozen calls from Carla, but nothing from Jim.

I grabbed a knife from the kitchenette drawer and sliced through the plastic box enclosing the charger. I plugged the phone in and sank back on the bed.

I'd just close my eyes for a moment, then call Jim.

Chapter 6

An electronic ring from the phone woke me, a tuneless reminder that Detective Bailey had pocketed my old one that played "Camptown Races." With sudden clarity, I remembered everything.

I rolled over and grabbed the cell. "Hello."

"Are you all right?" It was Carla, and she sounded anxious. "I've left you so many messages. You never called me back."

I had a cornucopia of excuses, but they'd all sound too weird. "It's been kind of a . . . long day."

As Carla's sigh came through the line, I sat up and scooted back against the headboard. Through the slats in the blinds, the portico outside appeared deep in shadow.

"There's something I need to tell you," Some emotion had ground a sharp edge into her words.

I didn't want any more bad news, but had a feeling it was coming. "Tell me."

Carla breathed in, and remained silent a moment, as if searching for the words.

"*Carla?*"

Her voice was hesitant and slow. "I never told you this, but . . ."

"Whatever it is, Carla, just say it."

"Thirteen years ago. I had a – a baby." Her words rushed now. "I gave her up for adoption."

"What?" This came out of *nowhere*.

"You *heard* me. A baby girl. I gave her away."

I heard a small sob. "Oh my God, Carla." Why was she telling me this?

"It's not something I'm proud of, Nikki. I was only

fifteen, still in high school. The father was a jerk, wanted me to abort. I would never do that."

"But you *gave* her away?" The words slipped out before I thought about them. I knew what it was to be motherless. That Carla had done this to her own child lit a flame in my stomach.

"What the hell is with your attitude, Nikki? You're lucky *you* didn't get pregnant at fifteen. Maybe you'd like to have given up being a jockey and everything else to raise a child!"

I'd never heard her so angry, and I deserved it. The woman had been a mentor to me, taken me under her wing, like Jim. It wasn't as if she'd abandoned the baby. *Get a grip, Nikki. This isn't about you.*

"I'm sorry, Carla. I shouldn't have said that."

"No, you shouldn't have."

"Have you found her?" I asked, to fill the icy silence. But Carla wasn't having it and hung up. *Good play, Nikki.*

My mother had died when I was thirteen, leaving me in the care of the monster she'd married not long before her death. I'd been left with some serious issues about abandonment.

The phone made its robot-tapping-a-tin-can sound. I answered.

"If you really want to know," Carla said. "I almost found her."

"You *almost* found her? What happened?"

"I hired a private detective. He found her family in Florida – in Boca. I was going to meet her."

She stopped like she'd hit a road block, and I waited.

"Her name's . . . Jade. She's only thirteen. Her parents are dead. The police think it was a burglary that went bad, and Jade is missing. I'm coming down there. I have to find her! You have to help me!"

"Jesus, Carla . . . of course. But how do you know she's –"

"She's alive, I know it, and one of her girl friends swears she saw Jade in Hollywood last night."

"Hollywood, *Florida*?" Holy shit. I gripped the phone so tight I thought my fingers might snap. "What does she look like?"

"I don't even know that." She paused a beat. "Have you heard something?"

I exhaled slowly, and chose my words carefully. "No, I don't know anything. It's just that Hollywood is right up the road from Gulfstream. She could be . . . she could be here."

She could be dead.

#

After we disconnected, I sat on the bed staring at the wall, my mind like a mill grinding the same thoughts out over and over again.

I shouldn't have been so hard on Carla. She'd had it tough, too. Her father had gotten involved with another woman when Carla was only sixteen, not long after she'd given up the baby. What a guy.

Then she'd lost her mother to cancer. Both of us were motherless – a shared emptiness that had bound us a bit tighter.

Scrambling off the bed, I went into the bathroom and turned on the shower. My nap had left me disturbed by vague dreams, and I felt stale and queasy. The story about Jade had left me reeling. I stripped and stepped into the tub again. Even though I'd washed the girl's blood away earlier, I had an overwhelming need to soap up, scrub, and let the hot water pour over me.

After pulling on clean street clothes and fluffing my hair with mousse, I grabbed my new cell and accompanying manual. The names and numbers I could remember I programmed into speed dial, then called Carla back to ask her about her travel plans.

She sounded hurried and nervous. "I've booked a US Air flight for tomorrow afternoon. It gets in at 1:30. I'm staying at the Diplomat Hotel. Apparently it's close to you. Can you pick me up at the airport?"

"Sure." I wanted to tell her to calm down, but knew it was pointless.

After ending the call, I reached Jim.

"It's me," I said. "You still coming down with the horses day after tomorrow?"

"Yep. Things okay?"

"Not exactly. Maldonista's horses showed up this morning. The colt's a bad actor. He almost killed a guy."

"*Killed* a guy?"

I explained about Diablo. "Did you know about this?"

"Would've told you if I did."

Of course he would have. Jim had looked out for me since he'd discovered me as a young runaway hiding in a stall years earlier. He'd given me a job as a hotwalker, and when he saw I had a gift with horses, he'd believed in me, taught me to be an exercise rider, and finally helped me get a jockey's license.

He broke the silence. "Horse didn't hurt *you* did he?"

"No," I said. "But what do you know about these three horses? I thought you'd be here before they showed up. I don't know anything about them. Don't even know if I can get that colt saddled tomorrow."

There was another brief silence. Then he said, "Maldonista was supposed to send me a packet of information. Hasn't come yet, but all three won stakes in Argentina. You know I verified that."

I did. Under normal circumstances, Jim would never race at Gulfstream. Competition at the Florida track was too tough. The old trainer was shipping down his two best turf horses, and even with them, he'd have to pick his spots. Maldonista's horses must have looked pretty good for him to uproot like this. He'd have to travel back and forth between

Florida and Maryland, too.

"You got their papers?"

"Yes," I said. "But –"

"Here's what I can tell you. You've got that three-year-old colt, Diablo Valiente, a four-year-old filly named –"

"What does La Bruja mean?" I asked.

"Look it up. Then the third filly, Imparable. She's a four-year-old sprinter. La Bruja and Diablo like to go long. When I get more, I'll either call or bring it with me."

Jeez, Jim was in a rare mood. Always spare with words, today he was one step short of rude.

"Are you okay, Jim?"

"Don't like that guy sending his horses in early. He's got a place somewhere in South Florida, but I don't have a number for it. Got one of those phones that blocks the ID. Have to wait for him to call me."

"Oh." I knew Maldonista had paid a month's day-rate in advance. For some trainers it was all they'd need to know. But Jim wasn't like that.

"Don't worry, Nick, we'll find out soon enough."

Jim disconnected. He had enough to deal with. I wouldn't tell him about the girl.

Chapter 7

Shoving the phone into my tote, I stepped outside and let the door swing shut behind me. The sunlight had faded on the back side of the motel, and the temperature was falling. The empty lot beyond the small paved drive lay deep in shadow.

On my left, the door to the next room stood open about six inches, and a slack chain hung across the opening on the inside. I glanced at the room's window. Crushed between the glass and yellowing Venetian blinds, a row of potted cacti and tall snake plants lined the inside ledge.

A dark calico cat with demented green eyes squeezed out through the gap in the doorway. She stiffened, then pounced, and a lizard fled up the wall, its colorful stripes illuminated by a florescent fixture hanging overhead.

The cat swiveled her head to look at me, her pupils such narrow vertical lines I didn't see how she could focus on anything. I'd had to leave my part-Persian feline in Maryland. Though he stayed with friends who doted on him, with a pang, I realized how much I missed him.

The calico lifted her head and emitted a deep yowl that made me take a step back. She must be unhappy about that escaped lizard.

"Scat! Stop that caterwauling." An elderly woman rattled the chain loose and swung the door wide. She stepped onto the concrete walk in a black nylon track suit. She had straight, chin-length gray hair and a widow's hump, but her eyes were bright and interested.

"My, you're young," she said looking me up and down. "I'm Stella, and this is Scat the Cat." Stella looked at Scat and shook her head. "She's a real operator. Snuck in one day when we was eating tuna fish sandwiches. Lou here," she gestured inside the room and I spotted an old man lying on a quilt-covered bed, "went and gave her a bite."

"If I hadn't, you would have," he said, working to sit up against a pile of pillows.

"That's neither here nor there," Stella said.

"It's somewhere." Lou looked at me and broke into a gap-toothed grin. "Say, you want a beer?"

"Maybe later." I edged away. Good to have friendly neighbors, but I didn't see myself sitting on a bed drinking beer with Lou. "Nice to meet you, Stella. Lou."

I beat it past the row of rooms to my right, down three steps, and onto the pavement running along the back of the motel. Several small businesses with store fronts next to the motel's lobby had rear entrances here. Small signs advertised a hairdresser, Harry's Gym, and a tiny French bistro.

The warm smell of baking bread and cinnamon drifted around me as my phone rang. Now what?

"It's Jim," he said when I answered. "Mello's been having one of his 'I *knows* things' spells, and I had to promise him I'd call you."

Suddenly nervous, I glanced around, not liking this deserted side of this motel. Mello, the old black groom in Maryland, had a touch of the second sight, and I could guess what Jim was going to say next.

"I'm in danger, right?"

"He wants you to call some distant cousin of his down there in Hollywood. A woman named Klaire. Said she spoke to him in a dream last night."

"Oh for God's sake," I said.

"You know how he is, Nick."

"Yeah." I knew, and it gave me the creeps. Thing was, Mello had been dead-on more than once. I picked up my pace and headed for the lights on Hallandale Beach Boulevard.

"He says you need to talk to her."

Oh boy. "What's her number?"

Jim read out a number, we disconnected, and I saved the number into my new phone before I forgot it. I'd call this person later. It was past time to move to the safety of the lighted street.

I hurried through an opening in a chainlink fence and onto the sidewalk of Hallandale Beach Boulevard. I only needed to make sure the horses had been fed, that they'd settled in, and were happy.

Traffic whizzed by in both directions. Night had set in, but plenty of people still walked along the boulevard, some carrying plastic grocery bags, some spiffed up for an evening out.

Heading toward Gulfstream, I saw the bus stop shelter a block ahead. A piece of yellow tape waved in the breeze of passing cars. My feet became leaden and I realized I'd stopped moving. Was the girl's blood still there?

I crossed the street. *Keep moving, you have to get past it.*

But what if she'd been Carla's daughter?

Chapter 8

The next morning, I arrived at Gulfstream before six. Low clouds scudded over the Hallandale Beach area, and a sea breeze chased after the warmth created by little bursts of sunshine. Warm in January. I still couldn't get over it.

Several doves, of a type I'd never seen before, perched on the roof of a nearby barn, their calls forlorn and unfamiliar. The mile-oval track opened for training at six, and a few horses with exercise riders aboard walked along the dirt aisle in barn number two. No doubt a brief warmup before they followed one of the paths leading to a racetrack entrance.

Eight hours of sleeping like I'd been in a coffin had put some life back into me and I was humming a Sheryl Crow tune as I stepped onto our shedrow in barn three.

A dark haired man of medium height, probably in his forties, stood a few feet from Diablo's stall. I approached him from the side and felt that little thrill I get at the first sight of an exceedingly handsome man. His profile displayed smooth olive skin, a well proportioned nose and jaw, and a dark eye with thick lashes. Even from the side, something about his bearing suggested a man who commanded respect.

The heavy, linked gold around his neck would probably have paid for my by-the-week motel for years. I bet his white shirt, black pants, and reptile patterned shoes didn't come from Walmart, either.

"Excuse me," I said. "This is Mr. Ravinsky's barn. May I help you with something?"

He turned, revealing an angry red-and-white scar, long and jagged, through the outside corner of his right eye. His lower lid drooped and fluid leaked from the corner.

As he pulled a white handkerchief from his pocket and dabbed at his eye, I tried not to stare. He put the kerchief back, and smiled, revealing strong, even teeth. He stepped toward me and held out his hand.

"I am Currito Maldonista. I see someone takes good care of my horses. You?"

"Yes," I said, and told him my name.

His handshake was firm and quick, but his dark eyes studied me a bit too long for comfort. Stepping back, I returned his smile. Poor guy, he must hate the inevitable reaction to his appearance.

By now it was almost six a.m. and Orlando, ready for duty and right on time, appeared around the corner of our barn. His steps slowed as he took in Maldonista's disfigured eye. Or maybe the gold necklace caught Orlando's attention. His own hair was pulled into a ponytail, revealing the gold flash of all four of his earrings. I introduced him to Maldonista, handed him the key to the feed room, and told him to get started. Before he unlocked the door, Orlando turned back for another look at the newcomer.

Mr. Maldonista," I said. "Tell me about Diablo."

The man's face lit up. "A powerful colt. Very swift. But you must call me Currito, and I may call you Nikki, yes?"

"Sure," I said, hoping for more information.

Currito turned, and we both looked into Diablo's stall. The horse stood with his massive hind end facing us, his head busy with his hay rack that hung in the corner.

"He has the fire," Currito said.

Straight from Hell. I forced a bright tone. "Yes, and he's a stakes winner."

Currito's eyes glowed with pride, but I found the right one extremely unnerving. I tried to focus on his mouth and failed. Damn. It looked like someone had gone after him with a knife. Yet the light in his eyes was a light I knew. This man loved his horses.

Warming to his subject, Currito relayed a race by race

tale of Diablo's prowess, finishing with, "So, you see, to be a true champion, he must run here. He must conquer the great American horses."

Diablo had come to the right place, but Currito hadn't answered questions about the simple stuff, like how was I supposed to get the colt saddled and out on the track?

"Currito, does Diablo pony?"

"Pony?"

"Will he allow a rider on another horse to lead him? To the starting gate, for instance?"

"But of course. You must be sure to use a gelding."

Did he think I'd use a filly with his horny devil? Smiling, I nodded. I'd learned the hard way that some owners didn't want to hear anything negative about their horse. You had to work around it, and until I knew more about Currito, I didn't want to risk angering him and causing Jim to lose this opportunity.

Diablo shifted from the corner, moved to the stall gate, and shoved his head out. Currito murmured something to the horse in Spanish, but didn't attempt to touch the colt.

I hadn't had a chance to study the horse the day before. Fierce, intelligent eyes stared at me from above the bold curve of a Roman nose.

"We had some difficulty with him yesterday . . ." I left it vague, hoping Currito would fill in the gap.

"You cannot fight him. He will battle you to the death," Currito nodded knowingly. "You must persuade him."

"Or outsmart him," I said.

"Exactly!" He smiled at me. "You will be good with him, I see that."

I didn't, but kept it to myself.

"So, he will go to the track now?" The man's expression was childlike in it's eagerness.

"After he's had some breakfast," I said.

Currito appeared disappointed and I thought I might have seen a little tick in his right eye. He glanced at his gold wristwatch.

"I have an appointment. Perhaps tomorrow I can see them train?"

"We'll be here," I said.

Currito pulled for his kerchief and dabbed at his eye, then slid on a pair of sunglasses with an interlocking crystal G on the frames. Guccis. He gave me a formal nod and strode away.

An interesting man. But who had cut him? And why?

Chapter 9

Orlando poured grain into two feed tubs and set them in the fillies' stalls. As the taller of the two fillies, Imparable, dug into her breakfast, I removed her water bucket, rinsed it out and refilled it to the brim. I stared into the swirling water and blinked suddenly. For a moment, I'd swear the glimmering eye of the sea horse appeared beneath the surface.

"Nikki, you spill water!" Orlando said, giving me an odd look.

"Sorry." Before I could shut the hose off, water splashed over the rim, down the front of my jeans and eddied in the dirt at my feet. I took a breath. *Stop thinking about the dead girl.* At least Currito hadn't stayed around for my water bucket performance.

I looked at Orlando. "What does *La Bruja* mean?" I asked.

"*La Bruja.* It mean the witch."

"Oh." I glanced over at Diablo, who glowered at me from his stall. How nice. A witch and a devil, just what every barn needs.

Impatient for breakfast, Diablo pawed at his straw bedding, stirring dust into the air.

"I'll get to you in a minute."

I stared at the rubber pan still lying in the straw at his feet. How would I remove it? When a brilliant plan failed to materialize, I focused on our equipment problem. Our tack wouldn't arrive until the two Maryland horses shipped in the next day, but we had to ride these horses today.

"Do you think you could borrow a couple of saddles and bridles?" I asked Orlando.

"Is just for today?"

I nodded.

"*Sí*, my friend will help." Orlando grinned, then trotted down the dirt aisle and across the pavement separating us from the barn next door. He disappeared inside the building.

Sighing, I glanced up and down our shedrow. The two fillies had their heads out, taking in the view while they ate. The mingled scents of grain, hay, and manure hung in the morning air. On the far side of our barn, someone played salsa music and sang along off key. I reached up and combed through Imparable's forelock with my fingers.

"I can hardly wait to get you two ladies out for training," I told her. "But first, I gotta deal with your buddy Diablo. You think the all-purpose rake will work?"

When Imparable responded with a silent, inquisitive stare, I grabbed the rake from an overhead hook and knelt in the dirt outside Diablo's stall. I stole an uneasy glance up at the colt.

I'd assumed he was a dark bay, but a bay's black lower legs always give way to some shade of brown in the body. Not this colt. Black as night, and not a white spot on him, either. Unusual in a Thoroughbred.

Diablo lowered his head, studying me as if curious to see what I'd do next.

"I'm winging it," I said.

Sliding the rake into the stall, I hooked the pan's lip. As soon as the feed pan moved, Diablo grabbed the side with his teeth and pulled back.

"Let go!"

Diablo shook his head, bared those big yellow teeth, and bit deeper into the rubber.

Hopeless. Maybe bait would work. I yanked the rake out and went into the feed room. A bunch of carrots lay on a metal table. Grabbing them, I hurried to Diablo's stall. Staying as far back as possible, I stretched my arm forward and offered him one. The black nostrils widened and narrowed as he sniffed. His lips, reminding me of rubbery fingers, worked the carrot into his mouth. When it disappeared, he flicked his ears toward me, and he gave me an expectant look.

"You want more? Here," I said, tossing three carrots into the far corner.

He snorted as they sailed past, but turned to follow them, moving into the corner.

Squatting, I grabbed the rake, hooked the tub, and whipped it out. Faster than a horse that size had any right, Diablo whirled and rammed the gate with his chest. The impact shook the barn walls, and a pitchfork fell to the ground from its hook. Somehow the stall gate held, and the pitchfork missed me, but I landed on my butt with the tub on my stomach.

Jesus! That was close.

I heard the jingle of metal and looked up. Orlando, lugging two saddles, bridles and a couple of different sized girths, stopped and frowned.

"Why you sit? You hurt?"

I gritted my teeth. "No."

"Wha' happen?" he asked his glance shifting to Diablo, the beginnings of a smile lifting his moustache.

"I don't want to talk about it."

As I stood up and dusted my seat off, Orlando's smile grew.

"Shouldn't you be adjusting some of that tack to fit Diablo?" I asked. Before he could answer, I marched into the feed room, grabbed my phone and called the woman named Klaire.

A soft, breathy voice answered.

"I know who you are," she said. "Let me give you a different number to use."

"But I'm – "

"This line is not secure! Use this number."

She read off a string of numbers, asked me to repeat them back. As soon as I did, the line went dead. This was ridiculous. But I punched in the new number.

"Nikki," she said, answering the first ring. "It is important we meet. I spoke to Mello. He wants me to offer you my services."

Her services? I exhaled slowly and stretched out my one-word reply. "Okay."

I waited, hoping she'd fill in the silence, but she didn't.

"These services Mello thinks I need," I said. "What would those be, exactly?"

"Even on this line, it is not safe. You must come see me.

"This is crazy!" I said. "I want to know what you're talking about."

"Tell me." Her voice slowed, then changed to an eerie whisper. "Did you touch the sea horse?"

I almost dropped my phone. "How do you know about that?"

"Will you come?"

"Yes," I said, gritting my teeth. "Where are you?"

I grabbed a piece of paper and a pen, and my hand shook as I wrote down directions.

Chapter 10

Orlando and I stared at the huge monster lumbering toward us. He looked like one of those Budweiser horses, tall as a skyscraper. I'd asked for a big "pony," but this was ridiculous. Probably a Clydesdale. The long tufts of white fur pluming out above the animal's ankles were a pretty good clue. That and the fact this walking mountain must weigh close to a ton.

"What is he?" I asked the heavyset pony girl on his back.

"Three parts Clydesdale, one part Quarter Horse. My recipe for bombproof. His name's Bullwinkle. I'm Beth," she said.

Curly hair peeked from beneath her helmet, and perspiration trickled down her neck. A burgundy safety vest protected her torso, and heavy leather chaps covered her jeans.

"Where's this colt we're ponying?" she asked, adjusting a protective rubber pad covering part of Bullwinkle's neck and withers.

I pointed at Diablo, who stared over his stall gate at Bullwinkle, seemingly mesmerized by the pony.

"That's him," I said. "A real prince."

Beth's mouth tightened. "Isn't this the one attacked that guy on the van yesterday" I nodded.

"How'd you get that saddle on him?" she asked.

"Used bribery carrots and got lucky." Only Diablo hadn't been that horrible with me. Maybe because I was female and didn't threaten him with a crop.

I slid the leather strap Beth handed me through the ring of Diablo's bit. I led him out, handed the strap to Beth, and stepped back. She nudged Bullwinkle with her boot heels, and the two horses moved away. I'd never seen two more massive sets of hindquarters. Bullwinkle, however, won the size prize and when Diablo tested Bullwinkle by purposely bumping against him, Bullwinkle slammed the colt back, causing him to stagger.

Orlando and I exchanged a look.

"Is just what he need," Orlando said. "That Boowink, he cut Diablo down to size, no?"

"*Somebody* has to." I watched Beth and her charges continue down the shedrow.   Further along, the trainer who shared this side of the barn with us started to bring a horse out. He took one look at the towering twosome bearing down on him and backed his horse into its stall. I shouldn't be grinning. I still had to ride Diablo. I slipped on my helmet and protective vest.

Moments later, Beth finished her circuit of the shedrow and pulled Diablo up next to me. Orlando stepped in fast and gave me a leg up, and before Diablo had time to think about me on his back, Beth moved us along the aisle way.

"You always hold your breath when you ride?" Beth asked.

"When I'm scared, I do." I took a deep breath, and forced my hands to relax on the reins. No sense in telegraphing fear.

We were nearing the end of the barn when two people walked around the edge of the building. A redheaded woman and a guy built like a squat gorilla. Detective Bailey and the partner who had driven us to the Hallandale Beach Police Department.

From my vantage point, Bailey looked short. She wasn't wearing pumps today, but flats with a black pantsuit. Maybe she wouldn't recognize me on the horse. Under the helmet.

She stared at Bullwinkle. But then, who wouldn't? Only her gaze settled on me.

"Ms. Latrelle, I need to talk to you," she called.

"Who is that?" Beth whispered.

"Damn," I said softly. "She's a cop."

Beth threw me a questioning look. I could do without the doubt flickering in her eyes. A couple of grooms cleaning tack outside our barn stopped working and stared.

"Detective Bailey," I said, as we drew closer. "I have to get this colt onto the racetrack. Only be a few minutes."

"You two stop right there," she said, holding up her badge.

Beth pulled Bullwinkle up. Then Gorilla Man went into action, rushing over with an outstretched hand like he thought he could stop us.

Instinctively, I grabbed the martingale strap around Diablo's neck and hung on. Diablo's muscles bunched beneath me just before he lunged at the detective. From the expression on the man's face, and the way he threw himself under the wood rail, I assumed the big teeth were bared. I heard them snap.

On my left, Beth white knuckled Diablo's lead strap, as an unconcerned Bullwinkle ambled forward and pressed his bulk into Diablo's shoulder.

My horse reared up. His front hooves sliced the air above me, then streaked down toward Beth's head and the pony's neck. Bullwinkle sidestepped neatly, and Diablo's hooves glanced off the protective rubber pad.

"Officer, no disrespect," I said, "but if I don't keep this colt moving, somebody's gonna get hurt."

Beth's lips were pinched, but she booted Bullwinkle, and we headed forward.

Bailey backed out of the way.

"Ms. Latrelle, do whatever it is you're doing with that horse, then get back here! We'll wait. There are some questions about your relationship with the victim."

I stared at her. *Relationship?* What was she talking about?

Bailey's expression hardened. "We think we know who she is."

Her words punched me in the stomach. I grabbed Diablo's mane to steady myself. *I didn't want to know.*

Beth guided up past Bailey's hard stare and headed for the racetrack.

"She looks really mad," Beth whispered. "What kind of trouble you in, anyway?"

"I witnessed a . . . crime." I swallowed hard. "Let's just ride."

Chapter 11

When we reached the racetrack that morning, Diablo surprised me. All business, he had the big loose walk of a pro, his ears and attention straight ahead. Beth kept him secure and snug against Bullwinkle by using her pony strap. She watched Diablo as she urged both horses into a trot.

"You know, he might be all right."

"I sure hope so." I breathed in his heady horse smell, then the sharper scent of sweat hit my nostrils as he warmed up. I felt alive. Worries about detective Bailey and the rest of it could wait until later.

A couple of horses sped by us in the opposite direction. Breezing along the inside rail their hooves kicked up dirt and scattered it behind them with little clinking sounds, like coins. Diablo took it all in stride.

Beth pushed us into a canter. "I've known a few that are lunatics in the barn but behave pretty good when you put them to work."

When Bullwinkle shifted into a gallop, his heavier frame made his stride ponderous. Diablo remained fluid, even with Beth's tight hold on the strap that forced the colt's neck to bow until his chin almost touched his chest. Amazingly, he accepted it. *For now.*

Beth's cheek's flushed pink and moist with heat. "I don't know how much good this is doing your horse. Most are smaller and get more out of pony work than your guy will."

"Take us a mile, and we'll see," I said.

"You got it."

I'd only missed one day of riding, but damn, it felt good to be on a horse again. This one gave me a strong sense of unleashed power, and an ability for self discipline I wouldn't have thought he possesed. Smooth, too. I was aching to turn him loose.

Beth took us the "wrong" way, purposely traveling clockwise on the mile oval. Races run counterclockwise in North America, and exercise riders generally go the "wrong" way for slower speeds. In Europe, they do the whole process backwards. If I ever rode a race in England, I'd probably end up cross-eyed.

By now, we'd covered most of the backstretch, staying closer to the outside rail, away from the inside where riders set horses down for speed. Diablo was still behaving.

"When you get us to the turn, let him go," I said. "But track us in case he gets tough."

"You got it," Beth said.

She held both ends of the smooth, slender pony strap in her left hand. Made like a long leather rein, the strap folded in half where it threaded the ring of Diablo's bit. As the horses approached the turn, she let go of one end. Diablo felt her hold ease, lengthened his stride, and the strap slid away easily.

Don't run off with me, you devil.

Once he reached an open gallop, I kept my hands near his withers, far from his head, taking what's called a "long hold" on the reins. This steadied Diablo. His stride reminded me of a stakes filly I'd ridden named Daffodil. She'd been a lovely mover. So was this colt, only more powerful. A lot more powerful, and still businesslike.

We motored along for a mile before I pulled him down to a jog, heading for the gap in the rail that would lead us back to the barn.

Just ahead, a chestnut filly sashayed down the track with her tail up in the air. Diablo's head lifted, and with a sudden squeal, he bobbed up and down beneath me like a giant rabbit.

What the hell?

The filly surprised her exercise rider by doing an about face, as if to check out Diablo. The rider, a young woman, took one look at my colt and frantically booted her filly.

This was not looking good. I drummed my heels into Diablo's sides, tried to get him moving forward. He bunched up beneath me, made a sound more like a scream than a squeal, and bolted toward the filly.

The rider wacked her filly with a crop. "Move it! *Move."*

Ignoring the whip, the filly planted her feet and whickered at Diablo.

Oh for God's sake. The filly was in heat, and Diablo was ready to oblige. "No!" I yelled, trying to turn his head.

I was used to fillies going to the track even when they were "in season" as trainers can't afford for them to lose a day of exercise. But colts at the track are inexperienced sexually and usually not studdish. Lucky me, I'd gotten a real Romeo.

"Get that freak away from us," the exercise rider yelled. "He's gonna try to mount!"

I glared at her. "Do I look like Superwoman?"

That filly of hers could use some cycle suppressing Regu-Mate. Both horses needed a cold shower, and I had no control. It was like the reins weren't connected to Diablo's bit.

The filly's rider screamed once and bailed, launching through the air. As soon as she landed, she scrambled away.

Diablo lunged at the filly and reared onto his hind legs. A large, bulky figure loomed in my peripheral vision. Bullwinkle rammed Diablo sideways. I flew through the air and landed on my side in the dirt. Rolling to my hands and knees, I saw Beth grab Diablo's rein. Like a cow pony, Bullwinkle knew just what to do and herded Diablo away from the filly.

The Gulfstream outrider showed up and grabbed the filly's rein. It was over.

As I stood up, a gray horse cantered toward me. Will Marshall pulled the gray to a stop, slid off and looped his reins over the horse's head. He walked toward me.

"You're lucky. You've got more lives than a cat, Latrell."

I wasn't hurt, but I didn't feel that lucky.

Beth glanced at Diablo and her eyes widened. "That's a pretty serious fifth leg he's got going."

I'd already noted the large companion Diablo had sprouted, but refrained from comment, dusting the dirt off my clothes instead.

"Need a leg up?" Will kept a straight face, but his lips compressed a little with the effort.

"Sure," I said, tightening the strap on my helmet.

Frustrated, Diablo stomped and snorted next to Bullwinkle. I ignored Diablo's tantrum and slid my boot into Will's cupped hands.

As he threw me into Diablo's saddle, he muttered, "I know just how he feels."

"*What?*"

"Nothing," he said. But his eyes gleamed with an unsettling intensity.

I looked away, and Diablo skittered forward until I tightened the reins and brought him up short. The colt must sense my emotions.

In an effort to calm down, I breathed in the warm air and took in my surroundings. A few horses jogged nearby, and a set of three galloped away on the wide expanse of dirt. The blocky outline of tall condos and fancy hotels broke the skyline in the distance, hiding the ocean from view. But I could smell the saltwater.

Above the skyscrapers, a jet flew silent and fluorescent white in the morning sun. God, Carla would arrive that afternoon, and I still had to have that talk with Bailey.

"What's wrong, Nikki?" Concern tightened the sharp planes of Will's face.

"Can you ride back with me? I should talk to you. I've got this little problem with the police, and . . ."

Will held up a palm. "Give me a second." He put his hands on the gray's withers and vaulted easily into the saddle.

Beth's mouth hung open. "How does he *do* that?"

I shrugged. "Beats me."

"I'll take it from here, Beth." Will grasped Diablo's rein and headed us toward the barn.

Chapter 12

As Will and I headed back from the track, we rode past half a dozen backstretch barns. Grooms were cooling out horses, cleaning tack, and raking the dirt aisles on their shedrows until the surface was clean and smooth.

Still grasping Diablo's rein, Will remained silent as he digested my tale about witnessing a murder, being questioned by the police, and the search for Carla's daughter.

I steadied Diablo when he spooked at a rack of green and pink bandages that fluttered in the breeze outside a nearby barn.

"So," Will finally said, "this detective's waiting at the barn?"

"That's what she said."

Will stared at me. "You're a trouble magnet, Latrelle. You know that?"

"That's not fair!"

He shrugged. "Fair rarely happens. But it might help if you were more cooperative with the police."

"But I didn't *do* anything."

"Do they know that?"

He was right. What cop wouldn't question a witness standing over a body? Still, I could never control my tongue. Something about authority figures bugged me.

And there was one over by barn three. I could make out Bailey's red hair and black suit, and she appeared to be tapping her foot as she stood outside my shedrow.

I was hoping she'd left. Seemed like I'd been gone for hours, but a glance at my watch confirmed it had been less than fifteen minutes.

"Is that redhead the homicide detective?" Will asked.

"Yep, and the guy who just joined her is her pet gorilla."

"See, that's what I mean. Your attitude, Latrelle. It needs an adjustment."

"Diablo doesn't like him either." I leaned forward and patted Diablo's black neck.

Closer to us, a roan horse held by a groom stood patiently under the spray of a hose, the sweat and water streaming down his legs, pouring onto the pavement.

"We're going to be on top of those two in a minute." Will's eyes were on the detectives. "When they were at the murder site, did they ask you about anyone connected to Gulfstream?"

"Gulfstream? Why are you asking?"

He shrugged. "Just curious. You said it happened only two blocks from here, right?"

"But why would the murdered girl have anything to do with the racetrack?" I glanced at him, curious.

"Here she comes," he said quietly.

As Bailey strode toward us, I could smell the big morning dig-out of stalls hanging in the humid air around us.

Bailey's nose winkled. Then her lip curled. Her suit would probably have to go to the dry cleaners. What a shame.

As I fought a smile, Orlando emerged from the tack room and jogged past the gorilla, then Bailey, stopping a few feet in front of us.

Will halted both horses, and we dismounted. I pulled the reins over Diablo's head and handed them to Orlando, and Diablo followed him along the grass growing next to our barn without fussing.

Probably thinking about that feed pan.

Reaching us, Bailey flashed her badge at Will. "You work here too?

"I'm licensed to ride here. Nikki's a friend." Will's expression was unreadable, almost like he had cop eyes.

"My partner," she tilted her head toward the gorilla,

"Detective Aguierro. We'd like to talk to Ms. Latrelle. Alone."

I glanced at Will. Silent understanding sparked between us.

"I'd like him to stay."

She shrugged, but Aguierro got into Will's face. "Shouldn't you put your horse somewhere?"

"This guy?" Will's long fingers stroked the gray's neck. "He's already cooled off. He can graze on the grass here."

Will wasn't easy to get rid of. I knew.

A flash of irritation flickered in Bailey's eyes, but she put on her game face and turned to me.

Only I was wound tight, and the big question blurted out. "Who was the dead girl?" *There went my tongue again.*

Bailey, cool as a frozen daiquiri. "Why don't you tell me, Ms. Latrelle?"

"I don't know. I don't *know* anything. But . . . she might the daughter of a friend of mine. Carla Ruben."

"Who is Carla Ruben?" Bailey's eyes narrowed.

"Tell her," Will said.

I poured out the whole story, starting with Carla giving up her baby up for adoption, ending with her flight into Fort Lauderdale that afternoon.

"I'm supposed to pick her up."

The tension seemed to ease from Bailey's shoulders. Maybe she believed Carla was my only possible connection to the victim. But she still watched my face closely as she took a half step closer.

"What does Ms. Ruben's daughter look like?"

"Nobody knows. I mean, Carla never had the chance to meet her."

I thought I saw sympathy in Bailey's eyes. "The victim probably isn't your friend's daughter. We think she's a local girl old who went missing a few days ago. We had trouble locating her parents at first, but the description fits, and they're going to ID the body at noon.

I sagged with relief. Will let out air like he'd been

holding his breath a long time. The dead girl belonged to *strangers*. Still, I ached for those people.

The soft light left Bailey's eyes. "I'd like you to bring Ms. Ruben directly to my office after you pick her up. We need to talk to her. And you. I'm having a vice detective join us."

A ripple seemed to pass through Will. He nodded as if something had been confirmed.

Bailey handed me her card again. "You call me if that flight's delayed. And don't even think about not showing."

Aguierro gave me his hard look, then followed Bailey, who was already walking away.

"How do you do it, Latrelle?" Will shook his head slowly.

"*Me?* I didn't do anything. But *you* know something. What is it?"

A whinny trumpeted from my barn, followed by a loud bang. I heard Orlando yell, "*Madre de Dios!*"

"You'd better see to that beast. We'll talk later." Will pulled on the gray's reins and led the horse away.

I still had to get those two fillies out and was running out of time. *Stupid detectives.* I jogged to our tack room and grabbed the second bridle, then the saddle with the smaller girth. I'd take Imparable out now, let Orlando ride La Bruja after he finished cooling out Diablo.

Opening Imparable's stall gate, I paused to study her again. A sturdy, dark bay with three white socks, she had the classic close coupled body and short legs of a sprinter. Orlando had done a good job grooming her. She was gleaming and ready for her tack.

As I adjusted the bridle down to fit her head, I realized Will had never told me what he knew.

Chapter 13

I waited in the Sand Castle's lobby to use the motel's only computer. They'd built it into the wall next to the receptionist's desk, and its printer – accessible only to the desk clerk – hid somewhere behind it. This is the kind of place I stay in – everything that can be taken by a guest is nailed down.

After printing out and examining a map to the airport, I discovered if I took the scenic route, Klaire's place would be on my way to get Carla, whose plane didn't land for a few hours. I could stop and meet this Klaire person first. The map showed her address on a side street that ran straight to the Atlantic Ocean off of a coastal road called South Ocean Drive. My luck was changing, Carla's hotel was on South Ocean, too.

I left the lobby, fired up my Toyota's engine and drove east on Hallandale, toward the sea, soon rolling onto an overpass. The Intracoastal waterway flowed beneath, and I almost ran into the back of an old Caddy when I got too busy watching a powerboat slice through the blue-green water below.

From the overpass view a flat blue horizon seemed to stretch out forever – *the Atlantic*. I hadn't realized the Sand Castle was this close to the ocean.

A delivery van honked behind me, the driver gunning past me with a rude hand gesture. I stopped rubbernecking and drove down the ramp, at the last minute crossing over South Ocean Drive instead of turning left toward Klaire's place and the airport. Directly ahead, stood the Hallandale Beach water tower, a giant red-and-blue onion on a turquoise stalk. The tower rose before a two-story fire and rescue station. The beach and the sea lay just behind it. I pulled to the curb outside the station, letting the car idle.

Why had Mello's cousin asked about a sea horse?

Could she know about the tattoo? I didn't believe she was psychic. Probably just listened to police radio.

Sighing, I stared out to where the water touched the sky. Massive ocean liners and container ships cruised without sound. Closer, a yacht powered through whitecaps, its prow dipping and surging.

Jim's horses would arrive tomorrow. Free time would evaporate, physical demands would increase. I twisted the horseshoe ring on my right hand back and forth. How could I help Carla without shortchanging Jim? I owed them both so much.

I closed my eyes and drank in the salty air, so like the breeze that had whipped up Hallandale early yesterday morning. It brought the memory a sea horse tattooed on the arm of a gunshot victim. *Don't go there.* I snapped my eyes open, shifted into drive, and headed north.

#

With my foot heavy on the pedal, I sang along to "We Were Dead Before The Ship Even Sank." The tune blasted out the Toyota's speakers, and I felt almost high as I sped up the coastal highway.

Ahead on my right, an impressive building, structured in gleaming shades of silver, white, and pale turquoise rose toward the sky. A sign read "Westin Diplomat." Carla's hotel. I'd like to stay in a place like that.

I started checking side streets beyond it. In a mile or so, I found Klaire's street, Blue Water Lane. Rolling the car slowly, I spotted her number on the left about three houses from the beach. I pulled to the side, shut off the engine and stared. What had Mello gotten me into this time?

The house sagged away from the ocean as if tired of being beaten by the wind. It was covered in asphalt shingles, some of which lay in the yard, scattered between pots of plastic flowers. Gold-and-silver tinsel hung from the edge of the one-story roof, and the neon-lit figure of a turbaned woman sputtered above the door. I gaped at the accompanying electric sign. "Klaire Voyante, Psychic Reader."

"Forget this," I muttered, ready to fire the engine and leave.

Just then, the front door swung inward and a woman stepped into the yard, her hand making a "come here" motion. Medium height and full bodied, she wore a palm print top with a long skirt.

I'd come this far, and truth be told, as much as I'd resisted Mello's psychic stuff, I was still curious. I climbed from the Toyota and walked toward her, noticing she'd worked amber-and-gold strings of beads into her dark, wiry hair. Her skirt, decorated with a gold foil pattern, glittered in the sea breeze riding in from the ocean.

She spoke in that same breathy voice I'd heard on the phone, "Nikki, I'm glad you've come."

"Klaire?" I asked.

"Yes, let's go inside." She looked around nervously, as if she sensed some danger lurked close by. She urged me through the front door, then quickly shut it behind me.

Up close, she looked much older than I'd expected. A hard life was written on her face, but the amber beads in her hair complemented large dark eyes and the tiny spots of color in her irises. With her dusky milk-chocolate skin and generous curves, I suspected she'd once been drop dead gorgeous.

Doors opened on either side of the foyer we stood in, revealing rooms with dim and murky lighting. Straight ahead a tiled hallway led to a kitchen at the back of the house.

After motioning me to follow her into the room on the right, she turned on a floor lamp – a carved female statue holding a flickering electric torch. The lamp cast moving shadows onto the tiled floor, revealing three armchairs. Carved sphinx heads watched me from the ends of the chair-arms. A long, low, backless-couch completed the set. The whole room had an Egyptian feel to it and smelled like incense.

The room seemed surprisingly chic compared to the tacky exterior of the building. Odds were, Klaire held numerous facades and layers.

"So why did you want to see me?" I asked.

She smiled and gestured at the closest chair. "Please, sit. All will be learned."

I glanced at my watch. "I have to pick someone up soon."

A frown deepened the creases around her eyes. "I know that."

"Of course you do," I muttered.

"Do you care about the girl in the sea, or not?"

I grew still. "What girl in the sea?"

"I do not know," she said quietly. "I only know she is connected to you, to the friend who will visit you."

Did she mean Jade was in the ocean? I sank into the nearby chair, my hands gripping the sphinx heads.

Klaire sat in the closest chair, and seemed to be staring at something I couldn't see. "The girl came to me in a dream. You know dreaming is a gateway to another world? "I saw you and my cousin Mello, too. But I felt a very strong connection to you."

I glanced around the room and peered deeper into the shadows. The walls were draped in fabric, and a large crystal ball glowed from a table on the far side.

"Oh for God's sake," I said. "This is so hokey."

Klaire's eyes narrowed "Don't be so quick to judge! Have you forgotten what Mello can do? Did he help you?"

I exhaled slowly. "Yeah, he did."

"And he knew things he couldn't possibly know?"

I nodded, remembering Mello's ability to "see" details of an eight-year old murder in Virginia. My fingers curled around the wood sphinx heads so tightly it hurt. I loosened my grip and rubbed my hands on my jeans.

Klaire stood up suddenly, the beads in her hair

swinging and twinkling in the light from the torch. "You must get the sea horse box. I know where it is waiting. I have *seen* it."

"So, you saw this box in a dream, or you were actually *in* a shop?"

"You have so little respect," she said. "Yet you are connected to the other world."

"No," I said, standing up. "I'm not."

"You will learn," she said, and pulled a piece of paper from a pocket in her skirt.

I noticed a number of strange carved rings on her fingers. The designs looked like astrological figures.

"This is the address. If you care about the girl who died, you will find this box. Look for the sea horse. I cannot tell you more."

Of course she couldn't. She probably didn't know anything. I took the paper from her hand, and left. The whole thing sounded like nonsense, but as I walked to my car, I couldn't shake the image of a tattoo needled onto on a dead girl's arm.

#

I drove to Route 1, and watched for the street number of the shop Klaire had told me to find. An endless lineup of "designer" furniture stores, real estate agents, car repair shops, and grocery stores crowded against the sidewalks on either side.

Though Klaire was probably a charlatan, I had time to check the shop out and too much curiosity not to look.

Driving with good tunes still blasting kept my foot on the pedal and the side street sign I searched for whisked into view. I slowed, saw the billboard for the strip mall I wanted, and pulled into its parking lot.

Sandwiched between a podiatrist office and a laundromat, a dozen or so pink flamingos with electrified eyes stared from the storefront window of the shop Klaire had insisted I go to. The birds encircled a plastic palm tree decorated with Christmas lights. Maybe Klaire had decorated this place, too.

Under different circumstances, I would have looked for a gag gift for Carla.

A bell rang in the back when I entered the store, and a tiny, Asian Woman with a lot of eye-liner appeared from the rear. She passed a display of refrigerator magnets -- palm trees, bikini-clad Barbie dolls and alligators. Closer, a table seemed to sway beneath the refracted light of a hundred paperweights, mostly fish and minature sea vessels sealed into turquoise glass.

The place smelled like carpet cleaner and dust, with a faint overlay of cat box. The Asian woman paused before me, rubbing her palms together.

"I help you?"

Should I mention the sea horse right off? Snoop around first?

"Just looking," I said, noticing a corner section marked "Pawn Shop" set off by a barrier of plastic palmettos.

Above the plants, two electric guitars hung from the ceiling. One was hot pink. A pearlescent beauty next to it had a sign claiming the guitar had belonged to Eric Clapton when he lived on Ocean Boulevard. My mom had owned the "461 Ocean Boulevard" album. Clapton's "I shot the Sheriff" started playing in my head. No doubt it would continue until overtaken by a radio tune.

From beneath her kohl-lined lids, the woman studied me. "Come, I have for you." She grasped my wrist and tugged me toward the pawn shop. I let her lead me past cameras, jewelry and a fine looking set of silver candelabra to a wooden cabinet in the far corner.

"Look." She pointed at the cabinet.

I stepped closer and stared. A small carved box lay on the second shelf. From the lid, the green eye of a sea horse glimmered at me. The design of the sea creature was so like the tattoo on the dead girl, a small gasp escaped me.

Gingerly, I picked up the box and examined it.

Maybe three by five inches, carved and polished in red-brown wood, it was inlaid with starfish and shells on the sides. When I tried to open it, I realized there were no hinges, only tight seams along the edges, which refused to budge. It must be one of those puzzle boxes

"Take with you." The Asian woman nodded, pushing the sale.

I stared at her. She barely reached my shoulder and a little bald stripe marked the top of her head. "Did Klaire call you?"

Her puzzled expression seemed genuine. "Who is Klaire?"

"Never mind. This box looks expensive. It's . . . beautiful."

"Yes, and it go with you!"

I glanced at the woman.

"How much?" I asked.

"For fine polonia carving? Hundred dollar."

How did I get suckered into this? I couldn't spend a hundred on some soothsayer's gibberish.

"I don't have a hundred dollars." But I pulled my wallet from my tote and opened it. "This is what I have."

The woman studied the two twenties, the five and assorted ones. Her long nails plucked them from my wallet.

I hurried from the store with the sea horse box, trying to shrug off an unpleasant tingling between my shoulder blades. It's the feeling I get when I'm being watched.

I yanked open the door to my car. Once inside, I locked the doors, cranked up the engine, and got out of there. At the next red light, I told myself I was being ridiculous.

From the lid of the box, the sea horse stared. I leaned over and locked the box into the glove compartment. I didn't need Carla asking questions about it.

Chapter 14

I steered the Toyota around a minibus and slowed outside the passenger pickup zone of US Airways. Exhaust from buses, cabs and cars, choked the air.

Glancing at the automatic doors, I saw Carla coming through. No mistaking her luminous blond hair and tall, knockout figure, as she pulled her wheel-mounted luggage behind her. She must have seen me about the same time, because she waved and broke a smile.

As I pulled up to the curb, I saw vulnerability in her expression I hadn't seen before. I got out, rushed over, and gave her a quick hug before stepping back to look at her more closely. Lines of tension etched the outside corners of her brown eyes. She was trying not to cry.

"Hey," I said, "it's gonna be okay."

She nodded quickly, but remained silent. I was so not used to this behavior from Carla. She was always upbeat and in control. I popped open the trunk, grabbed her luggage and flung it inside. My car rocked in protest, the trunk slamming shut from the bounce.

Any other time I'd have joked about the trunk being snappish, but the lost way Carla looked at me, I didn't know what to say.

She started to speak, but a shrill whistle cut her off. An airport security guard pierced the air with his metal whistle again and motioned for me to move along.

"We'd better get going." I climbed into the Toyota and popped the lock on Carla's side. She'd barely closed her door before I gunned the engine and pulled into the flow of cars.

Silence ruled until I turned onto Route 1 with its traffic lights and string of mom and pop stores. By then, Carla's gaze on me was so intense it unnerved me. I turned to her and set loose words I'd intended to phrase carefully.

"We have to go to the police station."

The color drained from her face. "They found Jade?"

"No! They haven't found Jade. But there's another girl. There's stuff I haven't told you." I wasn't looking forward to telling her about the girl who had died on the street. But I did.

#

"That's Bailey," I whispered, when I saw the detective step out of an office inside the police station, where Carla and I had been cooling our heels for some time.

Carla was responding to my tale about the dead girl with continued, total denial. It could *not* be Jade. I left it alone.

Detective Bailey, wearing her black heels, thumped softly toward us along the carpeted hallway. She must have changed out of the flats she'd worn that morning. Probably gotten horse manure on them.

I stopped pacing before the bench where Carla sat with her long legs crossed. She stood up quickly, and faced Bailey. She was taller than the detective, and twice as attractive. Bailey stared right back, her face giving away nothing.

"Detective Marcia Bailey," she said, shaking Carla's hand. She nodded at me and led us down a corridor in the opposite direction from the interrogation room I'd sat on my first morning in town.

We passed a doorway where uniformed officers worked at desks lined with computers, phones, and stacks of files and notebooks. Air conditioning spilled from overhead vents, and the smell of strong coffee overlay the sharp odor of cleaning fluid.

Bailey stepped into an office and pointed at two stiff and uncomfortable looking chairs.

Why don't you both have a seat?" She walked around her desk and settled into a leather executive chair.

A man in a well-made suit stood leaning against the back wall. He was close to 40, maybe younger. Hard lines etched a ruddy, attractive face. Beneath thick brows, his eyes were a warm brown as he watched us sit. Friendly.

A subdued interest flickered over Carla's face. She'd always had a weakness for good-looking, sharp-dressed men. Even now.

"This is Detective Rick Harman," Bailey said. "He's with Vice.

Something about the man seemed familiar, but I couldn't place him. Why was Vice involved, anyway?

Harman turned to Carla. "Ms. Ruben, we're sorry your daughter is missing. We're doing all we can to find her." He paused. A fleeting look passed between the detectives, as if they engaged in a second, silent dialogue.

Harman continued. "There are several teenage girls we're looking for."

"Detective Harman," I said, tilting forward on the edge of my chair. "Why is vice interested in Jade Paulson?"

Instead of answering me, Harman quirked a brow at Bailey. "I see what you mean," he muttered.

Carla had flinched when I said the name "Paulson," the name of Jade's adoptive parents. She probably thought of her daughter as Jade Ruben.

Still ignoring my question, Harman spoke to Carla.

"Some of these girls run away from home. When they find themselves on the streets, they have to survive . . . "

"I think Jade had a good home life," Carla said. "She wouldn't have been on the streets." Her glance darted my way, as if seeking my agreement.

Harman straightened from the wall and took a step toward her. "I'm not putting your daughter into that category, but we want to cover every possibility." He spread his hands, "Right?"

Carla nodded.

This Harman guy seemed kind, but he wasn't

answering questions, wasn't easing the anxiety that tightened Carla's face. She needed answers. I clamped down on an urge to launch myself from my chair, grab the guy and demand he tell us everything he knew.

"We understand from Ms. Latrelle that you weren't in touch with your daughter," Bailey said from where she stood near her desk. "You've never heard anything about who her friends are?"

Carla shook her head.

Bailey placed her elbows on her desk and leaned forward, her expression still impassive. "What about Jade's adoptive parents. You been in touch with them?"

Carla pressed her teeth into her lip. She'd been doing that in the car, too.

"No," Carla said. "I just don't know anything. You must think I'm awful."

But she *had* been in touch with them. Through that private detective she'd told me about.

"Not our place to judge." Bailey stared at a point over Carla's shoulder. "When did you give your daughter up for adoption?"

"Right after she was born." Carla's voice trembled and she inhaled as if to steady herself. "I – I only saw her for a moment. They took her from the hospital room."

"And you never saw her again? Never spoke to her?"
Again the teeth into the lip. Carla closed her eyes and shook her head.

Bailey's eyes narrowed, becoming almost predatory. "Interesting you would say that, Ms. Ruben. After we first heard about you this morning, I ran you through the computer, checked phone records against Jade Paulson's. We *know* she called you, Ms. Ruben."

Carla's lips parted, and her eyes widened.

Bailey placed her palms on her desk and stood. "Are you still denying you've spoken to Jade?"

Carla appeared to tune us out as if she were searching

for something inside. "Oh my God," she said softly, "that's what those calls were."

"What calls?" Bailey asked sharply.

"My voice mail," she said, her voice quickening with excitement. "I got several calls where someone stayed with the call until it went to voice mail. But they never said anything. There were background sounds, like conversation or a TV."

I noticed Harman's interest pick up. He seemed to follow the two women's conversation closely.

Carla rose from her chair, her gaze fixed on Bailey. "Are you telling me my daughter tried to reach me?"

"Did she?" Bailey asked.

"No, I just told you that. She may have been trying to call me but she never even left a voice mail message."

The two women seemed to reach an impasse, both standing motionless.

"What about you guys," I said, gesturing at Bailey and Harman. Haven't you found a picture of Jade Paulson?

Bailey held up her hand, as if to ward off a buzzing fly. "We first heard the name from you only this morning. The schools are still closed for the holidays. We'll have it later today, but we don't have it now."

I saw a tremor run through Carla. What would it be like to see your child for the first time in 13 years?

Bailey's expression hardened. "You came down here to search for your daughter, right?"

"Yes," Once more, Carla looked at me as if for confirmation.

"You felt guilty about giving her up? Never having a part in her life?"

"Yes, of course."

Bailey moved from behind the desk, closer to Carla. "And when she called you, you wanted her back in your life."

"I told you we haven't spoken!"

By now, Bailey loomed over Carla. "It could be argued you wanted her back in your life so much you'd do anything."

Carla's eyes darkened as the implication of Bailey's last words sunk in. "You think I was involved in . . . I was in Baltimore!"

This was ridiculous! "Carla –"

"It's all right, Nikki," she said, before turning angrily back to Bailey. "Are you charging me with a crime? Because if you are, I want a lawyer. If you're not, I want to leave."

This was the Carla I knew and loved. The one who'd taken an instant liking to me when we'd met and taught me how to get around and act like a grownup instead of a resentful child.

Harman gave Bailey a warning frown. "Take it easy Marcia. We have nothing to charge Ms. Ruben with."

Bailey eased back from Carla, her expression like a dog forcefully jerked off a bone. She returned to her desk, sat in her upholstered leather chair, and tried not to glare at Harman.

"Ms. Ruben," he said gently. "May I call you Carla?"

"Yes," she said.

"Okay then, Carla. The department has a task force working on this. We have a lot of contacts working the street, looking for Jade, and we've already put out an Amber Alert on her."

They hadn't had Amber Alerts when I'd run to the streets. But then I hadn't wanted to be found. Jade, though . . ..

I stood up. "But what about these parents that had a daughter go missing? Wasn't their name Booker? They were supposed to ID the murdered girl? It's way past noon. Did they do it?"

Bailey turned on me, her lips pursed tight with disapproval. "Ms. Latrelle, you need to back off. This is a police investigation, not a Pony Club meeting."

Carla was staring at me. I wished she wasn't so pale. Was she reconsidering, thinking now that the murdered girl could be Jade?

Bailey exhaled, blinked, then nodded at Harman.

He moved closer to Carla, raised his hand like he would touch her, but dropped his arm to his side.

A little spider of trepidation crawled up my spine.

"The murder victim on Hallandale Beach Boulevard . . . it was a negative ID. She's not the Booker's daughter. We don't know who she is."

Chapter 15

Carla and I sat at a table in the Westin Diplomat's restaurant. The hotel was way out of my league, snazzy and expensive, like Carla. The dining room had soft teal carpeting, matching velvet upholstery on the chairs, and sparkling wine glasses and cutlery laid out on white table cloths.

Our waiter appeared in a starched shirt with a black bow tie, and his shoes gleamed with polish. His greeting was formal. None of that hi-I'm-John-and-I'll-be-your-server stuff for this hotel.

We ordered drinks and shrimp salad. Our iced vodkas with cranberry juice and splashes of tonic arrived quickly. Our immediate plunge into wishful drinking saw the glasses emptied twice as fast.

Carla looked dazed. She stared out the plate-glass window where white sand faded in the gathering dusk.

Turning to me, she said, "I can't believe they didn't have a picture of Jade because the high school is closed."

"Did you ever look for her on Facebook or any of those social networks?"

She gave me a withering look. "Of course I did. I couldn't access her photos and her profile picture was a pop star."

How had Carla's private detective found the girl? I upended my glass, and rolled a melted ice cube into my mouth, a dozen questions rattling in my head. Did the police consider the murdered parents a higher priority than the missing teenager? Could they think Jade had murdered her adoptive parents?

I kept that last thought to myself, and said, "Why didn't you tell Bailey about the private detective?"

Carla picked up her glass, realized it was empty, and set it down. "Why should I? He's *my* detective."

"But if they find out about him, it will show you *have* had a form of contact with Jade and her parents. You told them you knew nothing."

"I *don't* know anything. The detective, George Turner, only found out about the family two weeks ago. I was going to fly down and meet them. George had arranged it, but then he called two days ago and told me Jade's adoptive parents were dead and Jade was missing. He knows what the police know, and they seemed short on information, to say the least."

Again, she reached for her empty glass. "Where is that waiter?"

"The cops are probably doing the best they can, Carla," I said. "That Harman guy seemed pretty cool. Sharp, and he acts like he wants to help." Carla so needed to find out about her daughter. One way or the other.

Our waiter arrived with a tray of shrimp salad. The tang of lemon and a whiff of garlic made me almost faint. He set down a basket of breads.

Carla stared at the bread with an offended expression. "We don't need the rolls."

"Wait," I said, as the guy began to whisk them away. "I'll take them."

As I reached for a roll, Carla told the waiter she wanted more vodka.

"No thank you," I said when he asked if I wanted another drink. I had to get up and ride Diablo in the morning and needed a clear head. I got busy buttering a roll instead and watched the man transfer salads with grilled shrimp, chunks of avocado, and other goodies from his serving tray to our table.

Across from me, Carla traced the carved wood on the arm of her dining chair with one finger. The vodka had put a little color back in her face, but shadows still bruised the skin beneath her brown eyes.

When the waiter left our table, she glanced at me.

"I feel so guilty. She must hate me."

I took me a moment to catch up mentally. "Jade won't hate you. You did what was right at the time. You provided her with a home and two parents."

Carla continued as If I hadn't spoken. "Stupid, getting pregnant like that. My father was so embarrassed. He started up with that woman, Tiffany, after Jade was born. My mother got sick and . . . you know the rest."

"Carla, stop it. You were young. You did not cause your mother to get cancer! It runs in your family."

"Thank you for reminding me."

Brisk movement near the dining room entrance caught my attention. The maitre d' was rushing toward two men standing in the entryway. The one in the foreground appeared to be Asian. He was tall and partially blocked my view of the second man. The maitre d' looked so anxious to please, I expected him to salute and click his heels.

Carla glanced over at them, and as the second man stepped forward, I heard her breath suck in.

"Look at his face!" she whispered.

I tried not to stare at the hideous red-and-white marks scarring the right side of Currito's face. "That's my new owner," I said.

"You're joking."

"Nope, his name's Currito Maldonista. He's the main reason I'm here."

"He looks like he was in a knife fight."

"I know, but he's okay," I said. "At least he loves his horses."

As the Maitre d' led the two men past us, several tables over, I checked out the profile of Currito's companion. Tall for an Asian, he was clean shaven with a small, smiling mouth and long, flat nose. Except for the smile, his face seemed almost immobile, the skin stiff. Something about his eyes seemed odd, but I didn't get a good enough look.

I swallowed the last bit of buttered roll, when Currito's head turned and his gaze flicked over us. His stride seemed to falter a moment, then the men disappeared past a fountain into another dining area.

After spearing a hot shrimp, I closed my eyes as the taste of shellfish, butter, and garlic hit my tongue. We were both quiet while we dug in, and I was pleased Carla had an appetite. The food seemed to revive her, and when her second drink arrived, instead of diving into it, she continued working on her salad.

Somewhere, a cell phone began playing a Sheryl Crow tune.

"That's mine." Carla reached for her black leather bag that featured a lot of silver zippers.

She found her phone immediately, she'd always been way more organized than me.

"Carla Ruben," she said in her business voice, then listened for a moment.

"Oh, George. I was just thinking about you. You do?" She closed her palm over the receiver and leaned toward me. "He's got a picture of Jade! No, I'm here George. At the Westin Diplomat. You *can?* That's wonderful. I'm in the dining room with my friend Nikki. I'm the blonde in black. Nikki has spiky dark hair. Yes. That's great, George! See you in ten."

I felt sick inside. Suppose the girl in George's photo was the girl who died on the street?

I squeezed my eyes shut a moment and when I opened them, I saw Currito Maldonista walking toward us. He came directly to our table, skirting halfway around, turning so the handsome side of his face was in full view – the ruined side partially hidden.

"Nikki, you must introduce me to your lovely friend." He smiled, flashing white teeth as he held out his left hand to Carla instead of the customary right. It kept the good side of his face to Carla.

I made the introductions, noticing how Currito couldn't take his eyes off Carla. She was a beautiful woman, but his stare seemed intense beyond that of a man admiring a woman. But I'm not a man, so what did I know?

"Have we met before, Miss Ruben?" he asked, finally dragging his attention from Carla and turning to include me, too.

"I don't believe so," she said.

Like she wouldn't remember if she'd seen *that* face before.

Carla frowned slightly. "You aren't involved with the hotel and restaurant industry, are you?"

Currito's focus sharpened onto Carla. He seemed fascinated by her. "What is it that you do, Miss Ruben?"

"She sells meat," I said, regretting my quick tongue when Currito started and took a half step back.

Carla's light laugh covered the momentary awkwardness. "I work for a Baltimore wholesaler. We sell quality meats to restaurants and hotels up and down the East Coast."

Currito appeared to relax, placing his hand on the back of an empty chair, smiling at Carla. "I see. A true businesswoman." Turning to me, he said, "And how are our horses, Nikki?"

When I gave him an update, his next words surprised me.

"I spoke to Mr. Ravinsky earlier. There is a race coming up for Diablo Valiente."

"There is? When?" I hoped I didn't sound as dubious as I felt. I had only galloped the horse and didn't even know when he'd last run. "Shouldn't we give him a work first?" I asked, referring to the morning speed works given to prep a horse for his next race.Unless, of course, the horse had run quite recently. I should have researched the past racing performances of Maldonista's horses and wished I hadn't spoken about the work. But too much had happened for me to keep on top of my game.

"There is no problem. I have arranged everything. Eduardo Carmanos will work the horse tomorrow morning. I will watch the work from the grandstand. The race is in four days."

This time I kept my mouth shut and simply nodded. Carla watched me – she knew me so well, I'd lay odds she knew I was fuming inside.

After taking a slow breath, I said, "Great. He's an excellent jockey. He'll ride Diablo in the race, then?"

Currito nodded, his glance resting again on Carla. "Jim Ravinsky knows the details." Of course Currito would want a top jockey. I didn't really want to ride that beast anyway, did I?

I could see fluid starting to leak from the outside corner of Currito's bad eye. He pulled his silk kerchief, but instead of dabbing at the liquid, he said, "But I interrupt your meal. It has been a pleasure to meet you." He nodded at Carla, then left abruptly.

"He's an odd one," said Carla.

"Especially when he's got that eye thing going on." I poked at my shrimp with less interest.

"He can't help that." She took a big sip of her second vodka. "Why were you upset about the race thing?"

"Because the horse just got here, I don't know when or how well he raced last, I don't know what kind of race he's in, and I don't like Eduardo Carmanos."

Carla leaned back in her chair. "And he's a male jockey and everyone making decisions for you is male, and you weren't included."

"Yeah, that too."

"What's wrong with this Carmanos guy?"

"His nickname is 'The Intimidator.' He's a macho man and almost ran me off the track one time in a race."

"Need a slug of this?" She held up her vodka.

"No, I'm fine. Besides, I beat the bastard in that race."

Carla grinned, but it faded quickly as a red-haired man in a wrinkled gray suit walked into the dining room, looked around, then made a beeline toward us. He carried a black briefcase.

"That must be George, the detective. I haven't met him, only seen his photo online. He –" she had to clear her throat before she could continue. "He'll have a picture of Jade."

Her upper teeth pressed into her lip so hard, I expected to see drops of blood.

George Turner looked rushed and rumpled in tired clothes, with his black-framed glasses sitting crookedly on his nose.

Carla frowned. "He looked better online."

Though tired and stressed, she didn't have a hair out of place, and her black knit suit was impeccable.

When George reached us, he held his hand out to Carla, and after introductions were made, he set his briefcase on our table.

I stared and felt a little kick of adrenalin. When I glanced at Carla, she seemed frozen in place, like she'd forgotten how to move or breathe.

"I have two pictures for you," George said, unsnapping the clasps on his case. "The first one is from the school. The second I was able to get from Mrs. Paulson's sister."

Why couldn't the police have done this for Carla?

George pulled out an eight-by-twelve envelope. "I don't know who the other girl is in the second picture, but it's the more telling of the two photos." He held the envelope out to Carla.

She stared at it, but didn't move.

"Carla," I said, "take a breath."

She did, suddenly coming to life and snatching the envelope from George's hand. She jerked the flap open, and two photos slid out.

I was out of my chair and looking over her shoulder by the time the pictures hit the table. I stared at the images, and my knees almost buckled with relief.

"It's not her! Carla, it's not the girl who died on the street!"

Carla bit her lip as she struggled to get a grip on herself. I exhaled slowly and studied the pictures. The first was obviously a school portrait. A lovely young woman who looked a lot like Carla gazed solemnly at the camera. Her hair was long and blond, her eyes brown and bright with intelligence. Like Carla's.

The second picture took my breath away. Jade had posed with the unknown girl friend. The friend was cute, but Jade was drop-dead gorgeous. Nubile and curvaceous, she wore a magenta miniskirt and skintight top. Lipstick covered full lips and shadow turned her eyes smoky and alluring.

But it was her expression that twisted my heart – wistful and lost, like a child alone on the street.

I shook my head to clear the image and looked at the legs beneath the miniskirt. Miles long and shapely, just like her mother's.

Carla's fingertips trembled where they rested on the edge of the photos. I could almost feel the electric shock coursing through her. She hadn't said a word, but tears were streaming down her face.

Chapter 16

When I woke up on January fourth, I stretched beneath the covers, then remembered it was opening day for the Gulfstream Park meet – the day Eduardo Carmanos would ride Diablo in a five-eighths-of-a-mile work. I scooted out of bed and sped into the bathroom.

When I arrived at the track, I stopped at the stable gate and picked up the new overnight sheet with a list of races scheduled for January 8. Scanning the page I found Diablo and Carmanos named in the ninth, going a mile and a sixteenth in an allowance race – the type a step up from a claimer, but not as classy as a stake's race. Diablo shouldn't have any trouble with the distance.

As I headed toward my barn, a restless energy filled the backstretch. For many of the grooms, trainers and jockeys, the waiting was almost over. The low hum of human excitement flowed into the horses, and a filly got loose in the next barn over. She ran free for almost five minutes, galloping wildly down our shedrow, snorting and bucking. Diablo almost broke open his stall gate, and I sighed with relief when they caught the runaway. Fortunately, she hadn't hurt herself.

Eduardo arrived on time, and he looked just the way I remembered, eyes predatory over a sharp, hawk-like nose, lips curled in an arrogant smile. For once, Diablo's behavior pleased me. He wiped the smirk right off Eduardo's mouth by shoving his large, Roman-nosed head over the stall gate, baring his teeth, and snapping them inches from Eduardo's face.

Eduardo's eyes narrowed, and he took a quick step back.

"Is he manageable?" he asked me, his glance flicking

toward the track.

"I rode him out there yesterday," I said.

Right about then, Beth and Bullwinkle showed up, and Diablo nickered at the huge gelding.

The previous evening I'd arranged for the pony-girl to bring the monstrous Bullwinkle to our barn this morning to escort Eduardo and Diablo through their warm up and on to the starting gate.

Taking advantage of Diablo's fascination with Bullwinkle, Orlando and I got the colt's tack on, Eduardo into the saddle, and the colt turned over to Beth who took them for a few turns around the shedrow. I climbed on the bay filly, Imparable, and followed at a safe distance. When Diablo and his rider turned a corner ahead of me, I could see the colt's eye rolling back to glare at Eduardo. Diablo's back was humped up, a clear sign of a pending explosion.

We made it out to the track, and Imparable's action -- smooth, quick and powerful -- lifted my spirits. When Beth eased Diablo into a slow gallop ahead of us, I steered Imparable closer to the rail, and she switched into high gear like she'd been released from a slingshot. She did not have a long ground-eating stride that needed to build on momentum, she produced speed in an instant. Like Jim had said, she was a sprinter.

I steadied her back to an open gallop. She was the kind of horse who listened and didn't live up to her name which translated to "unstoppable." Still, we blew by Bullwinkle and Diablo like they were parking meters. I planned to gallop my filly a mile, then jog her to the starting gate to see Diablo break. I would have preferred to watch the colt more closely, but I still had to get La Bruja out and didn't have the luxury of time.

After Imparable and I motored around the mile-oval one time, slowed to a jog, and walked toward the gate, I could make out Bullwinkle towering over a black horse on the far side of the starting gate. I still had time.

I could almost feel Currito watching his horses train from the grandstand with his top-of-the-line Leica binoculars. He could probably read my mind with those things.

I urged Imparable into a jog, passed by the side of the gate and into the chute behind. Several horses milled about with Diablo and Bullwinkle. A figure hurrying toward us from beyond the rail turned out to be Orlando. What was he doing here? Maybe he had a dark side with a taste for mayhem.

The head starter, a tall muscular guy named Greg Haskell, gave me a questioning look. "You working from the gate?"

"No. I just want to see how that black colt breaks."

Haskell nodded, and I rode Imparable to the back end of the chute close enough to watch, yet keep the filly out of trouble. I kept her moving in a wide circle so her muscles wouldn't tie up.

By now, Orlando had reached the rail, where he paused and stared at Diablo. Even his double gold-earrings that flashed in the morning sun weren't bright enough to lighten his dubious expression. Probably observing the humped back and Diablo's latest addition -- violent tail-swishing.

An assistant starter took the lead strap from Beth. Diablo resisted the man, bucking twice and rising in a half-rear. The starter held on, then tried to lead the colt closer to the gate. Diablo's bared his teeth and sank them into the man's arm. The guy screamed, and Eduardo's crop flashed as he struck Diablo's neck. The colt dropped the man's arm, then reared like a skyscraper, twisted, and fell against the gate. His weight pinned Eduardo against the steel cage.

Frozen in place, I watched Diablo scrabble away from the gate. Eduardo dropped to the ground like a squashed bug, but somehow staggered to his feet. His face was a mask of pain, and one arm and looked twisted and broken.

Eduardo was hurt bad, and my colt was going to be *ruled off.*

I jumped from Imparable. "Orlando! Hold this filly."

He did, and I ran to where Diablo stood, eyes defiant, lead strap trailing beneath him onto the ground. Three of the gate crew formed a loose circle around him. The one with the savaged arm was leading Eduardo to safety, and no doubt, they'd both head for the hospital.

"Hey big stuff," I said softly. Diablo's head turned. His ears pricked toward me, and his head lowered a tad.

"Beth," I called, "can you bring Bullwinkle over here?" She did, and Diablo pushed his nose against the giant horse's neck. Beth leaned forward in her saddle and grabbed the strap.

The gate crew guys stepped back and began to look around at the other horses and jockeys still behind the gate.

"I need a leg up," I said to the head starter.

Haskell turned and stared at me like I'd sprouted hooves and a tail.

"Are you serious?" he asked.

"Don't do it," whispered Beth.

"This horse needs to work." I said. "Will you help me out?"

Haskell's eyes were shadowed by the bill of his ball cap and I couldn't read them.

"If somebody take this filly, I do it," Orlando said, leading Imparable toward us. "I not afraid!"

Haskell shrugged, and gave a nod to a crewman, who took Imparable from Orlando. I walked to Diablo and put my palm near his nostril, sort of testing him. When he stayed calm, I stroked his neck, and he leaned slightly into my hand.

"Let's do it," I said to Orlando, and quick as a wink he lifted me onto Diablo's saddle.

I continued to pat the black neck as I spoke to Haskell. "I'm thinking we should open the front door as well as the back for this colt, and put his pony just outside the exit door. This colt might walk right in to see his buddy."

"We'll try it one time," Haskell said, his expression

hard. "But if he goes nuts, you're going to have to get him out of here." He glanced at the impatient faces of the other riders. "Those horses have to work, too."

Beth circled Bullwinkle around the gate and parked him outside the two hole after Greg opened the exit door. A guy named Fred took Diablo's strap from Orlando, who flipped back his long hair.

"Nikki, I go to barn now. Everything be ready when you come back."

Something about his expression told me he was thinking, "*If you come back.*"

But he was a godsend, and I told him so. He grinned at me. A crewman gave Orlando a leg onto Imparable, and he jogged the filly away.

I stared at the massive metal cage before me and took a deep breath. Patting Diablo's neck, I clucked at him and gave a light squeeze with my legs as Fred started to lead him in. Bullwinkle nickered at Diablo, and my colt strode boldy into the gate behind Fred. The crewman removed the lead strap, quickly hopped onto the metal rail beside Diablo's head, and held onto one rein.

When they locked us in, I swallowed and glanced at Fred. He looked a little shaky. A sour odor wafted from his skin. I kept stroking the colt's neck, choking back the fear when Beth reined Bullwinkle off to the side and away from us.

As they loaded three other horses, I could feel the rage draining from Diablo. I gathered the rubber-covered reins, crossing them over his neck. I held the cross with one hand, and grabbed a handful of mane with the other. As soon as the last horse was in, a gap opened in the traffic out on the track. Haskell hit the release.

With a clanging bell and a crash of metal, we exploded from the gate. Diablo broke well, but took longer than his companions to lengthen his stride. I'd been so used to seeing him next to Bullwinkle, I'd forgotten how big this colt was. I could feel his powerful hindquarters driving us forward.

Ahead, two horses ran nose to nose on the lead, and the third hugged the rail to our left, surging a half-length in front of us.

Diablo's body lowered to the ground as he stretched his neck out, found his stride, and began to run. We passed the third horse and quickly drew even with the two on the lead. Three across, we flew around the turn, and at the top of the stretch, I asked him. He opened up and tore past the eighth pole like a runaway train. I glanced back under one arm, astonished to see we were a good three lengths ahead. I sat real chilly and let the wire come to us, standing in the stirrups and asking the colt to ease his speed.

With a snug hold, I eventually got his nose down closer to his chest and his speed down to rapid gallop. I couldn't use him up with a race scheduled in only four days!

But I couldn't pull him up, and we passed by the gate and headed down the backstretch again. How do you stop a locomotive?

With relief, I saw Bullwinkle lumbering into a gallop ahead of us and crowding in close as we sped to him. Beth leaned over and grabbed Diablo's left rein, and soon we were cantering, jogging, and finally walking down the backstretch.

Gasping for air, I said, "Did you see *that?*"

"This devil can run!" she said. "Bite, too."

"Have you heard how Eduardo is?" I asked.

"Not yet, but bet you a bag of bagels he won't be riding in that allowance race.

Chapater 17

When I rode Diablo onto the shedrow and dismounted, Curitto and the tall Asian I'd seen at the Diplomat restaurant were waiting for us. Since they'd watched the work from the grandstand, they must have seen Diablo crush poor Eduardo into the starting gate, but they appeared unconcerned and asked no questions.

Orlando, halter in hand, grasped the colt's rein and led Diablo into his stall. I followed, closing the stall gate behind me. After unbuckling the girth, I pulled the small saddle from Diablo's back. By then, Orlando had removed Diablo's bridle and replaced it with his halter.

Currito stood outside the gate, staring with open admiration at his colt. "Good job, Nikki!"

He smiled broadly. I hadn't seen him do this before. The effect was horrible, pushing his jagged scar up, wrinkling and folding it until it looked like a red-and-white worm.

Had the guy never heard of plastic surgery?

"Thanks," I said, turning away quickly and pulling the bridle from Diablo's head.

Still holding my saddle, I followed as Orlando lead the colt from the stall to cool him out.

Currito moved down the shedrow to the two filly stalls, making a fuss over both of them, stroking Imparable's neck, and murmuring to La Bruja in Spanish. He surprised me by pulling several carrots from his suit pocket and feeding them to his girls. He was a sucker for horses, which was okay in my book.

But his companion loitered indifferently in the aisle way. Chakri's silky, midnight blue suit displayed a fabric so fine and fit so excellent, it had to be custom made. He caught me staring and though he kept his face immobile as plastic, his eyes revealed an intense energy. The same small smile I'd seen in the restaurant stamped his mouth.

"Nikki," Currito said behind me. "This is Tau Chakri,"

"My pleasure," Chakri said, with a stiff nod and a slight bend forward.

I might recognize a Chinese or Vietnamese accent, but Chakri's was unknown territory. I gave him my best fake smile.

"Is racing popular where you're from?"

"Not really, no." He turned to Currito. "Shouldn't we go?"

"You must pardon Tau," Currito said. "He just flew in from Bangkok, and is anxious to attend to business."

"Sure," I said. "I need to get La Bruja out, anyway." I spotted the smaller filly-bridle hanging outside Imparable's stall and moved to grab it.

"Nikki, wait. There's a matter I need to discuss."

I was really short on time, but turned back to Currito with my expression set on pleasant-mode.

"The jockey's agent called me," Currito said. "Eduardo is in the hospital. Crushed ribs, a dislocated shoulder." Currito paused, and studied me a moment. "You would not have been my first pick to ride Diablo."

Gee, thanks.

"But after the way you handled the . . . situation this morning –"

Situation? Eduardo and I could have been killed!

" . . . I want you to ride him in the stake."

His words caught me off guard.

"Um, really? I mean, that's great. I'd love to ride him!"

Wow, a ride in a Gulfstream Park race. On a really good horse. *Who might kill me in the gate . . . .*

Currito pulled a fancy stopwatch from his coat pocket. "Diablo worked five furlongs in fifty-nine and three. He went the last furlong in eleven flat! He will get the bullet!"

I understood Currito's excitement. This was a really good horse! The best dirt horse I'd ridden. Working five-eighths of a mile in under a minute was excellent. If he got the bullet on the charts, it meant he'd run the fastest five-eighths of any horse working that distance at Gulfstream that day, and –

"So," Currito said, "You'll do it?"

"Yes."

I could feel Chakri's stare. A weird light in his eyes intensified as if feeding off my excitement. I shrugged, grabbed the bridle, and double-timed it to La Bruja's stall, anxious to escape the weight of Chakri's stare.

#

When I returned to the barn after galloping La Bruja -- a spooky, long-striding grey filly with plenty of stamina – Currito and buddy were long gone.

Orlando, with a little help from a groom named Afilio, had the barn spic and span, Imparable already put away, and Diablo bathed and in the last stages of cooling out. Turned out, Afilio was the guy who had scrounged up feed and hay that first morning when Currito's horses had arrived.

I handed La Bruja over to Orlando and sighed. We'd gotten through the morning and were establishing a nice rhythm to our routine.

Around me, the scent of sea water, underlaid with the tang of horse liniment and the sweet smell of molasses, rode along the warm air. I wanted to lie down on a hay bale and sleep forever. But I had to feed first, then I could return to my motel and crash.

Except Carla strode around the corner in silver designer-sneakers, shrink wrapped in a sleeveless black top and matching capri-length pants. She didn't have any of those don't-look-at-me-I'm-having-a-bad-day ensembles like other gals.

"Nikki!" she said as she closed the gap between us, silver hoop earrings swinging on her ears. "George called. He has a contact in the Boca Raton police department. They got a hit on Jade and agency called White Sand Careers."

"What kind of agency?"

"They do career development for women – like marketing, modeling and name branding," Carla said. "Jade's name was on their applicant list.

"I have to go there, see what I can find out. Today. *Now*. Will you come with me?"

This sounded like a good lead, only I couldn't go with her. Color flushed Carla's face and purpose pumped her body. This was the old Carla, and I was glad to see it. She'd done so much for me. I couldn't turn her down. Maybe I could ask Orlando – The noise of a motor distracted my thoughts. Jim Ravnisky drove his Ford pickup truck and trailer toward our barn. *Now?* As he got closer I could see how tired he was. Had he always looked so old? His hair beneath his cap so gray?

I had to help him with his horses. *And make sure the bandages were washed and hung to dry. The tack cleaned, the water buckets topped off. The shedrow wet down with spray to settle the dust.* I twisted the ring on my finger so hard, it hurt.

"Carla," I said, pointing at the truck, "that's Jim. I have to help him unload and stuff."

"Oh," Carla said, and some of the energy drained from her face.

"I'll go with you a little later. I just can't right now."

"I could really use your support," she said, her expression starting to tighten.

"Carla, I'm sorry –"

Her lips parted and she held up one hand. "My daughter's not waiting on your schedule."

"Carla, let me talk to Jim. Maybe –"

"*Forget* it! I shouldn't have wasted time coming to ask you." She turned and stalked away down the long shedrow aisle.

I started after her, but Orlando stepped out of a nearby stall, blocking my path.

"Is Imparable," he said. "She got heat in her leg. You wan' to look before I put the bandage?"

All that riding her in circles behind the starting gate. Had I injured her leg?

"Cold-hose it for 20 minutes," I said to Orlando. "If there's heat in the tissue, we have to get it out before it does more damage."

Orlando gave me a "who doesn't know that" eye-roll as I heard the creak of Jim's truck door. Jim climbed out of the cab. And now I had to tell him his new owner's horse was injured?

"Jim," I called, "you're here just in time. Can you look at Imparable's leg before we do her up?" I referred to the lineament, poultice and support bandaging we still needed to put on her legs.

"Yeah." The lines on his face creased sharply. He knew I wouldn't ask him to look at the filly's leg unless something was wrong.

Just then, Carla, her back stiff with anger, reached the far end of the shedrow and disappeared around the corner of the barn.

Sometimes I hated my life.

Chapter 18

Later that morning, Jim and I sat at a laminated tabletop in the "kitchen" at Gulfstream Park eating an early lunch. Jim worked on a burrito smothered in salsa, while I munched on a grilled cheese.

Like all track kitchens – or cafes – this one was doing a brisk trade, the Latinos behind the counter baking tortillas, stirring pots of chile, rice and refried beans. On the grill, hamburgers sizzled, and french fries crisped in the hot oil vat nearby. Yogurt, salads, and cold sandwiches lay behind fogged-over glass in a refrigerated case.

I'd just brought Jim up to date about Currito and his three horses, and one question rode me hard. "It wasn't your decision to put Diablo in that allowance race so soon, was it?"

"Nope."

"I didn't think so." I took a sip of cold water.

He frowned, brows drawing closer. "Sure you want to ride him, Nik? I can put somebody else on him."

Jim had always looked out for me, he knew I could get hurt on Diablo. But I didn't want to ruffle Currito's feathers. The Columbian could pull his horses in a second. There were plenty of other trainers at Gulfstream. Top ones, too. Riding a horse like Diablo in a stake was a hell of an opportunity. And we *needed* the income.

"Yeah, I'll ride him."

Jim nodded, and after we finished, he pushed his chair back.

"How did you find this Currito Maldonista guy, anyway?" I asked.

Jim hesitated a moment. "Friend of a friend."

"What friend?"

He emptied his water bottle, then stacked it on his plate with his plastic knife and fork. He fidgeted with his napkin, wiping some crumbs into a pile.

"Jim, what friend?

"Amarilla knows a guy who knows Maldonista."

"Well *that's* a great reference. Most of her buddies are in *jail*."

I'd met and last seen Amarilla when I'd worked a meet at Virginia's Colonial Downs. I'd nicknamed her Yellow Jacket, because of her stinging personality and her fondness for yellow clothing.

Jim pushed his pile of trash to one side, pursing his lips. I could tell he was getting nervous. "She paid her bills, Nikki. You won good money riding her horses."

Hard to argue with that. We'd both made money, and deadbeat owners are no fun. At least Amarilla wasn't one of those.

"Yeah. But who was the other connection?" Anyone I know?"

"Doubt it. Fellow named Anthony DeSilvio."

"What? I *met* him. He's an arrogant piece of crap. Thinks women exist to please him!"

The way Jim was tapping his lip with one finger made me suspect he knew more about DeSilvio then he was letting on.

"Nikki, what's eating you? Has Maldonista done something?"

"No," I said. "He's fine. He really loves that colt. He's been nice to me."

"Then what?"

I didn't want to involve Jim in Carla's problems with her daughter, or for that matter, me with a murdered girl at my feet. I looked about the room, searching for a little white lie. The glass doors opened and Orlando walked in.

"Hey, there's our new groom," I said. "He's working out great." I waved him over and introduced him properly to

Jim. We'd all been like high-speed launches passing each other in the shedrow earlier. I didn't think they'd done more than nod at each other.

Orlando flipped his long hair back, and the sun shining through the glass doors lit the gold in his ears. His white teeth flashed above his moustache.

"Mr. Ravinsky, I am honored to meet you. Nikki is good assistant, but is better to have a man in charge."

His moustache twitched. Was he smirking?

"You know," I said, "it's a relief for me too. It's been tough not having a man around until now." I smiled at Orlando.

#

Outside my motel room, I set my plastic grocery bag down and worked my fingers into the inside pocket of my tote bag for my key. Next door, where Stella and Lou lived, the door opened as wide as the inside chain would allow, and Scat the Cat flew out the opening in a flash of orange-and-black fur.

I needed a quick nap, didn't feel like talking to anyone, and pushed my key into the lock before Stella or Lou unlatched that chain and came out. I slung my tote over my shoulder, but before I could grab the grocery bag, Scat sidled over and bumped it with her forehead.

"Stop that."

I grabbed the bag before the cat could knock over the sea horse box I'd carefully placed inside atop a loaf of bread, three oranges, and two cans of tuna fish. Could the cat smell fish inside a sealed can? I opened my door, she darted into the room.

"I'm not sharing," I said. "Forget about it."

After putting the groceries away, I scooped up Scat and set her outside my room. Her tail twitched, and she threw me a resentful stare.

"Check back later," I said, and closed the door.

A reflection from the sea horse box where I'd laid it on the small kitchenette table, drew me over. I picked the box up and turned it slowly. I traced the starfish and shells on the sides with my finger and looked for a way to get in.

This was stupid. This Klaire character had to be a charlatan. How could a box help me find Jade, or help Carla? A jab of guilt prodded me. I should have gone with Carla, but then I would have left Jim to do my work. I grabbed my phone and tried to reach her for the third time since she left that morning, but, again it went straight to voice mail.

I carried the box to the bed, where I set it next to me, before stretching out and closing my eyes.

#

I woke up with a narrow shaft of sunlight on my face. The beam had slipped through the crack between the window frame and the closed blinds as the sun slanted toward evening. The digital clock said three p.m. I'd slept for almost two hours. When I stretched and sat back against the headboard, it bumped the blinds and freed a slice of light to illuminate the sea horse box. Vivid, and in suddenly bright relief, a seam on the side just below the lid revealed itself.

I grabbed the box. After several frustrating attempts, and a bad word or two, I discovered that by pressing on the starfish inlaid on the side, I could move the whole panel forward. A four inch, black velvet bag lay inside. Turning the box over in my hand, I shook it gently. The bag slipped into my palm and a tremor of apprehension zinged me. Maybe there was poison or something inside. *Stop being ridiculous.* I pried open the drawstrings at the top and dropped a carved figure onto my pillow.

An exquisite jade mermaid clung to a rock as curling waves swirled around her, trying to sweep her away. This was no knickknack, the detail was incredible. I was certain if I touched her hair, my fingers would come away wet. Her skin would not be the cold of stone, but the cold of fear.

I leaned over and stared at the young face. Her eyes were wistful, not yet without hope. Was this how I'd looked to Jim at 13 when he found me hiding in a stall in his barn at Pimlico?

I stared into the stone face and felt my heart pounding. *She looked like the murder victim.*

I scrambled off the bed, putting distance between myself and the mermaid. What if I'd opened the box with Carla in the car? I grabbed my phone and called her again. Once more it went straight to her voice mail.

I paced the room with the phone for a moment, feeling anger build. Damn this Klaire woman. She'd set me up with this box business, and if she knew anything, she'd damn well better tell me!

As I scrolled through my address list, my phone suddenly vibrated and rang so loud, I almost dropped it.

"*Carla?*" I said.

Slow and breathless, a voice said, "Your friend Carla is in trouble. You must help her."

"Is this Klaire?" I didn't try to keep my tone civil. "Where are you? I have questions for you. I want to know –"

"I will be right there," Klaire said.

"But you don't know where –"

A distinct click sounded in my ear. She'd disconnected. Damn it. I called her back and went straight to voice mail. Didn't anyone answer their phone anymore?

From across the room, the mermaid stared at me.

Chapter 19

Klaire Voyante drove me down the exit ramp of I-95 in her black Jaguar XF and headed into the outskirts of Fort Lauderdale. I'd never have guessed the rickety garage next to her weathered beach-house held a fifty-thousand-dollar vehicle.

Like the unexpectedly nice furniture in her house, the car furthered my suspicions she made plenty suckering people with hokey information and false hopes. *But she'd known that Carla had gone to the White Sands modeling agency.* Unless, of course, someone had told her.

Klaire hooked a sharp left, making her bronze-and-silver bracelets clink and her long beaded hair swing in my direction.

After grabbing the leather handle by my head, I said, "So you're telling me you had a vision of Carla being at this White Sands place, and she was in some sort of trouble. Can you be more specific?"

"I told you," she said, swerving to avoid a Cadillac whose white-haired driver had stopped in the middle of an intersection for no apparent reason. "These things come to me in a wave. They are powerful, and then they are gone. I know what I see in that instant, no more."

We were on our way to the White Sands. "Are we on a rescue mission, or what?" I asked.

"I told you, we will help your friend, if we can. The vision was strong, she should be there."

Great, and I should be at the track soon. We passed alongside an industrial park with warehouses and boat-repair yards. Even here, palm trees sprouted from concrete planters and soared over the flat-roofed commercial buildings. I didn't think it would be wise to ask Klaire yet again exactly what she'd seen. The most I'd gotten from her since I climbed into her car was "Carla frightened, Carla grabbed by a man, Carla taken away."

If I wasn't so spooked by events since my arrival in Florida, I wouldn't have given two dead flies for Klaire's "vision." Or her suggestion I find a sea horse box.

I blinked and gave myself a mental head slap. I'd been so busy trying to worm information from her since she'd showed at my motel, I'd never mentioned the mermaid.

"Klaire, I found the sea horse box. But you probably already *know* that, right?"

"Yes. You found the box, you opened it, and I sensed your fear. I believe your fear brought on the vision of your friend, Carla. I told you finding the box would help."

"Oh, for god's sake. This is –

"And when you opened the box, you saw Jade."

"*Jade?* You're saying Carla's daughter is drowning in the ocean? This whole thing feels like a set up. How convenient to find a carving matching your dream about a 'girl in the sea.'"

"Listen to me," she said sharply as she turned the Jag into a long concrete driveway. "Maybe sometimes I tell people things they want to hear. It's not hard, people give so much away when they are searching for answers. They might as well give their money to me, right?"

Just like I'd thought. A charlatan. And now that she'd stepped out of her closet, she'd dropped the breathy, soothsayer voice.

She glared at me. "Don't look at me like that. Some people are happier – more at peace – if they can speak to a loved one on the other side. Fine, go ahead and roll those blue eyes. Believe you know everything." She paused, as if to get control and spoke more softly.

"But sometimes I *do* get visions. I can't control them, I can't make them come, they just do, especially when there is someone receptive involved like you. You are like a radio tower. You pass things on."

Oh great, now I was a radio tower.

Up ahead, several two-story buildings blocked the horizon. One, stuccoed in a cream color, displayed a black-and-white sign reading, "White Sands Agency."

"Okay," I said. "I get that sometimes you see things. But so what? Why are you helping us? I mean, what's in it for you?"

"Nikki," she said, "I've seen your childhood, how you fought to avoid wrong turns in the road. I . . . failed to avoid those turns." She stopped speaking, and her hands gripped the steering wheel hard as she stared at the cream building ahead.

A Broward County police cruiser was parked in front. A dark sedan with numerous short antennas sat next to it, and parked haphazardly before the entrance to the modeling agency was a big white van. The words "Broward County Vice Unit" emblazoned the side.

Klaire parked her Jag and left the engine going just as the door to the agency burst open and a bunch of uniformed officers herded and shoved a dozen or so young women toward the white van. It was noisy, the women yelling at the cops, and the cops shouting back and pushing some of the loudest female protestors hard.

"Crap," she said. "We're too late."

One girl fell onto the pavement. A cop leaned over to pull her to her feet, and I could see Carla just behind him.

"That's Carla!" I tried to find my door handle. But I was unfamiliar with the car, and groped a moment. I found the handle and grabbed it, only to discover I was locked in. "Klaire, open this!"

"No," she said. "That's a prostitution bust. You don't want to go out there."

"I don't care," I shouted. "Let me out."

A cop shoved the young woman who'd fallen and

Carla into the white police van. Quieter and more sullen now, the last few women were quickly herded inside. The cops slammed the double doors shut and three of them jumped into the front of the van. The other four rushed over to the cruiser, their polished, heavy boots clapping against the pavement. The whole entourage revved up and screeched out of the parking lot.

"Go after her!" I said.

"Honey, she's not going anywhere but the police station. The best thing we can do now is get her a lawyer."

"But she's not a prostitute!"

Klaire raised one brow. "Doesn't matter. I told you I took some wrong turns -- I used to be in the life. I don't have to be a psychic to know that gal's going to be processed."

"Could you unlock the door? I have to get out of this car!" I was about to go *psycho*.

Klaire pushed a button, and my door lock clicked.

I climbed out of the car just as the door to the "agency" opened and Detective Rick Harman walked out.

Chapter 20

"Detective Harman," I called, rushing to him. "Why was Carla arrested? You know she's not a hooker!"

"Hold on a minute," he said, leveling brown eyes at me. "Your friend was in that gang of hookers they just hauled out?"

"Like you didn't know!"

"I didn't." The lines around his mouth and eyes creased in confusion. "Why are *you* here?"

"Um . . ." I didn't want to admit my appearance was due to visions of a psychic prostitute. I turned and looked at Klaire. "That woman in the car told me –"

I was saved from further stammering when Klaire cut her engine and climbed out of the Jaguar.

A smile played at the corners of Harman's mouth. "Ms. *Voyante*. Imagine seeing you here. Thought you were out of the business."

"You know I am," she said.

"Hard to believe it when you show up at an escort service."

Escort service? Damn it. But I didn't want to stand around while Harman and Klaire caught up on old times.

I glared at Harman. "What about Carla Ruben?"

"Look, if she was up front with the officers that removed the women, I didn't see her. I came in the back with a couple of guys to secure the files and computers. Why don't you tell me why she was here? For that matter," he said, his gaze flicking from me to Klaire, "why don't you explain why *both* of you are here,"

The sun was heating up the pavement. Sweat trickled between my breasts and I could see beads forming on

Harman's forehead. I fanned myself, and Harman took the hint.

"Why don't we step inside where it's cooler, and you two can tell me all about it."

#

Inside the chilled reception area, misleading photos of attractive young women in conservative attire lined the walls above swanky furniture upholstered in plush taupe-and-brown fabric. The photos looked more like employee-of-the-month shots than girl-for-a-night rental ads.

I perched on a side chair, Harman sank into a big arm chair, and Klaire chose a love seat. I told him about George, the private eye.

"So," I said, "when George told Carla about this place, she came to look for Jade. She asked me to go with her, but I couldn't leave the track that early. Klaire was kind enough to give me a ride over."

Harman snorted. "That's Klaire, the milk of human kindness." Still, the gleam in his eyes was friendly as he glanced at Klaire. "What's the real story? You have a vision?"

"As a matter of fact, Rick, I did," she said.

Huh, first name basis. Since Harman was vice, they probably had a long history. I stared at her as she lounged on the love seat looking perfectly relaxed. All traces of the breathy, soothsayer voice had vanished. Still, she had the Voodoo priestess beads in her hair and all those strange rings on her fingers.

Harman turned to Klaire, his expression thoughtful. "You know anything about another young woman. One that might have disappeared?"

"I'm sorry," she said, "I don't.

I leaned forward. "You mean another girl is missing? Like Jade?"

"That's one of the reasons we're here," he said. "A gal

that was working out of this place went missing a few days ago."

"Is it . . ." I began.

He held up a hand. "It's not the girl who died on Hallandale. And I only mention this new case to show you how dangerous your involvement could be. Understand me, Ms. Latrelle?"

I let out a breath and settled back in my chair. "Sure, okay. But what about Carla? You know she doesn't belong in jail with those other women. Can you do something to help her?"

"I'll make a call for you," he said.

"And I already called Matisse," Klaire told Harman. Glancing at me, she said, "Before I got out of the car. He's my lawyer. He's on his way to the station."

"Then we'll get it sorted out," Harman said. "I'm sorry Ms. Ruben got mixed up in this. But this is what happens when you people try to play detective. Listen up," he said with a harder edge to his voice. "Stay out of trouble and let us do our job."

Tough voice, but his concern seemed genuine enough, so I nodded. As I stood, exhaustion overwhelmed me, and I pressed my hand against the chair arm for support.

A uniformed officer appeared in the hallway. If he was surprised to see Klaire and me, he didn't show it. "Detective Harman, those file drawers you found – and the two computers? We got 'em stowed in the van out back. Is that about it?"

"Yeah, we're done, and these ladies are leaving."

As Klaire and I left, Harman pulled a phone from his suit jacket. He'd better be making that call about Carla.

When I stepped into the heat with the acrid odor of tar rising from the blacktop, it hit me. Klaire's vision had been spot on. No denying it. Harman had even asked her if she knew anything about another missing girl, as if maybe the police consulted her, like I'd always heard they did with psychics. And he apparently *had* been in the back of the place with the files and computers. Maybe he hadn't seen Carla.

#

By the time Klaire drove me around the traffic circle in Hollywood on our way back to Hallandale Beach, the sun had slid toward the western horizon. Traffic was building and a train finishing its crawl across Hollywood Boulevard had made the congestion worse.

Outside the car, store front windows enticed the eye with decorative artwork, lingerie, and paintings. The canvasses on display seemed lit from within by vivid blues, greens and aqua colors. The lingerie favored hot pink, cream, and black satin.

At a stoplight, a woman who had to be at least seventy crossed the street. She wore a scoop-necked top, a snake-print mini-skirt, and fringed, black desert-boots. No one paid her any mind. Hard to tell the housewives from the hookers in South Florida.

Glancing at Klaire's hands on the steering wheel, I studied the carved rings on her fingers. A scorpion, a fish, a lion, a goat, and other astrological signs. Maybe they helped her read her customers?

"I'd go with you into the station," she said, "but I've got clients coming. Okay if I just drop you off there?"

"Sure," I said.

The light changed, and Klaire eased the car forward. "Carla is fine," she said. "I'd know if she wasn't."

My cell went off before I could reply with a smart comment.

Carla's voice. "Nikki, it's me."

"Are you okay? I saw them put you in that police van. "

"You were *there*?"

I explained the whats and whys of my presence at the scene. "I'm on my way to the police station now."

"Don't bother," Carla said. "We're just leaving. Detective Harman . . . Rick . . . made some calls. He got me released. He's driving me back to the hotel now. Thank your friend Klaire for that lawyer, but I didn't need him."

This had moved fast. Harman must have switched on the magic lights in his unmarked police car and whisked himself to the station to rescue Carla. Hell, they all fell for her.

"Nikki," she said, "why don't you come to the Diplomat and have a drink with me?

Thank God she was okay. But I had to get back to the barn and told her so.

"Can we get something to eat later?" I asked.

We made arrangements and disconnected.

Klaire glanced at me. "I told you she was all right."

Chapter 21

Looking for Carla and the hotel bar that evening, I tread quietly in my sneakers across the polished-to-a-mirror finish of the Diplomat lobby floor. The rectangular pattern of black-on-white lines resembled a game of tic-tac-toe. With all that was going on, I felt like a mobile X hoping to fill in the questions left by Carla's daughter. I just didn't know who else played on the board.

Ahead of me, the hotel lobby rose into an atrium, with palm trees growing from unseen planters beneath the tic-tac-toe patterned floor. The lobby ended in a glass wall. Outside, tiled terraces with tables, chairs, white cabanas, large blue umbrellas and multiple swimming pools descended toward the white sand that stretched to the turquoise ocean.

I found the indoor bar. I'd assumed it would be dark, with disreputable politicians and doctors' wives hidden away in the corners. But it was paneled in pale blond wood, with matching chairs upholstered in soft blue. Orange paper lanterns hung over the bar. No booths, no curtains, no place to hide.

I spotted Carla's luminescent hair and paused. She had her back to me and she wasn't alone. Harman, intent on her face sat opposite her, facing in my direction. When he saw me, he nodded, which made Carla turn. She waved.

Harman was a good looking man. Carla probably liked him.

"Buy you a drink?" he asked. "I think the department owes you one to make up for earlier. I think it owes Carla two." He grinned and turned to catch the attention of a waitress.

Carla must have found time for a refresher in the ladies

---

room. Her hair lay smooth to her shoulders. Her kohl liner highlighted her big eyes perfectly, but she'd missed a loose blond hair clinging to the fabric of her black top. I sat next to her, leaned forward, and picked it off.

"Glad you're okay," I said.

"Remind me not to go for any more rides in a police van." She shook her head but smiled in Rick's direction. "This guy was great. He pulled some strings and got me released immediately."

"I didn't want you entered into the system," he said. "It's hard to remove a name once the computers latch onto it."

"Thank you," I said.

"Just doing my job."

He did have a nice smile. I watched him turn to the approaching waitress whose uniform was the same hot orange as the paper lanterns hanging over the bar. Since Rick's department was buying, I ordered a shot of small batch Four Roses and water. He'd probably choke when the waitress presented the bill.

Carla was drinking Grey Goose and ordered another.

Harman looked at his wristwatch. "Ladies, I'm officially off duty." His smile included the waitress. Can you bring me a Heineken?"

"Detective Harman, can I call you Rick?" I asked.

"Absolutely," he said.

"I was wondering about Klaire Voyante. Is she really a psychic? I mean does the department ever use her?

"Vice doesn't, but I think missing persons may have had occasion to call her."

"Really?" Carla leaned forward, her expression intense. "Could she help us find Jade?"

"That, I don't know too much about," he said. "Don't know the extent of her abilities. But keep in mind, she was a prostitute for years."

"Everyone needs a job," Carla said.

This got another smile from Rick. "It wouldn't hurt to

ask her," he said. "Just don't let her take your money."

#

If the bar bill was astronomically high when the waitress handed it to Rick, his face never gave it away. He barely glanced at the paper before pulling his wallet from inside his navy-blue blazer.

After paying, he said he had to go, but his hand lingered on Carla's shoulder a moment before he left.

Carla asked the waitress for an appetizer menu, Rick went through the door leading out to the lobby, and three short, thin-faced men walked into the bar. Jockeys.

I stared a moment. Will was one of them. He saw me, said something to the other two guys, then split from the group.

He took the chair Rick had abandoned, and I introduced him to Carla. It was the first time they'd met, and after examining Will's honed, ascetic face, Carla raised a brow.

"Where have you been hiding him?"

"I haven't been hiding him," I said. Maybe too quickly.

"Nikki's lousy at keeping secrets, anyway," Will said.

Could everyone read me like an open book? Carla wasn't interested in Will, was she? I didn't want her putting her slick moves on him.

Will focused on Carla. "Nikki's told me about your daughter. I'm very sorry for your trouble."

The waitress showed up, and Carla and I ordered the "petit" tuna sandwiches. Then I surprised myself.

"Could I have a Wild Turkey 101 and water, please?"

Will set his menu down. "Bring me a shrimp appetizer, lemon, no sauce, and a glass of water.

As the waitress walked away, Carla stared at Will. "How much do you weigh?"

"The perfect amount," he said.

"I'll bet you do." She glanced at me. "I like this guy.

You should have him around more often, Nikki."

Carla, multitasker – matchmaking and flirting at the same time. I ignored her and watched a group of businessmen sit at the table next to us. Two of them stared at Carla.

When the waitress arrived with our orders, I took a swig of bourbon and watched Will slowly squeeze lemon onto his jumbo shrimp. *Jumbo shrimp.* One of those oxymorons. I giggled and took another swig of bourbon.

Will grinned at me. "I take it you aren't riding tomorrow?"

"Nope, don't have my first ride at Gulfstream until that big allowance race on Sunday afternoon. On Diablo."

"No wonder you're drinking," he said, then used his fork to carefully knock three lemon seeds off his shrimp.

Carla, who'd been watching him, turned to me with a wicked smile.

"I like a man who pays attention to detail."

I took another sip of bourbon, while the men at the nearby table stole surreptitious glances at Carla and me.

I smiled at Will. "I bet those guys at the table next door wonder why they're all alone and you're over here with two good looking women."

Will's eyes took on a gleam. "You want me to show them?"

A snort burst from Carla. I hadn't known she was capable of it. I was usually the one to embarrass myself and if I kept drinking Wild Turkey, I probably would because Will was entirely too cute.

I shook my head. I'd been up since four-thirty that morning, watched Carmanos get squashed at the gate, ridden Diablo, and seen a hooker bust. And now I was drinking? Time to go home. I set the bourbon glass down.

Chapter 22

A rough night's sleep, two aspirins, and several cups of coffee later, Jim and I watched Diablo stomp his hoof on the edge of his rubber feed pan until it flipped and spilled his breakfast grain into the straw.

"He's willful," Jim said. "Why use a pan?"

"We tried hanging a feed bucket on the inside of his gate. But he ripped it off twice. Besides, we can shove the rubber pan in there without getting our heads torn off."

Jim didn't respond, but I was used to that.

I looked up and down our row of horses. They all banged and shoved their feed tubs from time to time, but were not in the habit of tearing them off and stomping them to death.

Shaking my head at Diablo, I moved down the shedrow to the two horses Jim had brought in the day before. I'm known them both a couple of years. Imposter and Ambivalent – both geldings, both bays. Older and more seasoned, they sensibly licked the last bits of sweet feed from the bottom of their tubs.

Ambivalent had a crooked blaze twisting past his eyes that made his expression appear uncertain. He could also be ambivalent about racing. He could win a stake – if he wanted to.

Imposter was misnamed. The horse was quiet and patient, with an honest personality. He always tried. Jim had stalled these two on either side of Diablo, hoping they might buddy up, and Imposter had immediately befriended Diablo.

When I rode him and Diablo that morning with Beth and Bullwinkle, Diablo got along so well with Imposter, we agreed to shift Bullwinkle to an "as needed" basis. No question we'd still need him to pony Diablo to post for the upcoming race. No way I was going out there without Bullwinkle.

The morning seemed endless, long and hot. Afilio had to rustle up another groom to help walk two of the hot horses. After my final long, slow gallop, we cleaned stalls, washed bandages, and fed horses, while Jim did paperwork. By the time I topped off the last water bucket, I was barely able to stay awake.

#

Surfacing from my nap, I enjoyed a long luxurious stretch before someone knocked on the door of my motel room. I rolled off the bed and peeked through a slat of the Venetian blinds. Stella.

Maybe she wanted to invite me over for a beer with Lou. I opened the door, and her cat, Scat, rushed past me, making a beeline for the trash can in my tiny kitchen. She probably smelled the empty fish can. A true tuna hound.

Leaning against the door jamb, Stella said, "Ever since Lou gave her that sandwich, this is how it is. There is no controlling that cat. You want I should get her out of there?"

"No," I said quickly. "I'll take care of it. What's up, Stella?"

She was wearing a navy-blue jogging suit that screamed Walmart, but brought out the blue in her eyes. Her gray hair was stiff with spray, and a faint floral scent hung around her.

"I'm not one to tell tales out of school," she said, "but there was some Mexican nosing around earlier." She pointed at the concrete outside my door. "Standing right here. I came out, asked him what he wanted. Said 'never mind,' that he'd talk to you later. What am I, stupid? If he wanted to talk to you, he coulda knocked on your door."

"What did he look like?" I asked.

She scrunched her eyes half-closed. "Had a pony tail, earrings, and plenty of attitude. I'm telling you he was up to no good."

"Mustache?"

"Yeah, that's him. Friend of yours?"

I let out a breath. It was only Orlando. "Yes. He works for me."

"If you say so."

"I appreciate your keeping watch, Stella."

"Lou says I'm a busybody. But a girl has to be careful these days."

"Amen to that."

A noise from behind made me turn. Scat bumped the plastic trash can with her head and circled it like a submarine, her tail a raised periscope. Stopping, she gazed at me.

"I don't think so," I said, walking to her. As I scooped her into my arms she purred. She wasn't a squirmer, and her fur was silky as her long white whiskers tickled my arm.

"I am *not* falling for this."

I handed her over to Stella, who gave me a quizzical look. "Say, you wanna come over for a beer?"

"Maybe later?"

"Okay. If I see anymore creeps hanging around, I'll let you know." With the cat cradled under one arm, she opened the door to her room and disappeared inside.

I paused and gazed at the small slice of intracoastal water beyond the motel railing. Two long-legged white birds stood in the water. Egrets? In the distance, palm trees and condos rose against a soft blue sky.

At home, the Canada geese were probably standing on Laurel's frozen infield lake. I shivered involuntarily as I closed my door.

My cell rang. It was Carla, all worked up again. "I called George. I got him to give me the address where Jade lived . . . before the Paulsons were killed."

The adoptive parents. I didn't want to go to a murder

scene.

She must have read my thoughts. "The *neighborhood*, Nikki, not the house. We might find kids who know Jade. I got the sense from Rick yesterday that the police have very little information on her." She paused for a breath before rushing on. "I can't just sit here!"

Her last performance had put her in a police van. I didn't need any of that, still, I didn't want her going off alone again.

"Okay," I said. "Meet me at the barn. It's almost three now, and I have to start evening feed."

"But Jim's there, and he has Orlando . . ."

"It's my *job*, Carla. I have to show up."

She couldn't argue with that. We agreed to meet in a few minutes.

Chapter 23

During our drive to Jade's house, I got that weird prickly sensation on the back of my neck. Someone was watching me. I glanced in my rearview mirror. A white-haired woman drove a beige car on the residential street behind us. A black with darkened windows trailed behind the beige one.

Carla monitored the GPS system on her phone while I studied the neighborhood. The tile-roofed homes and tropical trees to my left were darkly silhouetted by the late afternoon sun, the houses on my right brightly highlighted. Another glance into my rearview showed the old lady slowing her car and turning into a driveway. The black car drifted along behind us.

"Turn right at the next light," Carla said. "The Palm Courts' entrance is on that street." Today her hair was pulled back in a silver and onyx clip, and she wore matching earrings.

We were about to see where Jade had lived, and I was curious to see if the car behind shadowed us through the next couple of turns. At the light, I swung a right. So did the black car.

"Carla, do you think your buddy George can run down a tag number?"

"He can do anything, as long as I pay him. Why."

"I think we're being followed. Can you sneak a look at the car behind us and jot down the tag number?"

"Sure," she said without jerking her head around to stare. Carla was the queen of cool. "This is one weird town."

She checked the side view mirror, then pulled a pen and memo pad from her patent leather bag. "Let me just get your jacket from the back seat." Rising up and swiveling around on her knees, she made a show of reaching into the back seat with both hands to get my jacket. "Got it," she said and pulled the jacket into the front seat.

I glanced at her. Her hand was holding the pen and pad as well as the jacket. Something was scribbled on the paper.

"Cool beans," I said.

"I didn't try to see the driver," she said.

"Just as well. The windows are too dark anyway."

"Nikki, on your left. The entrance to Palm Courts."

The community's developers had built a stone marker between the wide in-and-out lanes. The name "Palm Courts" emblazoned the structure's face in bronze letters, while white-and-gold flowers bloomed brightly beneath. I made the right, and when I glanced in the rearview, the black car sped up and kept on going straight.

Carla directed me through two more turns and told me to stop in front of a house that looked much like the ones we'd already passed – smooth cream or pastel stucco on the walls, with decorative archways, tiled roofs, and large windows abounding. Thick, green hedges or shrubbery partially hid most of the houses. Privacy was important in Palm Courts.

"I guess this is where she grew up." Carla said quietly.

I stared at number 7 Palmetto Way. Did I only imagine it appeared lifeless and abandoned? If only I could see inside the house, get a look into Jade's room, and meet the Paulsons. Except they were dead. How do you find a girl when you have no sense of who she is?

"So," I said, "you want to get out, or what?"

"Give me a minute." She drew in a long breath.

I gazed at the houses around us. What did Carla have in mind? This wasn't a community where neighbors hung out having cookouts and gossip sessions. We weren't the police. Why would anyone talk to us?

But I'd forgotten how Carla operated.

She exhaled, pulled out her makeup case, fluffed some

bronzer on her cheeks and used her lip gloss. "Would it hurt you to wear a little lipstick, Nikki?"

"We're trying to find your daughter, and you're worried about lipstick?"

"Perception is all. Put this on." She pulled another tube from her case and thrust it into my hand.

I know when to fight my battles and now wasn't the time. I put the stuff on. Of course, the tawny shade was perfect.

"You should get a haircut, too," she said, studying my face.

"Well, I can't get one *now*."

"No. At the moment, you are representing the state of Florida's Amber Alert System."

"I am?" But she seemed to have a plan. "Is that what it's really called?" I asked.

"I have no idea, but hopefully the people who live around here don't either." She pulled up the briefcase by her feet and rummaged a moment. "Put this on."

She held an official looking badge. I stared. It had "Amber Alert" embossed on the plastic, and my *photo*.

"How did you get this?"

"George has his uses. I took the picture yesterday while you were flirting with Will, then I sent it to George."

I knew she'd been texting the previous evening, but hadn't known she was taking my picture, only –

"I wasn't flirting with Will."

"You don't need to get indignant. The guy's adorable."

"You think?"

"I do. He likes you."

I stuck the badge pin into my thumb. "Ouch!" A bead of blood welled on my skin. "Good thing this top is black." I got the badge in place and looked at Carla.

Hers was already pinned to her jacket, and she was pulling a clipboard from the briefcase. "Since you don't want to talk about Will, take a look at this."

I leaned toward her. The board held another official looking Amber Alert document. It displayed Jade's high school picture.

"This one is real," she said, her fingertip lightly touching the photo. "And I have copies of that picture of Jade with her friend, too. Let's go."

#

No one answered the door at number 9 Palmetto Way. But after Carl knocked on number 11, the door swung open to reveal a slim, attractive, forty-something woman in a yellow-and-green tennis outfit. The afternoon moved closer five p.m., so as far as I was concerned, she had an excuse for the piña colada in her manicured hand.

I could smell pineapple and coconut and almost asked for one. Glancing down, I brushed at a flake of dried horse p9oultice clinging to my t-shirt.

Carla introduced us. "We're investigating the disappearance of the Paulson girl."

The woman took in Carla's face, the ID, the smart, black knit-suit and smiled. People usually did.

"Come on in," she waved us across a marble floor down three steps and into a large room whose windows faced a lagoon, probably fed by the intracoastal. "I'm Laura Wattley." She indicated a grouping of pastel upholstered armchairs next to the window.

"Have a seat." We did, and after taking a sip of her cocktail, Laura said, "I still get the creeps when I think about what happened to the Paulsons. So close to us! And when the police interviewed us that night, it was –"

"I'm sure it was terrible," Carla said, "but the daughter's missing and . . . "

Carla's lower lip started to tremble, so I jumped in. "Can you tell us anything that might help find her? You know, like who she hung out with?"

Laura shook her head. "I didn't really know the girl. She wasn't old enough to drive, so when I did see her, she was usually in the car with her mother."

"Carla, show Laura the picture of Jade's friend. Maybe she's a neighborhood girl."

Carla pulled the envelope George had given her from her briefcase and took out the two photos. She handed Laura the one of Jade and her friend.

Laura studied the picture. "Wow, I didn't realize Jade was so pretty." She glanced at Carla. "You know, she looks like *you*."

Carla stiffened.

"But what about the girl with Jade?" I said quickly. "Do you know who she is?"

Laura took a slug of her piña colada. "You know, she *might* live around here. I think I saw her, maybe more than once, walking with Jade toward the mall or someplace."

"Did you tell the police about this?" I asked.

"No, why would I?" She sounded defensive. "They didn't ask me anything about this other girl."

Why was I not surprised?

"Listen" Laura said. "I have things I need to do . . ." She stood. Apparently our meeting was over.

Carla cranked up her professional polish and thanked Laura as the woman ushered us to the front door. Then I thought of something.

"Laura, did you ever notice a black car or SUV with dark windows cruising around the Paulson house?

Laura stopped and stared at me. "There was an SUV like that around here recently. I noticed it because of that disgusting pounding you hear with loud music."

I took a quick step toward her. "Do you know *when* you saw it?"

"No. Is it *that* important?"

"It's hard to know what's important in a case like this," Carla said soothingly. "Laura, thank you again for your time."

We beat it back to my car, neither of us saying anything until I drove around the corner and stopped the Toyota. Didn't want Laura giving my tag number to the police.

"God," Carla finally said. "She saw the SUV. The one with the sick people who shot the girl!"

The memories rushed at me, dark and horrifying. I owed it to that girl to keep digging. I would never forget the look she gave me. I still didn't even know her name.

"Suppose those people have Jade?"

"Don't even think it," I said.

Carla's shaking hand caused the photos to rattle slightly inside the envelope.

"Let's interview more people," I said quickly. "We'll cover more ground if we split up."

Chapter 24

An hour later, I was starving, and still knocking on doors in the Paulson's cushy neighborhood. Carla, who pounded the pavement one block over, kept in touch on her cell.

Every house I'd seen in Palm Courts backed onto a strip of Intracoastal water. Small docks and boats crammed the canals and the odor of stagnant salt water, dead fish, and motor oil were strong. No wonder the residents planted so many flowers, blooming bushes, and trees.

Sighing, I studied the picture of the two girls again. Jade's friend had brown hair, knowing eyes, and a slightly crooked nose. Her lips were smothered in lipstick in a useless attempt to make them look fuller. I'd repeatedly shown this picture when I questioned people. So far, no one had recognized Jade's friend.

There had been the older beaky-nosed guy with pants suspendered almost to his armpits who peered down at me and said, "Miss, this is not a door-to-door neighborhood, you'll have to move on."

There'd been the desperate Scandinavian nanny who came to the door followed by two little boys throwing chocolate pudding at each other. A spoonful of the stuff had splattered my top, confirming my belief in the usefulness of black clothing.

I'd met spoiled dogs, bored housewives, and a precocious teenage boy who'd tried to lure me inside for a beer. Or something.

They'd all known about the Paulson murders, and I'd received an earful on the subject, but no clues on the girl in the photo with Jade.

A squeak and a door slam made me turn and look across the street. A girl with brown hair and plenty of makeup walked out the front door of number 10 Harbor Way. I'd already knocked there, but no one had answered. The girl moved down the sidewalk toward the street. She had a big pocket book on her shoulder, earbuds in her ears, and a slightly crooked nose.

Damn, it was her!

I used speed dial to reach Carla. "Get around here to number 10 Harbor Way. I've got Jade's friend!" I said, closing the phone before angling across the street to cut the girl off.

"Hi," I said, "I need your help."

She gave me a blank look. The music on her ear set was loud enough I could hear the strident voice of a female pop star. The girl pulled out one of her ear buds.

"Sorry, what?"

I gestured at the badge still pinned to my top, then held out the photo of her and Jade. "This is you, right?"

"Yeah," she said, dialing down her iPod while staring at the Amber Alert emblem on the photo. "Does anyone know what happened to Jade yet?"

"We don't. I'd like to ask you a couple of questions that might help us find her."

"It's about time somebody asked about her. The police never talked to me, and my parents . . . they told me not to get involved." She pressed her lips together. "But I don't know anything."

"Bet you know more than I do. Like your name."

"Tracy," she said. "Tracy Johnson."

I pointed at my badge. "I'm with the Amber Alert program." *Liar, liar.* "Okay, Tracy. So you and Jade hung out together?"

"Yeah."

"So when was the last time you saw Jade?"

"Um. Last week . . . I think."

"How was she then?"

"Okay, I guess." Tracy threw a look over her shoulder at her house. Probably worrying about the parents.

Getting this girl to open up was going to be like trying to win a race riding a rocking horse.

Carla clattered around the corner on her high heels and sped toward us. How did she move so fast in those things? She stopped in front of us, and Tracy's jaw dropped.

She stared hard at Carla. "You look like *Jade*."

"I'm her mother." Carla said.

"You mean, like her *real* mother? Like biological?"

"Yes," Carla replied.

"Wow. But she says she's never met you."

"No." Carla paused, twisting her hands together. "I haven't met her. But there's nothing I want more."

Tracy nodded, then opened up like a bottle of champagne. "Okay, I didn't tell you this, and you guys can't tell *anyone* – like my parents – but last week Jade and I went to this modeling agency place. The woman who ran it had a guy – I think he was like the manager – come up from the back. They tried to hire Jade, but she's pretty sharp and wouldn't sign anything. So they started talking about this party in Fort Lauderdale. She told them she'd think about it, like she was trying to figure out if she could get around her parents, you know?"

Carla seemed unable to answer.

"Sure," I said. "I know what you mean. Can you tell me what this guy looked like?"

Tracy thought a moment. "He was old, maybe thirty, but cool looking. Had long black hair and an awesome tattoo on his arm."

My body grew still. "Can you describe the tattoo?"

"Yeah, it was a guy driving, like, four horses out of the ocean. You know, just with reins."

"Poseidon," Carla said. "God of the Sea."

I was glad I'd never shown the mermaid carving to Carla, never described the sea horse tattoo on the arm of the girl who'd been shot. And what if the guy who'd come to my motel wasn't Orlando? This thing was starting to spook the hell out of me.

A quick mental note to call Rick Harman, and then I plunged ahead. "Was this agency guy white, Latino, black, what?"

"Oh," Tracy said. "Latino."

"Was he giving this party?"

"I don't think so, but it sounded so cool! Dagger and some of his band were going to be there and stuff."

The rock star. No doubt there would be all kinds of "stuff" at the party.

"Did Jade go?"

"I don't know," Tracy rubbed her arms like she was cold. "I . . . I haven't talked to her since we left the agency."

"What day was the party?" But I already knew the answer.

"It was the night her parents were murdered. The night she disappeared."

Chapter 25

"I'm calling Rick," Carla said as I turned the Toyota to the right out of Palm Courts a few minutes later. As she connected her call, I thought about talking to Klaire. With her past connections, she might know something about this Poseidon tattoo guy. If she was anything like her cousin Mello, she could help us.

Okay, I'd finally admitted it. I believed in this stuff. Didn't know how much, or how far I'd trust it, but I firmly believed in a human's ability to perceive things beyond the five senses.

Carla rolled her eyes. "Voice mail," she said in disgust. She left a message for Rick about Jade's friend Tracy, then turned to me. "What's next?"

"I'm starving. But I don't feel like a restaurant. I'm beat."

"That's why I'm ordering room service. You can lie down and rest while we wait."

"Can I take a shower?" I'd always wanted to try out the bathing options in a hoity hotel like the Diplomat. I even had clean clothes in my laundry basket in the trunk of my car.

"Of course," Carla said, connecting to the Diplomat.
As she placed an order, I drove past the famous restaurant, Billy's Stone Crab, on our right. *Someday*. A few miles farther, I took a left into the Diplomat's drive. We left the Toyota with valet parking – there were fringe benefits for hanging out with Carla – and rode the elevator up to the eighteenth floor.

Her room had a king size bed with a white comforter, a desk, a couch, and more importantly, a balcony with sliding glass doors. The terrace held a glass-topped table and four chairs. The balcony railing was paneled in glass so guests had a clear view of the Atlantic Ocean beyond.

I slid the door open and heard the rush of the sea. I collapsed in a chair and put my feet on the table.

"Carla," I called into the room, "do you think I could have a piña colada, too?"

#

By the time my drink arrived, I had already stuffed myself with salmon, pasta and spinach. Taking the froth-filled glass in one hand and my tote with a change of clothes in the other, I stepped into Carla's elegant bathroom.

White marble, huge fluffy towels, gold fixtures, and a whirlpool tub with ledges big enough to sit on. I set my drink down and turned the gold knobs, pouring steaming water into the tub.

The array of Carla's bath, body, hair and makeup products was staggering. I might never get out of this room. Moments later, I sank into the tub, poured citrus scented bubble bath into the water, and hit the whirlpool button. Sipping my piña colada, I closed my eyes.

Sex couldn't be this good. But as the bubbles swirled around me, I pictured Will's quick, sure fingers sliding the chain into Diablo's mouth that first day. *Maybe it could be as good.*

About the time I was dried, dressed, and spiking my short hair with mousse, Carla tapped on the bathroom door.

"Nikki? Rick's here."

"I'll be out in a minute." He sure was on the case. He must have called her back while I was bathing. And now he'd come to her room?

Stepping outside the bathroom, I saw Rick and Carla sitting on the balcony at the glass-topped table. He wore a white jacket over a black tee and slacks, apparently off duty. They were leaning toward each other, their hands almost touching. I drained the last drops of my drink, set it on the service cart, and stepped outside.

Rick noticed me first. "Nikki, good lead you got today." He frowned slightly. "I'm glad Carla called me, but you two have to promise me to stay out of this from now on."

"Sure," I said. "Can you tell me if this guy with the Poseidon tattoo was at the White Sands yesterday? Did you arrest him?"

"Any information I have about him is part of an ongoing investigation. Are you guys trying to get me fired?" Smiling at Carla and me, he made quote marks in the air with his fingers. "Hallandale Beach detective cited for injury to civilians in vice case."

"I don't want to get you in trouble, Rick," Carla said, "I just want to find my daughter."

"And I'm working on that, okay? You gotta trust me on this, Carla."

Beyond the balcony, the sea crested and foamed on the beach below. The Diplomat's long shadow darkened the image as the sun set to the west behind the hotel.

I nodded at Rick. "We trust you. I gotta get back to my motel and get some sleep." I felt like a third wheel, anyway. Rick had designs on Carla, and she didn't look too ready to beat him off.

#

The next morning, after finishing up stable work, I asked Orlando if he had come by my motel the day before.

He set down the rake he was using, drew himself up tall and said, "The men in my family don' go to motel to see woman. We take her to dinner or dance."

"Just checking, Orlando. Someone told me a man who looks like you was asking about me."

Orlando stroked his mustache. "He a lucky man if he look like *me*! Anyway, I not there."

"Okay. Later," I said, and gathered my things before

leaving the track and heading for the Sand Castle.

When I arrived at the motel, Scat was stretched out, sunbathing on the concrete in front my room. As I leaned over to pet her, the door to Stella's room clicked open a couple of inches.

"Hey, Stella."

"Nikki, you just get back?" she asked after widening the opening and stepping outside.

Like she didn't know. "Yeah," I answered. "Remember that Latino guy you saw hanging around? Did he have any kind of mark on his arms?"

She squinted, deepening the lines bracketing her eyes and mouth while she thought. "You know, he did. Had a tattoo of a guy looked like the devil. Holding this little pitchfork."

I'd bet my last two bucks the pitchfork was a trident. "Did this devil have anything else?"

"Yeah," she said. "Horses."

I swallowed. "This guy sounds pretty scary. Let me know if you see him again."

"Don't you worry, little bubala, he won't get past me."
"Thanks." Stepping into my room, I closed the door, hooked the flimsy chain and turned the deadbolt. Probably anyone could kick the whole thing in. I put a chair up against it and felt marginally better.

I made a cup of coffee and sat at my tiny kitchen table. I'd only been in Florida for five days. So much had happened it was hard to sort out.

A girl had died at my feet, her identity still unknown. Two girls were missing, one of them Carla's daughter. I'd been saddled with the horse from hell, a new owner with a horrible scar, and a psychic who had visions of Jade surrounded by water.

I touched the sea horse box, still on the table. Opening it, I withdrew the stone mermaid and stared at her face. Somehow Jade's disappearance was connected to the sea. But the mermaid wasn't revealing any secrets. At least not to me. Damn, I'd forgotten to call Klaire the night before.

Sliding the mermaid back into her box, I reviewed the most recent events: A vice detective pursued Carla, Will pulled at me like a magnet, and a creep that ran hookers was lurking around my motel room. In two days I had to race Diablo. No wonder I'd been tossing back the bourbon and piña coladas.

Chapter 26

The morning of the race we took Diablo's hay away and hand-walked him on the shedrow. He whinnied angrily when the two fillies, all decked out in saddles and bridles, sashayed out for morning exercise as if they lived to annoy him.

I sacrificed Imposter's morning exercise by leaving him in his stall next to Diablo. Keeping the colt calm was essential. A meltdown before his race would be a disaster.

Currito came by briefly to check on his colt, telling me he'd see me later in the paddock. By ten-thirty, we'd finished up, and Jim had left to run errands.

Orlando and I were drinking Cokes in the feed room when a loud crack resonated through the wall. I stuck my head out into the aisle way and saw a man with long, dark hair walking quickly away from Diablo and Imposter's stalls.

"Hey!" I called.

He looked back at me for a moment. Dark-glasses, taller than Orlando, and a full goatee instead of a moustache. A long-sleeved tee covered his arms so I didn't know if he had a Poseidon tattoo or not. But gold rings pierced in his ears.

"Orlando, who is this guy?"

Orlando darted from the feed room. "I don't know. I have not seen him before."

The guy had almost reached the far corner.

"Hey," I yelled again and took off after him. If he'd messed with Diablo . . . .

When I rounded the corner, the man had vanished. There were so many places he could hide among the barns, sheds and vehicles. Was this the guy who'd been at my motel? I ran back to check on Diablo, but Orlando, already in the stall, had beat me to it.

"I don't see no problem with him, Nikki. I think he kick the wall when the man walk by."

The loud bang *had* sounded like Diablo nailing the wall. Damn it. Strangers had no business in our shedrow.

"You got any peppermints on you?" I asked.

"*Si.*"

While Orlando crinkled off the plastic covering, I snapped a shank onto Diablo's halter. Palm flat, Orlando offered Diablo the treat. When his big equine molars crunched and ground the candy, the scent of peppermint oil drifted to my nostrils.

I handed the shank to Orlando and went back to look at Diablo's rear shoes. He'd always been good about picking his feet up, and when I checked the racing plates, the metal shoes were still on snug and square. Good. The slightest shift could cause a huge problem in his race.

Neither Orlando nor I found any sign the horses had been tampered with. Still, I didn't like the coincidence of this man showing up, whoever he was. I rubbed the small of my back and stretched my neck.

"Orlando," I said, "you need to stay with Diablo until Jim gets back around noon. Then you can take a break."

"Don' you worry, Nikki. Nobody bother this horse, not on my, how you say, 'my watch?'"

"Right, not on your watch. I guess I'll see you guys in the paddock. Beth is coming with –"

"You worry too much. Is my job to get Diablo to the paddock." He flipped his hair back and grinned. "*No problema.*"

"Thanks, Orlando."

I grabbed my kit and left for the jockey's room. At the grandstand, I found the side door that led to the jockey's room. Two riders stood outside smoking, probably to keep from eating.

I paused outside the building when my phone rang,

and stepping sideways to avoid the jockey's cigarette smoke, I answered.

"Nikki," Carla said. George didn't get much from that tag number. Car belongs to a guy who sells real estate in Broward County. He's clean, no record, lived here all his life."

"What's his name," I asked.

"Roger McAddis."

He didn't sound much like a Latino gunman, and I was pretty sure the guys we were looking for were either from outside the country or illegal immigrants.

"Are you sure he was following us,?" Carla asked.

"I don't know. I need to get ready for Diablo's race."

"See you in the paddock," Carla said.

#

Inside the jockey's room, two men sat at a desk with phones and big calendar-blotters where they kept track of the day's races, riders, silk colors, valets and who knew what all. One guy was gray-haired with a nicely clipped moustache and a snazzy Panama hat. In addition to his blotter, he had a clip board, colored Highlighters, Post-it notes and a tall glass of ice tea. His official title was "Clerk of the Scales." The other guy was younger, trimmer, and busy on his phone. Probably the assistant clerk.

The Panama hat guy checked me in and pointed out the entrance to the women's section.

"Let's see," he said, squinting at his blotter, "you're riding Diablo Valiente in the ninth, right?"

"Yes."

"You're in the seven hole?"

"Yes."

"Okey doke. Get yourself some towels," he waved at a long counter stacked with freshly laundered and folded bath towels. "Your valet today is going to be . . ." He squinted some more. "Juanita."

Not being a regular rider at Gulfstream, I didn't have a valet, but Juanita would receive a piece of anything I earned. Everything in racing is about slices of the pie.

If Diablo won – or placed somewhere in the first four or five – Currito as owner, Jim as trainer, me, and the valet got a percent. If Diablo finished out-of-the-money, Juanita still got a percent of the jock's fee I'd earn from Currito.

Glancing around, I saw the silks hanging on racks in a room to my right, and on my left the obligatory wall mounted video screen, where the jockeys could watch the day's races. A water cooler hummed beneath it, and beyond them, a woman stood behind a small snack counter fronted by stools. Green-padded armchairs surrounded small white-topped tables near the counter.

A couple of pieces of exercise equipment stood in the room, too, but no one was using them. A jockey, lounging on one of the armchairs, had pulled up another to rest his legs and feet. His eyes were closed.

I needed a shower and a catnap. After buying yogurt and a chocolate bar at the counter, I headed for the women's area.

The room was nicely outfitted with a steam room and dry sauna. It wasn't as nice as Carla's hotel room, but a far sight better than Laurel Park's accommodations for female jockeys. On the other side of the sauna's glass door a woman lay on a padded bench. She was covered by a green towel and beads of perspiration.

Large custom-made cabinets with cubby holes, drawers, and a working sink stood at each end of the room. Someone, probably the gal in the sauna, had placed a small stuffed lion, a jar of Johnson's shoe wax, a bottle of water and assorted bath products in one of the cubby holes. I touched the fuzzy mane on the little lion and put my things in the cubby hole next door.

Glancing again at the lion, I fingered the small San Raphael talisman hanging on a slender chain around my neck.

A jockey named Paco had given it to me when I'd been hurt once, and I'd had the medal made into a necklace and worn it often.

Playing the dangerous game we did, we took our good luck charms seriously.

Chapter 27

At four o'clock that afternoon, when the horses in our race had been saddled, the man with the snappy Panama hat called for riders to the paddock. In our shiny silks and polished boots, we filed through a door leading from the jockeys' room into the saddling tunnel.

At Gulfstream, they tack the horses inside this dim passage that runs through the base of the grandstand and connects the paddock with the racetrack on the opposite side.

As we walked the rubber-paved floor and skirted several fresh piles of manure, I glanced at the row of two-sided stalls built against one wall of the tunnel. The designer had capped the concrete stall walls with green metal railing and fronted each one with iron poles crowned by ornate brass finials.

Reaching the tunnel's end, we walked down a ramp into the bright sunlight of the paddock, where railing formed a circular dirt path for the horses. I spotted Diablo, proud and magnificent, on the far side. In the middle, pink flowers in planters bloomed around a putting-green oval of grass, and a fountain splashed in dead center.

I felt pretty snazzy in Currito's red and black racing silks, emboldened with a gold lightning strike between my shoulder blades. My black helmet cover even had a gold pom pom. Ahead of me, Jim stood near the rail. Currito, in a black suit with a red-and-gold pocket square, appeared to be my match mate.

Threading through the parading horses, owners, trainers and hangers on, I headed for the two men. As I reached them, Orlando led Diablo past us.

Up close, the colt looked calmer than I had expected, and I was glad to see it. Jim nodded at me, and Currito shook my hand.

"*Buena suerte,*" he said.

"Thanks," I replied. I needed all the "good luck" I could get – at least until we were safely sprung from the gate.

I glanced at the competition circling the paddock. Diablo was the standout as far as looks went, but the bettors weren't too high on him as it was his first start in North America. South American past performances were hard to read, and a lot of people didn't trust foreign stats, anyway.

Hammer and Stay Tuned, the four and the six, were the heavy favorites, ridden by two jockeys from the Florida New-York circuit. Their horses had won a number of good races, and I could see why they were favored to win.

As the paddock judge called for riders up, Jim drew me aside a moment.

"When you break, relax him. If you can. If he wants to go, let him. We both know what will happen if you fight him."

I nodded, and Jim gave me a leg up into the saddle. Then everyone walked from the paddock back through the tunnel.

I let out a breath when I saw Beth and Bullwinkle waiting for us on the track. Beth took the lead strap from Orlando and she and Bullwinkle escorted us away from the grandstand along with the other horses, lead ponies, and outriders. After a delightfully uneventful warmup, we paraded to the gate where the crewmen waited for us.

Beth leaned over and gave Diablo a pat. "He sure is behaving himself. Did you hypnotize him or something?"

"We didn't give him anything." I said, "Not even Lasix. He's just being professional."

"Let's hope he doesn't change his mind about that."

I followed her worried gaze to the metal contraption before us and swallowed. The head starter, Haskell, gestured at a crewman to lead Diablo into the gate.

"He's gonna put you in *now*," Beth said.

We'd drawn post position seven, but if they put Diablo

in first and he went loco when they tried to load him, the stalls on either side would still be empty and nobody else would get hurt.

Nice for *them.*

In a calm, almost dreamlike state, Diablo walked into his stall. The crewman stood on the narrow platform, holding Diablo's head while the rest of the field loaded.

Stay Tuned, with Patrick Graham aboard, loaded to my left. Graham's face was wizened by dieting and a long career in the saddle. A fractious grey horse loaded on my right. I ignored him, settled deeper into the saddle, and crossed the reins over Diablo's heavy black mane.

To my far right, the last horse loaded. I grasped the crossed rubber reins with my left hand and grabbed Diablo's mane with the right. Outside the cage door, the dirt track stretched ahead into the distance.

The voice of track announcer Larry Collmus blared from loudspeakers. "They're all in line."

When the bell rang and the doors crashed open, the screams of jockeys and the thunder of hooves almost deafened me.

One jump outside the gate, the grey to my right crashed into Diablo then bounced off like a ping pong ball. Diablo pinned his ears and charged forward. Hammer, quicker on his feet, took the lead on the rail. Stay Tuned clung to Hammer's flank on the outside, and several other horses with early speed closed in behind them.

We lay about sixth, the grey somewhere behind us. Diablo found his stride, and I rushed him forward onto the rail before the first turn. I could hear Collmus calling our positions.

". . . a ground saving trip for Diablo Valiente, fourth on the inside."

I sat chilly, riding a keg of nitro, cornering the turn into the backstretch. As we straightened, I tried to keep Diablo covered up behind Stay Tuned and a chestnut. These two ran together behind Hammer.

Diablo ducked to the outside, saw daylight, and exploded forward. No point in fighting. We passed the faltering chestnut.

"A half in forty-six and two-fifths. Diablo Valiente moving up on the outside. Hammer is hammering it out with Stay Tuned. Stay Tuned isn't staying. Diablo Valiente now challenging Hammer for the lead."

This was one fast son of a bitch! I did nothing to disturb Diablo's rocket move forward. As Stay Tuned came back to us, Diablo swept past him and set his sights on Hammer. Clearly, I was just along for the ride.

"At the top of the stretch, Diablo Valiente takes the lead. Opening up now, it is Diablo Valiente all the way. And it is Diablo Valiente by . . . seven!"

Holy shit.

We shot under the wire, and gasping, I stood in the stirrups, wondering how to stop my rocket. We went around the first turn again before I began to get some of my breath back. Ahead of us, a red coated outrider spurred his horse forward, getting up to speed so he could grab my right rein as we passed him.

He did, and I sagged a little with relief. I smiled at the guy.

He said, "Good job, Latrelle."

It had been so *easy.*

#

Diablo's neck arched with pride as he strode into the winner's circle, almost dragging Orlando. Jim and Currito beamed next to the Asian, Tau Chakri, who remained expressionless. Carla, in a mini-skirted red suit, stockings, and high heels, rushed to join us in time for the picture.

Diablo stood like a statue as the cameras whirred and flashed our animated expressions into a still-life.

When I slid off Diablo, I caught Chakri staring at Carla's legs. I wanted to hit him with my crop.

Jim stepped close and squeezed my arm. "Good ride, Nik."

Currito all but elbowed Jim out of the way as he grabbed my hand. "I told you he has the fire, no?"

"An inferno!" I said.

"Yes." Currito turned to Jim. "Nikki is very good with him, no? She did not fight him when he took the lead. Diablo, he shows me he loves Nikki. She will ride him in the Fountain of Youth."

The Grade II prep for the Kentucky Derby? The best three-year-olds in North America would be in that race. The best jockeys, too! But the race wasn't until February and a lot could happen between now and then.

"She'll do a good job for you and Diablo." Jim might have been talking about a $5,000 claimer at Charles Town he sounded so matter of fact.

"Good, it is decided." Currito said as he watched Orlando lead Diablo away to the test barn.

The requisite blood and urine samples would be collected from the colt in the test barn. All horses finishing first or second in every race had to test clean. I hoped Diablo wouldn't be too hard on the state veterinarian when the man came at him with the needle.

Currito turned back to our group, and thrusting a hand into a pocket, he withdrew a white handkerchief and wiped his scarred eye. I hadn't noticed it was dripping. Amazing the things I could get used to. Especially after a win.

He became expansive. "I have a table at Christine Lee's upstairs. Everyone is invited."

Going to lunch with my safety vest on under Currito's silks seemed a sure road to hot and sweaty. But I wasn't going to disappoint Currito, not with a Fountain of Youth in the wings.

"Sure," I said, nodding at him.

Jim, who hated socializing, produced a weak smile, and Carla said, "I'd love to go!"

Chakri frowned. "I have some business to attend to."

What a loss. I noticed Currito's eye twitch as he watched Chakri walk away from us. Probably annoyed by the man's rude behavior.

When our group headed toward the grandstand, I ended up walking next to Currito.

"Mr. Chakri isn't much of a racing fan, is he?"

"He is a friend of a business associate. I thought I should invite him. It was a mistake. I won't make it again." He jerked open the door to the grandstand and gestured me inside.

I wouldn't want to get on the wrong side of Currito.

Inside we walked through a slots parlor where much of the light came from the machines. The people hunched before these video devices were so focused on the flashing screens, and so insulated by the sound effects of bells, music, and crashing noises, they operated in a parallel universe.

I couldn't get out of there fast enough.

Ahead of us, Carla and Jim reached the elevator. Currito pulled out his handkerchief again, and I looked away.

"My scar, it bothers you?"

"Not really," I said.

He laughed. "It bothers most people!"

He seemed almost proud of the damn thing. My question slipped out.

"How did you get it?"

He answered without hesitation. "My brother cut me. When I was younger."

"*Nice* brother." I almost bit my tongue.

"It is no longer a problem. He is dead."

"Oh . . . I'm sorry."

"Don't be."

The elevator bell rang, and the doors slid open. I moved inside and stood next to Jim.

Chapter 28

The 10 Palms restaurant at Gulfstream Park takes up much of the second floor of the grandstand. Christine Lee's was one floor and one price hike up from there.

When the elevators opened on the third floor, the maitre d' led us into the restaurant toward tables set against a glass wall overlooking the track. Carla and I trailed behind Currito and Jim. We passed through a sharp dressed crowd of diners with plenty of cash for extras, like bottles of Voss sparkling water and Dom Perignon.

Way down the ladder, two floors below us, the noisy crowd we'd just left in the grandstand ate french fries from cartons and slurped beer from cans. Up here, people behaved with self restraint, and the waiters served beer in tall crystal glasses. Lots of sparkling and bubbling. Diamonds fractured light on the necks and hands of the women, and several fat pinky rings winked from the fingers of the men.

"Armani, Escada, St. John," Carla murmured as we passed tables in the center of the room.

"Is this a fashion tour?" I asked.

"It's always good to know what you're up against." Carla returned a diamond pinky man's glance with a dazzling smile.

"Are we at war? I asked, watching the man flush.

"If there's money to be made, always."

No wonder she had a Mercedes Roadster in her garage.

Several people discreetly studied our group. Me in my red-and-gold racing silks complete with safety vest lumps, Currito with his ghastly scar, and Carla, easily the best looking woman in the room. Nobody ever paid much attention to Jim. He liked it that way.

Reaching the table, I hung back waiting to see where Currito would sit. When he did, I dove for a chair catty corner across the table from his. I needn't have worried. Once he settled next to Carla, he never took his eyes off her.

Fine, let her deal with him.

Currito insisted on ordering champagne and poured each of us a glass. Something I'd only heard of called Veuve Clicquot La Grande Dame. Probably cost $200 a bottle.

Pulling his gaze off Carla, he held up his glass. "To Nikki and Diablo Valiente."

We clinked glasses, and I took a sip. The old dame was pretty good, but I didn't drink much.

After we ordered entrees, I searched for the ladies room, ending up in a long hall lined with prints of racing scenes painted by a guy named Robert Clark. Truly fine images of stars like Smarty Jones, Barbaro, and Lookin at Lucky. The artist had captured Lucky pulling away from the field to win Maryland's 2010 Preakness at Pimlico. I'd watched Lucky win that day. I'd ridden a race on the Preakness undercard.

Someday, I wanted to own a painting like that.

Laughter and the buzz of conversation came from behind several closed doors. Must be parties going on in the private suites. At the far end of the hall, a small lighted sign indicated the rest rooms. They seemed a long way from the restaurant.

A door beside me opened and Chakri stepped out, the smell of cigars, booze and perfume rolling into the hall with him. He stopped abruptly when he saw me, eyes widening ever so slightly. It was the first time I'd seen his face move.

"Oh, hi, Mr. Chakri. I thought you'd left."

A few shrieks of high pitched girlish laughter reached me, and my eyes followed the sound to a couple of girls in strappy dresses. As I took a half-step forward to get a better view, Chakri reached out and closed the door.

"Congratulations again on your win, Miss Latrelle.

Excuse me."

"Thanks," I said to his retreating figure.

Apparently we were both in need of a restroom, but I wasn't going to follow him down that long empty hall. I turned and beat it back into Christine Lee's where I saw another ladies room near the elevators and entrance. Probably smart not to tell Currito that Chakri had received a better offer.

#

I left the restaurant as soon as I'd eaten, anxious to change and shower in the jockey's room. As agreed, I met Carla outside the grandstand and we waited for a valet driver to bring around her car. She'd rented from Hertz that morning, no doubt tired of riding around in my wreck-on-wheels Toyota.

Taxis, limos, cars, and a shuttle bus jammed the driveway in front of the grandstand. The last big race had run and a mass exodus was underway. The crowd brought the scent of stale cigars and perfume with them into the ocean air. Overhead, the palm fronds rattled as a gunmetal gray cloud edged out the sun.

"This is bogus!" said a man standing next to us in a short-sleeved Hawaiian shirt. He scowled at the sky. "Temperature musta just dropped ten degrees."

"Beat's Baltimore," I said.

Carla reached into her patent bag and withdrew a small umbrella. She popped a button and raised it just as the first drops of rain fell on my head. The umbrella spread out, bright and red. Of course, it matched her suit.

I took a few steps back out of the rain and into the shadow under the grandstand's portico. I could smell the cold water as it hit the pavement and steamed on the hot, black asphalt. I leaned against the side of a stone column. Why hadn't I brought a jacket to put on over my thin gray hoodie and jeans.

On the other side of my column, two men emerged from under the portico and moved ahead of me to my left. One of them was tall, and when he turned sideways to glance at Carla beneath her red umbrella, I recognized the flat nose and tin smile of Chakri.

I'd never seen the other man before. He had a short neck, humped shoulders, a sharp nose resembling a vulture's beak and eyes just as empty. He turned back, searching for a spot out of the rain. His looked foreign, maybe eastern European, maybe with a touch of Asian about the eyes.

Neither man noticed me. With my short, still damp hair and dark clothes, I blended into the shadows on my side of the column.

The men stood on the other side, speaking softly, and I couldn't hear them at first. Then the man who looked like a vulture laughed.

"Yes, they are good girls. But Lena, I find exceptional. You will see."

"The private school girls," Chakri said, "are like hot house fruit."

Both men laughed, and I hated the way they talked about women. Even if these girls were willing participants, the conversation felt dirty.

Ahead of us, the man in the Hawaiian shirt was using his *Daily Racing Form* to shelter from the rain while he talked to Carla. She stood by the curb and turned her head to glance at a black stretch limo as it pulled in front of her a moment later.

As Chakri and his companion hurried to the limo, I darted forward and stood behind Carla, peering around her to stare at the men. The vulture opened the second of three side doors and climbed inside. He slid across the long seat and Chakri followed.

Through the space between the two men, and because the interior lights were still on, I saw two people behind them in the last seat. A tough, thug like male and a young girl with hair the color of cinnamon streaked with raw sugar. Her eyes were half closed and her head lolled to one side, like she might be drugged.

I came from around Carla to get a better look, but Chakri pulled the limo door closed and cut off my view. I stared at the limo as it worked its way through the traffic. Grabbing my tote, I found my racing program and pen, and scribbled down the tag number before my view was blocked by a shuttle bus.

"Did you see her? Carla said, grabbing my arm.

"See who?" the man in the Hawiian shirt asked.

"Nobody," I said, stepping away from him. Carla, still latched onto my arm, came with me.

Ducking under Carla's umbrella, I said. "Yes. I saw her. I think they were talking about her. Her name is Lena."

"She's Jade's age!" Carla's whisper was harsh. "She looked like – like they'd kidnapped her."

Her hand covered her mouth for a moment, her thoughts apparently receding into a dark place.

"I got the tag number," I said quickly. I hadn't seen anything below her shoulders, but there had been something awkward and unbalanced about the way she sat that made me think her hands or feet might be restrained.

I shook my head. "We can give the license number to Rick. Vice will have a real interest in this." *And if they didn't, maybe the FBI would.*

"Right." Her focus came back to me. "Yes. I'll tell Rick. But first Im going to call George and get him to run that limo's tag number."

Typical of Carla to rely on more than one source. With George on her payroll, she could call the shots. With Rick, she'd only learn what he was willing to tell her. I had a feeling George would have better luck with this trace. No way these guys were local real estate agents and native Floridians like the one I'd thought was following us in Jade's neighborhood.

"Here's my car," Carla said as a red Mustang convertible rolled up.

Carla tipped the valet, and we scrambled inside away from the cold rain. Glancing at Carla's profile, I could see she wasn't having much better luck than I was escaping the image of the girl in the back of the limo.

As she drove through the backstretch security gate, Carla reached George, told him what she wanted, then handed me the phone. I recited the limo's tag number to him and closed the phone.

I glanced at Carla. "He'll call back as soon as he gets anything."

"I'm seeing Rick later," she said. "I'll talk to him about Chakri. I'll get more out of him if I do it in person." She blushed slightly.

"You like this guy, don't you?" I had an idea what she was "getting out of him in person."

"He's been very nice to me about Jade. And he's a very sexy guy."

"Sharp dresser, too," I said, as she braked outside my barn. "But hang onto your heart, you'll find Jade and be leaving Florida." I climbed out of her car and ducked through the rain onto the shedrow.

As Carla drove away, Diablo's head appeared over his stall gate. He pricked his ears toward me and nickered.

"You never like anyone except Bullwinkle and Imposter," I said. "What's wrong with you?"

"Nothing wrong with this horse." Jim's gruff voice came from Diablo's stall.

I peered inside. Jim squatted by Diablo's left hind leg, rolling a stable bandage over leg hair damp with liniment. The other three legs were already done up.

"How are you doing that without Orlando or someone to hold him?" I asked.

"Trade secret," he said with a rare smile. "Besides, I gave Orlando the night off."

"I'm not falling for your nice guy act," I said. "You've finally got a good horse and you don't want anyone else putting hands on him."

The corners of Jim's mouth twitched almost imperceptibly. "Run to my office and get that condition book off my desk. We've got other horses to run."

I got the book from the tack room that also served as Jim's office, and when he came out of Diablo's stall, we sat together on a long, sweet smelling hay bale with the racing schedule. The dark rain bank had moved east behind our barn leaving pale, puffy clouds overhead. The receding storm stained one side of the clouds an India ink blue, while the sun fading in the west gilded the other side with streaks of pink and gold.

I wondered where Will Marshall was.

"Now here's an allowance race for La Bruja," Jim said pointing at a page he'd already marked in the book.

Pulling my attention back to the horses, I studied the race in the condition book. "For fillies and mares, three and up. A mile and an eighth on the dirt." The race was five days later, on Sunday. I nodded.

"Want you to work La Bruja five-eighths of a mile in the morning. If that goes well, we'll enter her in this allowance."

"Imparable," Jim continued, "tested negative on her vet scan earlier. Both her soft tissue and bone results looked good."

I was relieved. I'd been the one riding her before her leg heated up and worried us so much the day Jim arrived at Gulfstream.

"Still," he said, "I don't want to work and run her just yet. The other two can wait a while."

He referred to Imposter and Ambivalent who'd just raced in Maryland.

Jim creaked to his feet, stretched, and disappeared into his office. Overhead, the pink-and-gold streaks on the clouds had deepened to purple.

Diablo watched me from his stall. He might be hard to work with, but he confirmed my belief that nothing taught the lesson "you get what you give" as clearly as a horse did. These animals structured my world. They kept me sane.

And the naughty boy had just run a big race that would pay me almost $3,600. I felt pretty lucky, like things were taking a turn for the better.

Chapter 29

On the horse path leading to the track for her morning work, La Bruja spooked at a stable goat and shifted sideways under me. The goat was tethered outside the corner stall of a barn, and in the early morning sun, its hair and horns glared white. La Bruja froze and stared hard, snorting in alarm.

"You pass that stupid goat every day," I said. "Now move."

I squeezed her sides with my boot heels, and she moved forward. As we stepped onto the track, her walk became looser and her long gray legs covered the ground as we moved clockwise around the mile oval toward the green-and-white starting gate.

I eased her into a jog and we rolled along the track, passed the chute, and were almost to the clubhouse turn before I stopped and turned her around.

Once La Bruja headed counterclockwise in the direction horses race, her head came up, her legs dancing beneath her. I shortened her reins.

Not yet, wait for the gate.

A blue billboard with the words "Gulfstream Park" lettered in gold stood on top of the starting gate. Beneath the sign and above each stall, numbered placards marked the post positions. Each card was a different color. A black numeral eight stamped on pink marked the eight hole, a black seven on sunset orange came next, followed by a black card with a yellow numeral six. These colors were standardized throughout most of North America. Twelve stalls, twelve cards, twelve color combinations. When the horses ran, their saddle towels would match the cards.

In the distance, palm trees waved against the sky and behind them, tall condos gleamed in the morning sun and hid the ocean beyond. But I could sense its presence in the salt air and the vastness of the horizon that stretched endlessly into the distance.

La Bruja walked up to the gate without spooking, loaded, and broke like a charm. Five or six strides out, she was in high gear, her head lowered, her neck stretched long.

I didn't whip or drive her, preferring to see what she could do on her own. When we hit the wire, I was out of breath and grinning, thinking about some of the claimers I'd ridden with nicknames like Chokey Pokey and Potted Plant. I could get used to riding horses like Diablo and La Bruja. Used to earning real money.

My filly's walk remained loose and long-striding on our way back to the barn. The sun was warm on my back as I stroked her damp, grey neck. She should run well in five days.

Nearing our barn, my euphoria evaporated.

A security truck idled outside our shedrow, its yellow roof lights flashing. A uniformed guard and a tough-eyed man in a suit stood with Jim, who tapped his lip nervously with one forefinger.

As Orlando hurried to grab the reins, I booted La Bruja onto the shedrow, stopped short of the group, and kicked my feet from the stirrups.

At my unspoken question, he shook his head. "I don' know. Is not good. They just come here."

Removing La Bruja's saddle and bridle, I gave her a pat and left her for Orlando to cool out. Then I hurried toward Jim.

All three men turned to look at me.

"This is Nikki Latrelle." Jim's Adam's apple slid up and down as he spoke. "She rode the horse."

"I know who she is," the man in the suit said as he stepped closer. He held out a hand. "Mike Stonehouse, investigator, Florida pari-mutuel wagering division."

His grip wasn't as hard as I expected, more like the iron hand in the velvet glove. Just under six feet tall, his gray eyes were as different from Jim's as a block of granite is from a dove feather. I'd seen a lot of track investigators and many of them developed that mean look in their eye. Probably due to the lies and greed that coalesced at their end of the racing business.

His gaze fastened on me, as if trying to read me. "The horse you rode, Diablo Valiente?"

"Yes."

"He tested positive for cocaine."

"What? That's crazy. We were with him before the race. With him the whole time!"

"Exactly," Stonehouse said.

Staring at the dirt in the aisle or maybe the piece of straw near his boots, Jim still tapped his lip.

Could the state vet have mixed up the blood samples? Orlando wouldn't do something like this would he? Why would anyone?

"Look at my record," Jim said. "I don't get violations because I don't use drugs on my horses."

Stonehouse rounded on Jim. "I'm only interested in yesterday's incident. The track steward's office, tomorrow morning at 10:00 am., Mr. Ravinsky. See that you're there. And I'll want to talk to you." He pointed a finger at me. "And," he paused, opened a small brown notebook, and said, "Orlando Castellano."

Oh shit.

He put the notebook in his suit pocket. "I'll be in touch." He turned to leave.

"Wait," I said. "There was a guy that was on our shedrow just before the race."

Stonehouse gave me a weary look. "There always is."

"No, really. Orlando saw him, too."

Stonehouse sighed and opened his notebook. "Describe him."

I wanted to ask Stonehouse if he was as fed up with his job as he appeared. Maybe not a good idea, so I described the man I'd seen outside our stalls instead.

"He was wearing dark-glasses, had long black hair, olive skin, and earrings in both ears."

At that moment, Orlando led La Bruja around the shedrow corner. Stonehouse glanced at him and back at me. "This is Castellano, the groom right? Did you mean to implicate your groom?"

"No! The guy I saw had a full goatee, not a moustache like Orlando. And he was taller."

Orlando halted La Bruja. His eyes widening as he took in the situation.

"Keep her moving," Jim said.

He would say that if he had a gun muzzle pressed in his back. The horses always came first with him. To think he would have given a horse cocaine was absurd. And if there was ever a horse that didn't need an enhancement, it was Diablo. Except . . .

I turned slightly away from Stonehouse and watched La Bruja's long, grey hind legs move away from us down the shedrow. Diablo had been so good, so well behaved. Walked into the gate like . . . *like he was in a dream*. Was it possible?

I arranged my face before I turned back to look at Stonehouse, simply nodding when he left. I didn't want to telegraph anything.

Cocaine was normally used as a painkiller. Could it have been used to take the angry edge off Diablo? Wasn't it even more likely to have made him ballistic? I couldn't make any sense of it.

#

The four of us finished the morning in strained silence and then Jim had us come into his office to see if anyone had any answers. No one did.

"None of you," Jim asked, "know who this guy with the dark-glasses was?" His question was rhetorical.

"I tell you. I never see him before," Orlando said, fidgeting so hard with one side of his moustache, I was afraid he'd pull the hairs out.

I couldn't stop twisting the horseshoe ring on my finger, and Afilio kept shifting his weight from one leg to the other.

"Okay," Jim said to Orlando and Afilio. "You two are done for the morning. I need to talk to Nikki."

"Yeah, boss," Afilio said.

"We see you later, Papa." Orlando had gotten in the habit of calling Jim "Papa," an affectionate term a lot of Latinos used when they liked or respected an older man. The two headed out, speaking softly and rapidly in Spanish.

Jim sank into a metal chair, removing his cap and rubbing his eyes.

"You all right?" I asked. *What kind of a dumb question was that?*

He settled his cap in place. "Not really.

"I don't get it," I said. "Why would anyone give Diablo cocaine?"

"Before your time," Jim said, "they'd give it to stimulate horses. But it's so traceable nowadays, nobody uses it. All those -caines. They won't use Procaine Penicillium on the track anymore. Even if a groom rubs himself with Lidocaine, his horse could show positive for trace elements."

"Who do you think would do this?" I asked.

"Currito might have, or more likely someone who didn't want the horse winning the purse money." He shook his head and a long sigh escaped him.

"This thing goes the wrong way, Nik, they'll rule me off."

I hadn't thought that far ahead. But he was right. All tracks were the same. Legally, the buck stopped at the trainer. It didn't matter who committed the violation, the trainer was always held responsible.

As the repercussions began to sink in, I closed my eyes.

Chapter 30

I was driving out of Gulfstream, making a right onto Hallandale when it hit me. The stewards would void Diablo's win. The purse money would disappear along with my $3,600. *Damn.*

I almost ran a red light when my cell rang. Glancing at the caller ID, I saw Will's name and felt a tiny punch in my gut.

"Can I buy you some dinner later?" he asked when I answered.

Why not? "Sure," I said. I agreed to meet at a restaurant called Casa del Mar, Will said was in Hollywood on the boardwalk.

My little charge of happiness lasted until I passed the bus stop where the girl had been shot. I still hadn't called Klaire. I scrolled to find and ring her number.

She surprised me by answering her cell immediately using her breathless soothsayer voice. I understood when she said, "I have a client here now. May I call you back?"

If a client was with her, she must be at home.

"Wait. When will you be finished? I have a friend I want to bring by."

There was a slight pause and I could hear her muffled voice, speaking to someone. The she came back on.

"Yes, bring Carla. I want to meet her."

I rolled my eyes. Of course she knew it was Carla. Who else would I bring? Cleopatra?

We agreed to meet at two, and before I disconnected, she said, "I have a bad feeling for you."

Of course she did.

Hallandale was jammed up with traffic and it took me

ten minutes to reach the Sand Castle. After almost rear-ending a beer truck, I decided not to call Carla until I parked in the motel lot. In my present state, a ninety-year-old with one eye was a better bet behind the wheel than me.

When I did reach her from the safety of my room, Carla said, "Of course I want to meet the psychic. Ever since we talked about her with Rick the other night. Maybe she can help us!"

I said I'd pick her up at the Diplomat since it was on the way, then had a quick shower, a change of clothes, and a tuna sandwich.

#

When I parked the Toyota near the end of Blue Water Lane, Carla stared at Klaire's asphalt shingled house with the neon-lit, turbaned woman above the front door. The words "Psychic Reader" still sputtered beneath the figure.

"I understand her not wanting potential clients to think she's pricey, but this is ridiculous," Carla said.

"I know. And she has a Jag in her garage."

Carla's gaze moved over the plastic flowers in the yard. The stray shingles that had littered the lawn during my first visit had been picked up, but the tinsel still hung from the edge of the roof and fluttered in the ocean breeze.

"This property is worth some money." Carla tilted her head toward the ocean only three houses away. "It's practically on the beach. She's probably just holding on for the value of the land. I wouldn't fix this place up either."

Carla could have a knife in her and she'd be wondering if the weapon had resale value.

"It looks better inside," I said as we moved to the front door.

It opened and Klaire stepped out wearing amber beads in her hair and the astrological rings on her fingers. A long tawny dress flowed down from her shoulders, almost covering her ankles. Gold flip-flops and several toe rings adorned her feet.

"Come in," she said, turning and leading us through the foyer and into the room on the right where I'd been before. The heavy scent of incense assaulted my nose. The same dim electric torch held by the statue of a woman flickered at the side of the backless couch and the sphinx heads stared from the arms of two chairs.

Klaire's kohl-lined, dark eyes never left Carla as I introduced the two. Carla perched carefully on one of the armchairs. I sat on the other one, and watched Klaire who seemed to be reading something about Carla. Was there such a thing as an aura?

"Klaire," I said, "we –"

She raised a hand, stopping me, without ever breaking her concentration on Carla.

No one interrupted the silence and its intensity seemed to build. Then Klaire started, as if suddenly waking up. Rising, she took three quick strides and stood in front of Carla.

"Your daughter is alive."

"And you know this," I asked, "because . . .?"

Sarcastic, but I was tired of messing with this woman. She'd admitted to being a con artist, and Carla needed false hope like she needed an axe in her head.

"Because it's true," Klaire said, her eyes widening as if surprised.

"Jade? Jade's alive?" Carla's voice was so soft I barely heard it.

"Stop it!" I said to Klaire. "You don't *know* that."

"I may be a liar and I've taken people's money. But I know this to be true. This time, I really do." Klaire wasn't looking at us, she was staring at a point just above Carla's head. "I saw her. The image was so *strong*. I could feel her. She's very frightened. But she's all right."

Klaire blinked her eyes and shook her head. She was either the world's greatest actress or truly astonished by what had just happened.

"I *saw* her," she said again.

"But *where* did you see her?" I asked, unable to keep the frustration from my voice.

"On the sea, surrounded by water."

"What, on a boat?"

Klaire staret at the same spot above Carla. "Or a small island. The image is gone. I wish I could tell you more."

I felt like shaking the woman!

"Wait," Carla said to me. "I believe her. I believe that Jade is alive." She turned to Klaire. "Thank you." She broke then and started crying hard.

Klaire retreated to the couch, sank onto it, leaned forward and put her elbows on her knees, her head in her hands. Her shoulders slumped in exhaustion.

I stood up. This stuff was too much for me. "Klaire, can I bring you a glass of water from the kitchen?"

She waved at me to go ahead. "There's soda in the refrigerator, glasses in the cabinet on the left." Her voice sounded weak.

I beat it out of the room, paused in the hall, and took a deep breath. I needed caffeine. Or bourbon, or – I took another deep breath.

When I stepped into the kitchen, a large tawny cat that could have been Scat's distant cousin, arched its back on the kitchen table and hissed at me.

"Get over yourself," I said.

Opening the refrigerator, I grabbed two cans of Coke, put them on the counter and found three cut glass tumblers in the cabinet on the left. I pinged one with a finger nail, and it rang nicely. Crystal. I filled the glasses with ice from the dispenser on the front of her new looking refrigerator. She'd probably stashed away some of her psychic hooker cash in a mutual fund.

I took a long, cold sip and rushed the Cokes back to the parlor, where I found Carla had moved from her chair to sit next to Klaire on the couch. She had a bamboo tissue-holder on her lap and was dabbing her eyes.

I passed out the drinks, and when I was settled back with the sphinx heads, I said, "Klaire, we need to tell you what we've found out about Jade."

"And the girl in the limo," Carla added, looking annoyed when her cell started ringing. She answered, her eyes rounding slightly. She pointed at the phone with her free hand and mouthed the word "George."

"You've got a name on the limo?" Carla said, standing up. "Who is it?"

"Okay. Wait a minute." She sat again and grabbed her patent bag. Sliding her fingers into an outside zippered compartment, she withdrew a small notepad and pen. "Tell me."

As Carla scribbled words onto paper, Klaire studied the blue ink scratches as if she were trying to divine a message forming on a ouija board.

Catching her eye, I whispered, "We'll fill you in." No point in her straining her abilities when we could just tell her what we knew.

"Got it," Carla said to George. "Thanks. I'll let you know." She ended the call and leaned toward me.

"The limo's tag traces to a Fort Lauderdale rental agency. The company that rented the limo is called Worldwide Enterprises. And get this," she said her voice rising, "the company's incorporated in Bangkok. It took George a while to uncover him, but guess who the CEO is?"

I didn't need the second sight to answer this one. "It's Chakri, isn't it?"

"Yes. Worldwide has offices in Fort Lauderdale."

"Wait," I said, "let me guess. They're an import/export firm."

"Exactly, but mostly import. Fabrics and high end decorative arts."

I wondered if that included jade figurines of beautiful

young women. Did Maldonista know his associate had an interest in American girls? Had maybe even abducted one?

"Who was this girl, and who is Chakri?" Klaire asked.

We started filling her in between sips of Coke and a move to her kitchen when Klaire told us she had grapes and cheese. When we entered the room, her large cat glared, hopped from the table to the floor, and then stationed himself near my feet as soon as I sat down.

Ignoring him, I told Klaire about finding Jade's friend, Tracy Johnson, and the party Jade had supposedly attended. About the guy seen outside my hotel room, who may have been the man Orlando and I saw before Diablo's race, and who may or may not have given the colt cocaine.

Then I told her about Currito Maldonista and Tau Chakri. "Chakri doesn't seem that connected to Currito," I said. "He refused Currito's invitation to lunch and then wound up next door in a Jockey Club suite full of girls in sexy dresses and high heels."

"Those ladies were call girls," Klaire said. "Business women doing a job. They've always had them at the races. But the girl in the limo, she was something else."

Klaire's words jogged my memory, flashing on hair like cinnamon and raw sugar framing a child's face that looked drugged. At my feet the cat's ears flattened and the tip of his tail jerked in time to something I couldn't hear. I pushed myself on.

"The men I saw in the SUV, the night that girl was gunned down? They were Latino, too. The guy with the gun had long hair and dark-glasses."

"You need to be very careful," Klaire said. "There are Cubans in Fort Lauderdale that run hookers, drugs, gambling, and things I try not to know about."

"This is why we need Rick." Carla rolled the last purple grape back and forth on the serving plate with one finger. "He'll know something about organized crime and who might be involved. If there could be a connection between

Worldwide Enterprises and Chakri."

"I will talk to some people I know who are involved in the business," Klaire said. "Rumors and gossip can be very useful. When I get people talking, they often say more than they mean to."

"That's your specialty," I said. At least it beat looking into a crystal ball.

Chapter 31

At six that evening, I headed for dinner with Will at the Casa del Mar. After finding a parking space on a side street near the beach, I saw a sign for the Hollywood boardwalk and followed a paved path between a new condominium and an old wooden hotel that had a café facing the walkway. The smell of hot french fries and onions made my mouth water.

As I approached the ocean, the wind strengthened. At the boardwalk, a cold, hard gale hit me as it blew down the coast from the northeast, reminding me it was still January. Getting my bearings, I into the face of the wind. It drove so hard against me, I had trouble making headway.

Mist blurred the outlines of shops and eateries to my left. The moisture beading my jacket and slicking my face and hair felt more like sleet. On the beach, the ocean frothed with white caps and endless, beating waves. I shivered and wrapped my jacket tighter, wishing I'd found a parking spot closer to the restaurant.

I walked almost a half mile before I found the Casa del Mar. Shivering, wet, and tired of the battering wind, I pushed through two sets of glass doors, almost stunned by the sudden, quiet warmth and glow of candlelight inside.

"Good evening, *Señorita*," said a man in a dark suit behind a wooden stand that held a phone, a reservations list, and a large, gold dish filled with foil-wrapped chocolates. "The weather must be terrible."

"It's okay, I said, pushing my wet bangs and hair back from my face.

He reached behind the counter, withdrew a starched, cloth napkin, and held it out to me, his eyebrows raised in question.

"Thanks." I grabbed the napkin. "I'm supposed to meet Will Marshall."

"Let me check for you."

While the man consulted his reservations sheet, I swiped at my face and hair, then glanced at the long, polished wooden bar on my left. I spotted Will about halfway down on a burgundy padded stool with a tall glass of beer in front of him. I'd know his profile anywhere.

"That's him," I said, pointing. "I'll just go over."

"As you wish, *Señorita*," he said.

I walked to Will, stood behind him, and waved at his reflection in the bar mirror.

His face lit with a slow smile. "Hey. You swim over?" he asked.

I climbed onto a stool. "One-horse open sleigh," I said, rubbing my cold hands together above the gleaming surface of the bar top.

He slid his fingers over my hands. "Man, you need something hot. Irish coffee?"

I nodded, and he ordered. When he pulled his hand away, he left mine warm and tingly.

"Nice win you had on Diablo earlier. I watched the replay."

'He was awesome. I didn't do anything but sit on him."

"I was worried about you at the gate. At least there weren't any fillies in that race with you."

Remembering Diablo's "fifth leg" display in front of Will, I felt a flush of heat in my cheeks. My coffee arrived, and I cradled the hot mug between my hands and buried my lips in whipped cream. I wiped off the excess cream with one finger and licked it clean.

He smiled, turned slightly pink, then looked away. "So . . . what's going on with Carla? Any news on her daughter?"

Stressful subject, but probably safer than whipped cream and thoughts that made him blush.

"A lot," I replied.

I brought him up to date on everything, including Diablo's positive test for cocaine. How could it only have been five days since Diablo had misbehaved on the track with the race filly? Five days since the morning Detective Bailey had shown up at the track and I'd told Bailey and Will about Carla and her missing daughter.

"So let me get this straight," Will said quietly. "You think there might be some sort of slave trade going on in South Florida?"

I nodded.

"What does Detective Bailey say about this?"

"I haven't talked to Bailey. She's with the homicide department. This seems more vice-related."

While I told him about Rick and Carla's budding romance, I sipped Irish coffee. Carefully.

"So Carla's in contact with this vice officer?"

"In a manner of speaking."

"That's good," he said. "Do you think any of this is connected to the race track?"

"You asked me that before. The day Bailey showed up. What are you after?"

"Just trying to figure out all the angles."

I wasn't sure I believed him, but before I could press the point, Will asked me if I wanted to move to a table or eat at the bar.

"I like it here," I said.

He had the bartender bring menus, and after we ordered sea bass, Will turned toward me. I felt his fit, hard thigh touch mine. Damn, it was like a branding iron!

"You mentioned Maldonista," he said. "What is your gut feeling about him?"

"What? Oh, Currito's a strange dude, but he's really into his horses. He adores those two fillies. I think he's okay. It's Chakri that's bad news."

Will nodded.

"But," I said, "Currito creeped me out earlier. Said his

younger brother gave him that scar. Now the guy's dead."

"You think Maldonista killed him?"

"No! I mean, I don't think so." But the thought had occurred to me.

"So what does he do for a living?"

"Jim says he owns a coffee plantation, gobs of family money."

I paused, studying the ice in my water glass. I'd accepted Currito as just another rich owner. They were all strange in some way. But a plantation in Columbia and cocaine in Diablo's test? How could that be a coincidence? But why drug his own horse?

I glanced at Will. He was so cute. "What do *you* think he does for a living," I asked.

He grinned and drained the last of his beer. "Probably the same thing that just occurred to you. He may grow more than coffee."I

Will's steady gaze unnerved me. I needed a powder room break. The large mirror behind the bar had so many bottles of vodka, whiskey, and liqueur blocking it me, I couldn't see myself. My trek through the boardwalk gale might have left mascara streaks under my eyes.

"Be right back," I told him before sliding off my stool.

I found the bathroom, used the facilities, then stared into the large mirror, surprised to see I looked good. No mascara runs and a healthy glow on my cheeks. I fluffed my almost-dry hair and stepped back into the dining room.

A large fish tank bubbled on the wall to my far right. I hadn't noticed it on the way in. I took a detour to check it out, but as I got close, I couldn't see any fish darting about, only ocean grasses waving inside.

When I reached the tank, I grew still. A small herd of green-and-gold sea horses swayed on the grasses and coral, their tails curled and hooked onto the plants. Some were tiny, some almost as big as my hand. They reminded me of the dead girl's tattoo.

Trying to leave her behind, I read the card on the wall above the tank.

THE SEAHORSE

The Seahorse is a rare ocean animal found in shallow tropical and temperate waters throughout the world. They are upright-swimming relatives of the pipefish, and unlike most other fish, they are monogamous and mate for life.

Because of their body shape, seahorses are rather inept swimmers and can easily die of exhaustion when caught in storm-roiled seas.

Population data for most of the world's 35 seahorse species is sparse. Worldwide coastal habitat depletion, pollution, and rampant harvesting, mainly for use in Asian traditional medicine, have made several species vulnerable to extinction.

I wished I hadn't read it. Harvesting? How disgusting. I turned from the little sea creatures and beat it back to the bar.

"What's wrong?" Will asked when I reached him.

"They have a tank over there. With sea horses. They're beautiful, but they look like that girl's tattoo. I read about them. People *harvest* them. Will. They're becoming extinct –"

"Whoa, whoa, whoa." He grabbed my hands. "Sit. Take a deep breath."

I did, and let the intensity in his green eyes blot everything out for a moment.

"Thanks," I said, and drained the rest of my coffee.

"So you and Carla are going to talk to Detective Harman?"

"Yeah," I said. "Maybe he can help the girl in the limo. Maybe he can find Jade before it's too late."

"You need to back away from this a little," he said. "I don't like to see you so upset."

Just then, the bartender brought our dinners, and we dug in. The meal sobered me up, and by the time I finished, I was trying not to yawn. I just wanted to lie down and sleep.

Will put his hand on my shoulder. "You got a lot going on, Nikki. My car's only a block away. How about I drive you to yours?"

He did, and when I got back to my room, I sank into a deep sleep like a heavy stone dropped in the ocean.

Chapter 32

I woke up the next morning restless and uneasy. Throwing my tangled covers back, I stood up quickly, as if I could distance myself from the recurring nightmare that haunted me.

Once again, I'd been thirteen, running through the dark streets of Baltimore, desperate to escape a pedophile stepfather. Stanley.

Had fear for Jim brought the dream back? I hated to think of the stewards going after Jim. Was it the sea horses and missing young women? Or had my feelings for Will stirred up bad memories? Whatever, I hated it when that pervert Stanley came back.

Shake it off, Nikki.

I got the coffee maker going and splashed cold water on my face. After pulling on stable clothes, I poured hot caffeine in a to-go cup and headed for Gulfstream.

I worked through the morning, and when Jim returned from his meeting with the stewards around eleven, he was escorted by Investigator Mike Stonehouse.

Jim's lips were tight and angry. He stepped away from Stonehouse and motioned Orlando and me over.

"They ruled me off. Six weeks."

I squeezed my eyes shut. "This isn't right!"

I'd been in Jim's shoes. It worked just like when office employees are fired, and management forces them to surrender their key and security pass, then watches them clean out their desk and immediately escorts them off the premises.

As assistant trainer, without direct evidence against me, I would not be held accountable. I could stay.

Stonehouse watched us with a cop's unreadable expression. I faced Jim, turning my back on Stonehouse.

"You told me this might happen," I said. "But I didn't believe it."

Orlando glared at Stonehouse. "No one here give Diablo cocaine. Is *estupido*!"

"Easy son, he'll be talking to you next," Jim said quietly, before pulling his truck keys from his pocket. "You know where my trailer is out in the main lot?"

"*Sí.*"

I glanced toward the big lot where trailers, trucks, and cars were required to park to avoid choking up the backstretch stables during training hours. The sun burned with heat already and reflected off the few metal vehicles visible beyond the hedge and chainlink fence that surrounded the backstretch.

"Take my truck, hook up the trailer, and bring the rig over. We'll load Ambivalent. Take a little of the load off you. Found some races for him in Maryland." He put a hand on my shoulder. "You're in charge, Nik. You know what to do."

His hand felt light, almost withered, on my shoulder, but his eyes held strength and integrity. I didn't want to run the show without him. I felt like I was in charge of the whole world – training Currito's horses, riding races, finding Carla's missing daughter. "I'll take care of it," I said, then swallowed. "Did they void Diablo's win?"

He withdrew his hand. "Yeah, they did."

"Sorry." He could have used the bump up in his win percentage.

So much for paying off my credit card debt. I would have no time for anything now that Jim wasn't managing the training schedule, handling the paperwork, or taking care of the endless details involved in a racing stable. *Damn it.*

I let out a breath. "I won't let you down, Jim. Besides," I said, glancing at Stonehouse, "we didn't do this. You'll be cleared, and Diablo we'll get his win and the money back."

Jim nodded and headed into his office. I trailed behind him to help, and Stonehouse followed us with a last word.

"Ravinsky, I'll leave you to finish up and load. You've got two hours. I'd better hear from stable gate security that you've vacated the premises and turned over your trainer's license or I'll be back. You don't want to make me do that."

#

When Jim's rig pulled away from our barn early that afternoon, the wheels underneath the trailer spun up puffs of dust, and Ambivalent whinnied unhappily from inside. Imposter, still stalled next to Diablo, answered Ambivalent's call with a frantic neigh. Diablo chimed in with something that sounded more like an angry scream. He was furious to have one of "his" horses taken away. He backed away from the stall gate, then charged forward and slammed his chest against it.

Orlando hurried over to close the wooden door over the wire gate. We had enough troubles without Diablo getting loose and running amok. Though the colt had indirectly caused Jim's exile, the old trainer had left Diablo's buddy, Imposter, to keep Diablo happy once he settled down from Ambivalent's departure.

The two fillies pawed at the floor of their stalls, staring as the trailer rolled away. I stepped to La Bruja and stroked her grey neck.

"Look at it this way," I said. "You'll get more attention now."

I heard one last lonely call from Ambivalent, then the truck and trailer disappeared from sight.

No sooner were they gone than Stonehouse rang my cell with orders.

"I want both you and Orlando my office at two," he said.

"Yes sir." I hung up.

Glancing at my watch, I saw we had only a few minutes. The man believed in keeping the pressure on full throttle.

As we walked up the paved road to the track kitchen, Orlando looked as nervous as I felt.

"You do have a green card, don't you, Orlando?" I asked.

"Sí, of course. But I have nothing to say to him. I don' know what happened!" He punctuated his last sentence with spread hands, palms up.

And I knew exactly what he did – *nada*.

I shook my head and studied the concrete building ahead. Palm trees ringed the white high rise, and an emerald-green roof with green-and-white ventilation cupolas crowned the top. White columns ran from the roof to the ground five or six stories below, supporting open balconies that wrapped around each floor.

The structure housed grooms and other stable help for free during the meet. The track kitchen and the security offices were both on the first floor of the building -- one of the most attractive I'd seen for stable help.

The whole complex had been built with a plan. Its eye-pleasing architecture and matching color scheme contrasted sharply with the straggling motels, box stores, and strip malls that uglified so much of America.

But Will had told me I shouldn't judge this particular book by its cover.

"Security," he'd said, "has a master key to every room in the grooms' quarters. They bust in unannounced at any hour and check for drugs, or other prohibited items.

I was glad I had the money to stay at the Sand Castle. Orlando and Afilio didn't, and I hoped the remainder of their stay wasn't marred by gestapo-like middle-of-the-night invasions.

When Orlando and I reached the kitchen, we paused inside the entrance. This far past lunch time, the dining area was almost empty. Air conditioning chilled the room, and the hum of refrigeration equipment seemed louder than the morning I'd had breakfast with Jim. A faint smell of grease laced the cool air.

A number of office doors appeared beyond the kitchen's tables and chairs in the back. Next to me, Orlando fidgeted with a lock of his black hair, his fingers worrying with it repeatedly.

"Let's get this over with," I said.

The security office had a closed steel door and a window like a bank teller's. I'd never really noticed it before. Funny how I could be surrounded by things and not acknowledge them until forced to.

On the other side of the thick glass, only a narrow hall and closed doors were visible. Maybe the hall linked to the other offices I'd seen in the back. The guard behind the glass shield called to someone we couldn't see, and then unlocked the door and motioned us to come inside.

He put me in a small room with two chairs facing each other across a metal table bolted to the floor. I knew an interrogation room when I saw one. At least he didn't lock me in, or cuff my wrist to the metal ring on the table.

Orlando threw me a worried glance as the guard led him out of sight down the hall. Probably to his own little happy room.

I sat on one of the chairs and waited. A moment later, I heard footsteps and Stonehouse entered the room, closing the door behind him. He gave me a nod, then sat in the other chair. He placed a manilla envelope on the table between us.

"Thank you for coming in," he said, pulling out the same brown notebook he'd used when he'd notified us about Diablo's positive test.

I refrained from pointing out I'd had no choice. Wouldn't do to antagonize the man.   "I'll help you any way I can," I said.

"Good." He opened his notebook. "We're investigating

how cocaine came to be in Diablo Valiente's blood." He held my gaze. "This is a very serious matter. I'm sure you realize we'll be keeping a close eye on you and your barn in the meantime."

I had a wild image of an eyeball with little feet following me down my barn aisle. "Yes, sir."

"I something wrong, Miss Latrelle?"

"No sir."

"The man you saw on your shedrow," he glanced at his notes. "The one who almost matches the description of your groom, Orlando –"

"Except he was taller than Orlando," I said.

"I *got* that," he said, his eyes hardening back to the granite I noticed the first time I met him. "Have you ever seen him before?"

"No, sir. But he must work here. Wouldn't he have to have a pass to get on the backstretch?"

"Not if he's accompanied by someone with a track badge."

Oops, that was true. Still, it narrowed it down a little.

He leaned back in his chair. "Did you see the horse's owner, Currito Maldonista at the barn the morning of the race?"

I thought back to that morning, squinting. "I think he stopped by briefly. But I can't swear to it."

Stonehouse stared at me, weighting the room with silence.

"He's kind of creepy," I said. "But he adores those horses and seems like . . . like a sportsman. You know, the kind of guy who believes in good horses, not ones that need drugs."

Stop babbling.

Stonehouse opened the flap on the envelope, withdrew a photograph, and handed it to me.

Diablo's win picture, everyone smiling, me in the saddle. I hadn't even seen it yet.

"This man," he said. "Who is he?"

I'd been dying to tell someone in law enforcement about Chakri and I may have babbled again.

I explained Chakri was supposed to be from Bangkok, had an import export business, knew Currito. Stonehouse didn't seem surprised about the call girls, but leaned forward slightly when I mentioned the young woman I thought was named Lena.

When I finished, Stonehouse let the small room fill with silence again.

Had Carla reached Rick the night before and told him about Lena? Carla and I had played phone tag but hadn't connected yet.

"Listen," I said, "I've talked about most of this to a Hallandale Beach vice detective named Rick Harman. You should ask him about Chakri. See what he can find out." I sure intended to.

"Tell me how you've come to know a local vice detective, Miss Latrelle."

I'd stepped in it now. I sighed, then told him about the girl that had been killed, and about Carla and Jade.

Stonehouse listened, then shook his head. "You're having quite at time here in Florida, aren't you? Maybe I should have shipped you out with Ravinski."

I stared at him, almost holding my breath.

His stone eyes softened a fraction. "I checked you out. My counterpart at Laurel Park seems to think it's safe to let you stay."

He must have meant Maryland racing's chief investigator, Jerry Offenbach. We had what you might call an uneasy relationship. But I'd heard from several people that Offenbach said I was trustworthy, although I doubted I'd ever hear him say it to my face.

"And Offenbach will tell you Jim Ravinsky might be the most honest trainer he's got at Laurel Park," I said.

"We don't know how the cocaine got into Diablo

Valiente. Probably, Ravinsky had nothing to do with it, but rules are rules." Stonehouse leaned forward and held out a business card. "Both my numbers are on here. You hear *anything* about cocaine or any other violations on the backside, you call me immediately. Now, go back to your barn, Miss Latrelle. Try to stay out of trouble."

He stood, and when I left the room, he came out behind me and headed down the hall to the left, no doubt to talk to Orlando.

"Orlando's my right hand," I called. "I know he's not involved."

Without turning, Stonehouse continued down the hall.

I pushed through the door of the security office into the kitchen dining area. My cell rang. Carla.

"I'm with Rick," she said. Can you come over to the HBPD office and talk to him now?"

Chapter 33

The approach to the Hallandale Beach Police Department looked different in the intense south Florida afternoon light than it had in the small hours of the morning Detective Bailey had brought me in for questioning.

The last time I'd been there they'd taken me through a back cop entrance. Today I hurried through a set of glass doors in the front that led into a waiting area. A female officer, protected by a tall counter, grillwork, and a bullet proof layer of glass, glanced up as I approached.

"I'm here to see Detective Rick Harman," I said and gave her my name.

A scratchy speaker came on, and I heard her voice.

"I'll call up there for you. Hold on a minute." She picked up a phone and punched buttons.

I looked at the ceiling and spotted a couple of video cameras covering the room. One of them pointed right at me. Too bad they hadn't these things on Hallandale Beach Boulevard the night that girl had been shot.

The officer hung up her phone. "Take a seat. Detective Harman will be right down."

I glanced at the elevator, remembering my ride down from the second floor after Detective Bailey grilled me. Across the room, near the glass entry doors pictures of officers who'd won awards or been killed defending justice lined the wall. Their eyes were watchful and steely.

A uniformed officer entered the lobby, walked to the elevator, and slid a pass key into a side slot. When the steel doors yawned opened, he disappeared inside.

Bullet proof glass, locked elevator. Were they afraid drug dealers would rampage in from the mean streets and riddle them with bullets? I rubbed my arms. Did they have to keep the air conditioning so cold in this place?

The elevator returned, and Rick walked out with Carla at his side. The gleam in his eye reminded me of the look I'd gotten from Will, and I thought electricity might arc through me if I tried to walk between them.

Carla rushed over and gave me a quick hug, her warmth and citrus perfume wrapping around me like a down comforter.

Under her breath, she said, "We're going to talk about this outside."

"Okay" I said, wondering why Rick wouldn't want to be in his office where he had access to computer files and network information. I'd been curious to see if he was located on the same floor as homicide, too.

"Hey, Nikki," he said.

No question, the man had a sexy smile that rose right up to his brown eyes. When he turned back to Carla, I caught her gaze, fanned myself with one hand, and mouthed the word, "hot." She winked.

"What?" Rick asked. Then the two of them grinned at each other like high school kids, before Rick ushered us out the glass door into the parking area.

The warm humid air pressed down on us immediately, but it was late enough the air held a hint of coolness. Between us and South Federal Highway, a donut-shaped concrete walk ringed a tightly mowed area of lawn, an island in the middle of the asphalt parking lot. Shade from palm trees criss-crossed the area, and the city had set up a few benches there, too. Probably for citizens to collapse on after unpleasant visits to the cop shop.

Rick led us there and we settled on two benches, with him next to Carla and me opposite.

"First," he said, "we're meeting out here because we might have a leak in the department and I'd rather not talk about this inside.

He touched Carla's forearm. "So you were going to tell me about this guy Chakri and a girl you think –"

"So Carla already told you about this," I said.

"Actually, no. Carla started to tell me about it, but I wanted to keep it out of the department, and it made more sense to wait for you. So let's hear it."

Carla started describing the scene outside Gulfstream's grandstand, and Rick shifted on the bench as he listened to the details about the drugged appearance of the girl in the limo.

Glancing at me he said, "You got a first name for Chakri?"

"Yes, I said, he was introduced to me as "Tau Chakri, from Bangkok."

"From Bangkok," he said, as if to himself. "Huh." He was quiet for a moment.

Carla said, "You know I've used this private detective, George Turner?"

Harman nodded, but hips lips twisted as if dismissing the private eye.

"I got George to follow up. He traced the tag number to a company in Bangkok, Worldwide Enterprises."

Rick listened quietly at first, but when she mentioned Worldwide's Fort Lauderdale office he looked worried, like Fort Lauderdale was too close to his new girlfriend.

"Damn it, Carla!" he said. "You've got to stop chasing this stuff."

Carla straightened on the bench and drew away from him.

"Easy," I said.

He scowled at me. "She could get *hurt*." He took a breath, then turned back to Carla. "I'm sorry. I've seen a lot of bad shit and I don't want any of that happening to you."

"I appreciate that, I do." she said. "But this could lead me to Jade."

Rick shook his head. "You two want to disappear like she did? Then just keep it up. You have no idea how bad some of these people are."

"I do," I said. "I saw those men gun down that girl."

Rick blinked, took a breath and nodded. "Yeah," he said. "You did. I'm sorry."

Carla stretched her hand out and he closed his fingers around hers.

The steady click of high heels caught our attention. Detective Bailey strode from the police station entrance across the parking lot in a black suit, her hair fluffed up like an angry red hen. Although she was on a diagonal away from us, Rick shifted as if uneasy.

"Work with me a sec, Carla," he said putting his arm around her, pulling her close, and nuzzling her cheek.

I watched Bailey as she reached her unmarked and jerked the door open. She was such a bitch. Was she the leak?

"Don't stare at her," Rick said. "She might be trouble, and I'm just a cop on a break enjoying the company of his girl."

The engine in Bailey's car came to life, and she drove from the parking lot in a hurry.

"Is she the leak?" Carla asked.

"I'm not at liberty to say. This is why I want you two out of this. If anyone in the department is on the take, it becomes that much more dangerous." He withdrew his arm from Carla slowly, as if reluctant to lose contact. Then he took a deep breath. "I'm going to run a check on Tau Chakri. He must be new in town. Nikki, who introduced you to him?"

"The man that owns most of the horses in our barn. Colombian. Owns Diablo, the horse I won that race on." *And tested positive for cocaine. But that story could wait.* "Didn't we ever tell you his name, Currito Maldonista?"

"Don't think you did," he said. "Huh." He seemed to recede inside himself a moment, then snapped back. "I'll run a check on both of these guys." He glanced at the police station, then hugged Carla again, and she kissed him on the mouth.

"*Wow,* he said after she pulled back, probably fanning himself mentally. "If you two don't have anything else, I need to get back to the office. And please," he said to Carla, "don't call the private eye. Don't drive around anymore looking for people and putting yourself at risk. Let me handle this."

Then he grinned. "If I have to, I'll put you in a cell to keep you safe."

We said goodbye, and I watched him walk away. He carried a lot more size and weight than Will, but still had the athletic figure. Although I understood Carla's attraction to him, he didn't have the kind of appeal for me that Will did. But Rick sure liked Carla.

"You know, Carla, I think he was halfway serious about that jail cell. How do you do it, anyway? You're driving the guy crazy."

"I didn't do anything," she said, her gaze locked on Rick's receding back. Then she turned and gave me a just-ate-the-canary smile, before standing up and stretching.

"Of course you didn't," I said.

"You should see his office," she said. "He has so many awards and commendations framed on the wall." Then her smile faded and her expression became doubtful. "He *was* pretty angry, wasn't he?" she asked.

"Yeah, but I think he's half crazy about you. And he's right, we don't really know what we're messing with."

The palm shadows over our grass island were thickening and growing longer. I needed to get back to the barn and help Orlando. I wanted to check the bandages on Imparable's legs. Make sure that one leg was tight and cold.

"What?" Carla asked. "You look like you just stubbed a mental toe."

She'd always read me too easily. I hesitated, choosing my words.

"Now that they've forced Jim out, I have way less free time. I owe Jim so much, Carla. I can't let him down. Maybe Rick is right, you know, let him take care of it."

Carla's gaze dropped. She seemed to be considering my words.

And maybe Klaire was right too. She wasn't a total charlatan, after all. Was I in danger?

"Carla, don't you think we've done enough? We seem to be running into walls, anyway."

"I don't know," she said. "I can't just stop looking. She's my daughter!"

Hard to argue with that. "But we're not professionals, Carla, and I have no idea what to do next. And if we do get more information, we'll have to tell Rick first. Before we do *anything*."

"But George could follow up. *After* we tell Rick, of course," she said.

Just what Rick had told her not to do. "I guess that wouldn't hurt," I said.

Chapter 34

In the morning, under a chilly, leaden sky, I rode La Bruja into the barn after jogging her around the mile track. A few moments later, Currito showed up. He wore a black leather jacket over a white woven shirt, dark pants, and those expensive reptile shoes. The heavy gold necklace I'd seen before glinted from his neck.

"La Bruja looks good," Currito said, after Orlando passed us leading the filly on her first turn around the shedrow.

"She *re*ally is. She had such an amazing work yesterday, I didn't want to do too much with her this morning. Just a long, steady jog, you know?"

He nodded, his expression bright, and filled with enthusiasm.

"But," I continued, "I have to tell you, Currito, it was a struggle to hold her to a trot. She wanted to stretch out again *so* bad."

Currito moved in close and laid his hand on my arm near my shoulder. "*Excelente*. And she will run in what, three days?

I stepped back, not liking Currito's strong musky aftershave. Uncomfortable being that close to him.

"Yes. Entries are due in the secretary's office this morning."

The man moved right back into my space. "And you will be all right without Mr. Ravnisky, yes?"

"Sure," I said.

"A most unfortunate occurrence. I don't like them tainting the colt's reputation with a disqualification. How could it happen, cocaine in my Diablo's blood?"

173

"I don't know," I said, taking the opportunity to turn away from Currito and his growing anger by moving toward Diablo's stall. "But he seems fine, see?"

Currito followed me closely, then hung back when the colt pinned his ears, and bared his teeth.

I held an open palm to Diablo, and when his ears flipped forward and I judged it to be safe, I stroked the smooth silk of his neck. Diablo turned his head, butted his nose into my hand, then blew warm breath on my skin that smelled like peppermints and hay. Apparently, Orlando had already been at work with the candy the colt loved.

"Nikki, you are doing a wonderful job with my horses. You too, Orlando," he said as the groom led La Bruja around the barn's corner for her second turn. "Hold on a moment. I want to show you how pleased I am."

He thrust his hand into a pocket of his dark pants and withdrew two wads of bills. He handed the larger one to me. I stared, but when someone gives you a gift of cash, you don't count it in front of them. You wait until later.

"Thank you!" I said.

"Gracias, Senor!" Orlando said, dipping his head and sliding the money into his jacket. Then, he clucked to La Bruja, and he and the horse continued along the shedrow.

As I moved to pocket my cash, Currito's fingers lightly grasped my wrist and stopped me.

"Wait, *querida*. I wanted you to have this. You see?"

He turned my hand over. I'd been aware that some kind of clip held the money, but was surprised to see the other side widened into a half-inch silver band with the engraved letters CM. A stone glittered from a gold setting placed between the two letters.

This is beautiful," I said, staring at the stone.

"I wanted to make up for the lost purse money." He smiled. "A Diamond from the heart of Columbia. A young woman such as yourself should have a fine money clip. You will do well in life and should be given the gifts you need."

He leaned closer.

The gift was really nice, but if the guy tried to kiss me, I might consider suicide. Then I remembered how angry he had been when Chakri refused his invitation to lunch. I gently pulled my wrist from his grasp, took a half-step back, and holding the clip near my face, pretended to study the stone.

"Thank you, Currito. This is so sweet. You are a wonderful owner, and these horses," I gestured at Diablo and Imparable, "are already a tremendous gift. I feel lucky to have them in my care."

Currito beamed, and I glanced at my watch.

"Where has the morning gone? I still need to get Imparable out."

I had that filly tacked up and out of the barn so fast, I was gone almost before Currito knew it. Moments later, when Imparable and I moved onto the track, the low sky overhead opened up, and tight drops of cleansing rain poured down.

#

Currito was gone when we returned to the shedrow, and Orlando was silhouetted in the door to the tack room by the light bulb hanging from the ceiling behind. He appeared to be counting his wad of cash

He saw me and grinned. "Currito," he said, rolling the two "r"s in the name for longer than I cared to hear it, "he give me five hundred dollars! He the man!"

I still hadn't counted my stash. I was glad to have it, but gifts rarely came without strings. I didn't want strings tying me to Currito. Orlando stuffed the cash back into his jacket and took Imparable to cool her out.

After he finished, I hosed the filly down with warm water in the wash stall, scrubbing her coat with a big soapy sponge while Orlando held her. Imparable was scheduled for a visit by one of the track veterinarians, and I wanted her in good order.

By the time she was dried and groomed, a woman veterinarian fresh out of vet school showed up at our barn. She was tall and thin and lugged a scanning device, which she used to recheck the filly's leg that had showed heat a few days earlier. Jim always liked to check and re-check.

"The leg still looks good," she said. "But the scan will have to be read by a technician in our office."

If the report came up clean a second time, I would schedule a work for the filly. When the vet left, I called the blacksmith and pinned the man down for an appointment to pull La Bruja's shoes, trim her feet, and re-shoe her just before she raced.

While Orlando and I finished up the morning, the rain gurgled gently in the gutters overhead. By the time we were done, it was late, and the breeze that is so constant in South Florida strengthened to a wind, blowing the clouds away and releasing the heat of the sun. After one last look up and down the shedrow, I called the racing secretary's office and entered La Bruja in the allowance race.

"Do you think the race will go?" I asked, knowing if too few trainers entered horses, and the secretary didn't have the runners to make a proper field, the race wouldn't run.

"We've got quite a few in there already," he said. "You should be all right."

I thanked him and disconnected. I'd wait for the "overnight" sheet that would be printed late in the day. At most North American tracks, when the secretary's office finished filling the race card, they printed the schedule. It could be picked up in the racing office, or more conveniently, from the guard at the stable gate.

After walking to my Toyota, I revved up the engine and the AC. Then I counted the money.

Currito had given me a thousand dollar tip! The ten one-hundred dollar bills smelled new, looked freshly inked, and felt crisp. I slid the cash in my wallet and slipped the diamond clip in my pocket.

Powering up my cell phone, I found two messages. Jim had called to let me know he'd made it to Georgia the night before and was heading for Maryland.

"Don't forget to enter La Bruja. Glad you're there, Nik. You can handle those four horses."

Yes, I could. But could I handle Currito?

There was a pause, then the message continued. "Call me if you need anything."

I heard a disconnect and played the second message.

"Nikki," Klaire's voice, "I have new information that concerns you. You and your friend need to hear this. Call me right away."

I did, but Klaire gave me nothing on the phone.

"It is not safe, and it is better if no one sees us together," she said. She referred to Carla only as "your friend," as if using the name itself was risky. Her paranoia was contagious, and after she hung up, I found myself glancing around at the cars surrounding me in Gulfstream's public parking lot.

I cranked my Toyota up and sped away from the race track parking lot, driving the few blocks to the Sand Castle. Once parked there, I dialed Carla and told her about the call from Klaire. Two calls later, the three of us had agreed to meet in Carla's room at the Diplomat Hotel.

I should probably start a load of laundry, and take a nap, but I wanted to shake off the case of nerves that had grabbed me after talking to Klaire. I turned on the radio looking for an upbeat song only to land on an old Stones classic about rape and murder being just a kiss away.

Chapter 35

I stepped off the elevator on the eighteenth floor of the Diplomat and walked down the carpeted hallway toward Carla's room. Behind me, a second elevator chimed, and I heard the doors slide open. Still rattled, I glanced back, only to find a woman wearing a conservative, brown pantsuit, head scarf, and large sunglasses emerging into the hall. What had I expected? A drug dealer with a machine gun?

Walking toward Carla's room, I heard the brushing of pantsuit legs in the hall behind me. I darted another look behind me. The woman's dark glasses had a of lot eye-catching bling and hid almost a third of her face. Her hair was pulled up and hidden beneath the scarf. But something about her mouth rang a bell.

"Klaire? I asked.

A quick nod, then a finger to her lips and a hand wave that motioned me to keep moving.

I would never have recognized her if I hadn't looked twice and been expecting her at the hotel.

"Is this necessary," I whispered.

"Wait until we are inside."

It seemed so silly, but I knocked on Carla's door. Carla opened it immediately, and I stepped in with Klaire on my heels. Klaire closed the door fast.

"What's going on, Klaire? I asked.

Carla stared at Klaire's disguise, then waved toward the table and chairs on the balcony. The sliding glass door was open and salt air drifted in.

"Nikki," Carla said, "why don't we sit outside?"

"No," Klaire said. "Inside. We could be watched out there."

Carla and I exchanged a glance, and I said, "Fine." I pulled the desk chair around and sat, leaving them to the white couch.

They settled, and Klaire removed her sun glasses. The lines around her eyes had deepened, but a tense energy filled her as she leaned forward and spoke.

"I asked around about a party that might have been given the night Jade disappeared. I have friends in the . . . entertainment business. They're no longer active but they have contacts. There was a party, like you thought. With the rap star, Dagger. My contacts, they gave me the name of a woman who attended. I went to see her. She didn't want to talk, but I . . . convinced her."

Klaire had probably scared the woman to death with premonitions.

Klaire startled me by saying, "I *heard* that."

"Heard what?" Carla asked, with a confused look.

"Just go on, Klaire," I said.

Klaire's lips pursed, but she continued. "The woman talked to me because I showed her copies of Jade's pictures and told her the girl has been missing for days. I told her another girl was killed on the street. She knew what I was talking about. The party she attended was not a nice one. She finally admitted she saw Jade that night."

I leaned forward. We were getting close!

"She *saw* her?" Carla clutched the black sleeve of Klaire's jacket. "Was she all right? Did the woman say?"

"Jade was okay. At least at the beginning, but like I said, this was not a nice party. There was a lot of booze, and drugs.

Carla's mouth twisted, and her eyes darkened. "But what happened to Jade?"

"The woman is not certain, and – "

"Does this woman have a name?" I asked.

"I can't tell you her name or the name of my friends. I promised them. They need to be protected. You can't *tell* anyone. These people are in fear for their lives."

A cold knowledge hit me. This thing was turning into a nightmare, maybe the same nightmare I'd seen when the nameless girl had been gunned down at my feet.

"But, Klaire," Carla pleaded, "we have to tell Rick!"

"You can't," Klaire said. "I won't give up the name, I will deny knowing anything. I will stop helping you if you do that."

A seagull rose and hung in the air outside Carla's balcony, riding the warm, breeze. He seemed to stare into the room before emitting a harsh cry, dipping a wing, and plunging from view.

Carla slumped against the back of the couch, and I caught Klaire's gaze. "Can you at least tell us what this woman thinks happened to Jade that night?"

Klaire exhaled slowly. "Some men at the party got Jade high. They took her."

Carla's hands clutched wildly at Klaire's arm. "What? They took her? Who took her?"

"Two men," Klaire said. "My contact said Jade didn't look like she wanted to go with them, but was too out of it to struggle. They were . . . a little rough with her."

Carla's hands fell to her lap. "Oh, God."

"Did this contact tell you what these men looked like?" My voice sounded as harsh as the seagull.

Klaire glanced at Carla who was rubbing the fingers of one hand mindlessly against the nubby white fabric on the couch. Klaire hesitated a moment, as if unsure what she should or should not say. Maybe she just didn't want to cause Carla more pain.

Then she met my gaze. "Both men were olive skinned, with long black hair, and tattoos. One of them was the man Jade's friend saw at the White Sands agency, the one who first mentioned the party to Jade."

Carla started to speak, but Klaire cut her off. "Let me finish. I won't tell you the name of my contact, but I will give you the name of this man who worked at the White Sands."

I thought about Rick's warning. He would already have the name of this man. Did Carla and I really need to know it? But I stayed silent, staring at Klaire, waiting to hear it.

"Carla, I understand you have to mention this name to your friend Rick in vice. Promise me you will say it's a rumor you heard from one of the girls when you were locked in that police van. You only just remembered it. You cannot say you heard it from me."

"Of course," Carla said.

Klaire glanced at me.

"I promise," I said.

"His name is Hector Gonzales. He's not at the White Sands anymore. He cleared out after that raid. But he's run girls out of Fort Lauderdale for years."

"But how can we find him?" Carla asked.

"We can't," I said. "Jesus, Carla, Rick will kill us. Just give him the name. Tell him you just remembered it, like Klaire said."

Klaire rose and walked to the balcony doors. The wind had whipped up out there. The roar of the surf had grown louder while we talked. Klaire glanced back at us, and it hit me. She wasn't *reluctant* to tell more, she was afraid. I could see it in her eyes.

"I can't stop what will happen," she said.

"What are you talking about?" *I didn't want to hear this.*

"Dreaming is a gateway to another world." Klaire faced the sea again, and I had to strain to hear her. "Especially that place where the mind connects to many things, those moments before the subconscious finally submerges again and the mind rises up."

"You're creeping me out." I said.

"Nikki, wait," Carla said. "Let her finish. You know something, don't you?"

Turning toward me, Kaire continued. "I will be honest with you. I don't know how much credit to give these dreams.

Nikki, you know I feel you are in danger, but this morning, I saw Carla, too. You are both heading down a road that frightens me, but I believe you must follow this road –"

"To find Jade," Carla finished the sentence.

"Yes, so I will tell you what I know. This man, this Chakri? My contact tells me his company, Worldwide Enterprises, will have an event tomorrow night, in Fort Lauderdale. Gonzales will supply the girls."

"We're going," Carla said.

"*No*," I said. "We can't!" *This had to stop.*

"If you want to do something," Klaire said to Carla, "buy a throwaway cell phone. I know someone with a voice changer. You know, those things that distort your voice? Use it and leave an anonymous tip for Hallandale Vice."

"Just one little problem," I said. "Hallandale is not Fort Lauderdale."

"It will work," Klaire said. "Both departments are in Broward County. Harman will be given access."

Was there no end to Klaire's talents?

Chapter 36

Carla and Klaire were still talking about the throwaway and the voice distorter when I had to leave for evening feed.

After finishing with the horses at Gulfstream, I grabbed a sandwich from the deli on the boulevard. I planned to retreat to the Sand Castle and shut the world out with a hot bath and maybe a rerun of "NCIS."

Except Will was waiting for me outside my room. He was sitting with my neighbor Lou, who'd brought two folding deck chairs and a six pack of Bud from his room. Will had a beer in his hand and Scat the Cat in his lap. Lou appeared to be settled in for the next century. There was no sign of Stella. She'd probably already checked out Will and decided he wasn't a threat.

Will saluted me with his beer can.

"Hey," I said to them.

Lou broke into his gap-toothed grin when he saw me. "Say, you want a beer?"

"Please!" I turned to my room, unlocked the door, and threw my tote bag on the bed. Then I rolled my desk chair outside.

Will popped a beer and handed it to me. It was cold and went down nicely. I sighed and sank onto my chair.

"How's Stella?" I asked.

"She was here a minute ago," Lou said.

"Has she seen that fellow with the tattoo again?"

"Oy, him. She's always going on about something like that. Nah, he hasn't been around."

"You're talking about the man with the Poseidon tattoo?" Will asked.

"Enough already with the tattoo man," Lou said, before taking a long pull on his beer.

But Will gave me a sharp look, and Scat suddenly jumped from his lap. She flattened her ears and darted into Lou's room.

"Yeah, him." I said.

"Something else has happened, hasn't it?"

I nodded.

Stella appeared from a cut-through to the motel's courtyard. She was carrying a basket of clean laundry. I took a sip of beer and watched her progress.

As she got closer, she said, "I thought this stuff would never dry. They got schlock equipment in there. Somebody should clean the lint filters." She reached us and set her basket down.

"I ask you, would it hurt them to sweep the place? Lou, you gonna help me put this stuff away or drink beer all night?"

"All right, all right," he said, rising slowly. He bent over even more slowly to lift the laundry basket."

Stella gave Will the once over. "My," she said, "he's a cute one."

"Stella," Lou grumbled," you gonna help me fold or what?"

She followed him inside, and the cat slipped out before she closed the door to their room.

"Now that we've had a look at marital bliss," Will said, "why don't you tell me what's going on."

I glanced around at the lengthening shadows. "How about we go inside." I didn't wait for him to answer, just stood and rolled my chair back into the room up near the desk and sat on it again.

Will followed, closed the door, and flopped on the bed. He looked at me perched on the desk chair and a slow smile spread across his face. "You could get in trouble letting me into your room, you know."

I had to remind myself to breathe. "Except you're in here so I can tell you what's been happening with Carla and

Klaire." I launched into a description of my afternoon at the Diplomat.

He listened, and when I finished, he said, "I like Klaire's idea about the throwaway phone. It might be wise to keep your distance from this." He studied the top of his beer can. "Now that we have a name, I'll check with security to see if Hector Gonzales is licensed."

"But will they give you that information?" I asked, surprised. "Stonehouse is pretty tough."

"I know him," Will said.

"What do you mean? I asked.

"Why don't I get you another beer?"

"I don't think so." I rose to my feet.

In one lithe movement, Will stood and closed in. Momentarily startled, I stepped back, but he edged closer, placing a hand on the wall near my head, then watched my face.

My body responded to him, rising with heat. Then Stella knocked on the door.

"Nikki, you got Scat in there with you?"

Will exhaled, and stepped back.

"No," I called. "I don't have the cat."

"You might be wrong about that," said Will, tilting his head toward my closet near the bathroom.

Scat was sitting on a pile of clean tee shirts on a shelf above the hanging clothes. She must have snuck in when I rolled my chair back.

"Wait a minute, Stella. Oh, for God's sake." I marched back, retrieved the cat, and carried her to the door. I opened it and handed Scat to Stella.

"Cat's a regular busybody," Stella said as she stared at Will.

"I'd better get going," he said.

"Yeah, I guess," I sighed.

He walked through the door past Stella, who finally moved out of the way as I shut the door.

Chapter 37

Carla and I sat in her red Mustang across from World Enterprises in Fort Lauderdale. At nine p.m., the street lamps left shadows, and the headlights of passing cars distorted the shape of pedestrians on the sidewalk.

"We'll just watch," she had said that morning when she came to the track to hit me up with her plan. "See who comes and goes."

Looking across the street now, she said, "I'm surprised that World Enterprises owns so much concrete on Atlantic Boulevard."

I stared, taking in the circular driveway and awning. A glass atrium rose above the entrance. On either side and above, polished marble walls climbed to dizzying heights. Footlights in the thick, tropical foliage at the base illuminated the marble walls and made the glass shine and reflect like the surface of a lagoon.

"I hope Klaire's right, and Hallandale Vice raids this place," I said.

Carla and Klaire had made the call with a voice changer the night before, and I'd been amused that Klaire hadn't trusted the untraceable status of the phone and had made Carla drive up I-95 almost to the airport to make the call. Still, it pays to be careful, and who knew what Broward County police might do?

Across the boulevard, cabs and limos pulled up to the main entrance. Men in hot-colored Hawaiian shirts or solid tees entered through the glass doors. A few had long-haired women in high heels on their arms, and I caught the glint of a gold necklaces or bracelets on a couple of the men.

A group of Asian guys approached along the sidewalk on our side. They were loud, joking, as if they'd just come from a bar. They wore well-cut suits with a fine sheen. They were not speaking English. We had the convertible top up, and the late model Mustang's darkened windows provided cover. The men didn't notice us as they jaywalked across the street in front of the car.

The group drifted into the flow of people getting out of cabs and limos across the street. It was like opening night for a movie. Except there weren't many women.

"You think the girls are already inside?" I asked.

"I don't know. But we're not learning anything sitting out here."

"We're not going in there!"

"I know, I know." Carla said.

"Besides, with your hair and that red dress, everyone would see *you* coming a mile away." She had on high heels, too. I'd worn a plain black skirt, a red tee, and flats.

As we watched, the crowd moving into the building eased. Bye nine-twenty, it was a trickle.

"Where is Rick?" Carla said.

"This thing will probably go on past midnight. Vice probably wants to let it simmer for a while."

A last limo rolled into the half-circle drive. A white stretch. The doors on the entrance side opened, and a man with a dark ponytail pulled a young woman out. Her hair was the color of cinnamon and raw sugar.

"It's her!" I said. "Did you see the way he jerked her?"

"Where the hell is Rick?" Carla's voice was tight and grating.

The glass entrance doors opened, and Chakri came out in a hurry, yelling something at the long-haired man. Chakri made a sharp get-in-here motion, glanced nervously up and down the street, and the three of them disappeared inside the building.

"What are they doing to her?"

Carla didn't answer. I hadn't seen the shorter man the peroxide blond hair hair who'd been with the girl before at

Gulfstream. Maybe he was finished with her. I pushed the Mustang's passenger handle and started to open the door, but Carla grabbed my arm.

"What are you doing?"

"I'm going in there," I said. "This is bullshit!"

"But you're the one who said, 'no way,' and we promised Klaire . . ."

We stared at each other a moment. "You got those fancy, dark glasses in your bag?" Turning to the back seat, I grabbed her red straw hat. Perfect with my red tee.

Carla opened her bag and withdrew a pair of tinted glasses with graduated lenses I could see through at night. After handing them over, she checked her face in the rearview.

"No, Carla." I said, "You gotta stay here and keep watch. If anything happens to me . . . I need you out here with a phone."

She started to protest, then sighed. "I guess you're right. "But wait, your hair. You'll need this. She withdrew a small bottle of Bumble and Bumble spray. "Hold out your hands."

I did, and she pumped wet glue onto my palms.

"Yuk, Carla, I could use this stuff to shoe horses!"

"Stroke your hair back and up with your hands. Hurry, before it dries!"

I did, and when the hat went on, my short hair disappeared. The glasses hid my eyes.

I put my hand back on the Mustang's door.

"Wait!" Carla said, and pulled her favorite weapon from her purse. "When you put this red lipstick on, you'll look totally different. Besides, it goes with the hat. Chakri will never recognize you."

"Yeah, well let's hope Rick doesn't, either." I swiped on the lipstick, swung the door open, and climbed out of the car.

#

I paused just inside Worldwide's lobby, uncertain of my next move. The glass atrium soared overhead, and palm trees in bronze planters dotted the tiled floor. On one side, a door led to one of those little coffee/sandwich/pharmacies you see sometimes in office buildings. Across the way, a fountain gurgled and splashed.

Ahead of me, three men stood behind a table covered with white cloth, cream-colored envelopes, and what looked like a computer-printed checklist. All three men were tall and fair, and though not especially threatening, they blocked my access to the elevators. Apparently, I needed an invitation.

I didn't see Lena or Chakri, but two male guests in tropical flowered shirts waited for the elevator. One of them turned briefly, revealing a printed name tag. When the chime sounded and the doors opened, the two men disappeared inside. I watched the floor number lights to see where they got off.

"Can I help you, miss?" One of the reception guys stepped from behind the table and walked toward me. He got close enough for me to smell his expensive cologne. He gave me a cool stare. Probably saw me watching the progress of the elevator. I looked away from the number lights. I could always drop Chakri's name, but then this guy would discover I wasn't on his list.

"Hey, is there a coffee shop anywhere around here? I got a killer headache." I cupped the back of my neck with one hand and rubbed, grimacing like the pain was brutal. "I need some caffeine."

The guy paused a beat, then smiled. "Yeah right over there, behind that palm. You lucked out. They're open till ten. They have pain meds, too."

"Great." I bailed out of the lobby through a swinging door and entered the coffee shop. The guy behind the counter was reading a magazine and yawned as he looked up. Mid-thirties, balding, with a patch of scruffy beard under his chin.

I ordered a small cup of black coffee, and when I had it in hand, I grabbed a magazine off the rack, then stood by the door, sipping the bitter liquid and leafing through the magazine without seeing the pages. From my new position, I could read the numbers on the elevator. I waited while one of the check in guys handed a couple of stragglers name tags from inside the envelopes. The elevator took them to the tenth floor.

I walked back to the sandwich counter, set my cup down. I started to put my tote down, too, but noticed a gummy mix of spilled coffee and sugar on the counter. I set the magazine in a dry spot and pulled my wallet from my tote.

"You want the magazine?" the guy asked, scratching at his beard.

"Actually," I said pulling a twenty-dollar bill from my wallet, "I want to go to the party next door, but I forgot my invitation."

He laughed. "Twenty bucks ain't gonna get you up there."

"But, I really need to go." I pulled the glasses off and gave him a pleading look. "I think my boyfriend might be up there . . . with somebody else. You know what I mean? I really need to find out."

His expression softened, his eyes wandered to parts of me where they had no business.

"So what will get me up there?" I asked.

"Normally I'd charge a hundred, but with you being so cute and all, I'll give you the cut rate. Fifty bucks."

Damn it. Then I remembered the way they'd jerked Lena into World Enterprises. I pulled out another twenty and a ten. He reached for it.

"Wait! You get it when I know you can get me in."

I was a little uncomfortable when he motioned me into the storage area behind the counter, but he led me through a locked door into a hallway, then opened a door to a concrete stairwell. I craned my neck back. The stairs spiraled upwards as far as I could see.

"You can't get to this hall from the street without a key pass, but once you're in you can access the whole building. You look like you won't have any trouble climbing up ten floors."

"I'll be fine," I said. "But how do I know the door to the tenth floor will open?"

"It will," he said. "Fire regulations." He held out his hand for the money, and I gave it to him.

#

I stopped on the second floor to make sure at least this first door was unlocked. Peering at the names of offices visible through the narrow opening I'd made, I realized even if Worldwide owned the building, it didn't use all the space. The second floor appeared to be the law offices of Smith, Hammer and Goldstein.

I sprinted up the next eight floors, and my breath remained steady. I might not ride as much as some jockeys, but I could still prove the experts who consider us the world's fittest athletes are right.

When I reached the tenth floor landing, I stopped and tried texting Carla, but couldn't get reception through the concrete. I heard music, but not close by. I cracked the door. The music grew louder, and bits of conversation rode the female pop star's electronic beat.

Peering into the carpeted hall, I could see the elevators halfway down. Across from them, light and noise poured from a wide opening into the hall. Must be the party room.

I eased from the stairwell. A few people stood near the elevators chatting with drinks in their hands. Nobody paid me any mind, so I called Carla.

"I'm in. On the tenth floor."

"Who's there? Do you see Lena?"

"Not yet. I'm at the far end of the hall. I'm just going to stroll to the party room and see what's going on. Anything happening out there?"

"Nothing," she said. "Nikki, be careful."

"Plan to," I said and disconnected.

I put the phone away and catching my reflection in the glass covering an old ship print, I made sure my hair was still tucked beneath the red hat. Walking toward the music, I smiled at three guys with drinks near the elevators, then entered a large room.

Party time, only not the drunken debauchery I'd feared. The crowd seen on the street earlier was lined up at two bars on either side of the room and at a long table laden with finger food standing in between.

A number of men and women in dark business suits and gold badges appeared to be working the crowd. One of them, a woman, stood close enough for me to read the badge pinned to the lapel of her suit.

"Teresa." Below that, "Worldwide Enterprises." She wore her dark hair long, but neatly pulled back. Her makeup was expertly applied and conservative.

Catching my glance, she approached.

"Hi, how are we doing tonight?

"Fine," I said.

Her smile flashed with perfect white teeth. "You should get something to drink, and eat. The shrimp is to *die* for. And please, if you have any questions about the various ways that Worldwide can benefit *your* company, just ask."

She handed me her business card. "Call me anytime."

I examined the card. An "executive associate," probably one step up from coffee server.

She smiled again. "Of course you know how many US businesses are prospering from partnerships with Worldwide. Going forward, we see at least an eleven percent increase in sales of fabrics, green tea, and electronic equipment from Thailand and South East Asia. And that's just the tip of the iceberg when it comes to products and raw materials available through Worldwide!"

"Really?" I asked, stifling a yawn. "Uh, my company *loves* working with Worldwide. You know, I'm just going to take you up on your offer of a drink."

I smiled, turned away, and headed for the closest bar.

Three men in Hawaiian shirts with their drinks already in hand grinned at me. One wiggled his brows.

I kept going, speared a shrimp off the food table, then stopped to watch a woman walking through the crowd in a dazzling yellow dress. She must be modeling imported Thai silk.

Nearby, a dark suited man with a gold badge spoke earnestly to the Asian men I'd seen outside. I couldn't understand a word he said – all Chinese to me – but his promotional body language and tone duplicated the spiel I'd received from Teresa.

This crowd was entirely too business like. Where was the action? Where was Lena?

As I approached the bar, I noticed a permanent display of framed, color photographs on the back wall of the room. I eased past the people in line for drinks and studied the pictures.

The first one looked like an interior shot of a fabric mill, with workers busy handling textile machinery. In the background, some of the employees looked like children. Another photo showed the docks, with a massive crane offloading a container while people in hard hats operated forklifts and other equipment. Another, displayed a long run of stockroom shelves holding computers and software equipment. Was there anything Worldwide *wasn't* in to?

The largest picture, centered on the wall, drew me closer. A massive, container ship plowed straight toward me through a roiling sea. The words "Worldwide" were stenciled on its dark prow.

My understanding of Chakri's business gelled, and a

chill swept along the hairs of my forearms.

Traffickers used container ships to move humans as slaves or indentured workers. Was Chakri a slavetrader? Glancing around the room, I didn't see him.

Since liquor loosens tongues, and bars are a great place to eavesdrop, I moved back toward the line for drinks.

A muscular guy in a tight black tee shirt near the head of line, motioned at me.

"Ladies first." He stepped back leaving a space in front of him.

"Thanks," I said and moved in next to him.

"I'm Ned, and this is Ted," he said grinning at the guy next to him, who also looked like a weight lifter.

"I'm Mary," I said, doubting these two guys were really named Ted and Ned.

Glancing at the other people in line, I saw only one woman. She wore a dark green suit with pumps, not strappy stilettos like the women I'd seen going into the building. A guy with an equally business-like attitude was with her. He even carried a briefcase. Ned and Ted seemed more like fraternity boys out to have a good time. Their reason for attending was the one I wanted to learn about.

I ordered a tonic water, and the iron pumpers had something called a "curl" which involved multiple bottles and different colored fluids. I caught the smell of carrots, oranges, and rum. One of those health drinks with plenty of booze. The three of us drifted from the bar and sipped from our tall glasses.

"So, Ned," I asked, "are you in the computer industry?"

"Ted and I run a barge company. We like to help the big boys move in and out of port."

"Cool," I said. "You mean like cruisers and container ships?"

"Yeah," Ted said before taking a slug of his drink. "Like that. What do you do?"

I'd already thought about this one. "I do marketing for a lingerie manufacturer."

"Really?" Ned appeared interested. "Which one?"

"Triangles," I said. "It's new, just about to launch."

"You got any, like, glossy photos or anything on you?" Ted asked.

"Sorry, no." Time for me to lay down my bet. I smiled and arched one brow. "But if you're seeing some of the girls here tonight, they might be wearing our product."

It hung there for a moment until Ted bought it.

He grinned. "We are all over *that*! We'll have to take some of those triangles home as souvenirs!" Then he made a sound like a donkey braying.

I tried to smile amiably while they hee-hawed and slurped down more booze. Ned darted a look at a closed door in the corner. A small sign next to it said, "stairs." Only there was no matching red "exit" sign.

"I should mingle," I said. "You guys have a good time."

"Don't you worry, cutey. We will."

I walked back and spoke to the woman in the green suit.

"Hi, I'm Mary. My company is interested in partnering with Wordwide. Have you had luck doing business with them?"

"Hi," she said, shaking my hand. "I'm Louise, with the Grafton Company. We're in high end electronics, and yes, we've had great luck importing parts through Worldwide. Super prices."

"Cool," I said, wondering if the parts were assembled by children.

Louise launched into a lecture about getting the best bang for your buck with imports, and I glanced back at Ted and Ned. They had emptied their glasses and were heading toward the door with the "stairs" sign.

"Excuse me," I said to Louise, then took a quick breath and followed the iron pumpers.

Chapter 38

When the door closed behind Ted and Ned, I set down my tonic glass on a nearby table, then walked to the door and opened it. Inside, carpeted stairs and a carved wood railing climbed upward. I'd bet they'd built this addition after the main construction was finished.

I heard a door close above me, and glancing up, was dismayed to see a big guy in a gray suit staring down at me from the landing. His arms were folded across his chest.

"I think you're going the wrong way," he said. "You need a name tag to come up here."

I giggled and headed up the stairs toward him, stumbling a little as if unsteady from too much rum. "I'm with the two guys who just went up there."

"They didn't say anything about you."

"That's because they thought I was right behind them. They got me one of those curls they're drinking. That's a mean cocktail! Mixed me up a little, you know?"

"That may be true, but why would they need *you* up there?"

I smiled, gave him a wink. "Because we do *everything* together."

He looked at me with more interest. "Well, come on up, honey."

When I lurched past him, he grabbed for me, but I jerked away and sprinted up the stairs. Fortunately, he didn't come after me, but a glance back showed him using some sort of communication device.

I made a U-turn and followed the second flight of stairs to the next floor. Once there, I found myself in a hallway. I could smell cigars and cigarettes and something sour like sweat. I suspected I was in a section of the eleventh floor blocked off from the rest of the building.

Ned and Ted had their backs to me as they spoke to a man and two women sitting at a horseshoe shaped, carved desk against one wall. From their positions, the threesome could watch every angle of the hallway, especially the long row of closed doors on the opposite wall. The women were pretty, but worn, about thirty-something. Acne scars pitted the man's face, and behind him pictures of girls, like the ones at the raided White Sands agency, lined the wall.

Pit Face nailed me with a cold gaze. "What can we do for you?"

I walked toward him. "I'm a friend of Ned and Ted, here. I forgot to tell them they should look up Lena tonight."

The iron pumpers turned around, and I waved. "Ned, Lena's really hot, has this gorgeous body and . . . I fanned myself with my hand, then looked at the guy behind the desk. "She's here, right?"

"Who are you?" Pit Face asked.

"She's in lingerie," Ned said, apparently too fueled by his rum to think about distancing himself.

"I'm sorry. There is no *Lena* here." But his gaze shifted to a closed room across the hall, a little farther down.

Nearby, a door opened, and a man about forty walked out patting his hair into place. I glimpsed a girl lying on the bed, naked under some sort of sparkling, sheer covering. She stared mindlessly at the ceiling, never glancing our way. She was Jade's age.

I must have shown my disgust. The man paused when he saw me, dropped his gaze to the floor, and hurried past. He moved into the stairwell and disappeared. Pit face was giving me the hard stare. "This is a private club up here, lady. What people do is their business. Turn around and go downstairs." He rose from his chair.

I couldn't help but look at the girl in the room nearby, then at the door where I hoped to find Lena. I took a step toward it. Big mistake.

Pit Face circled from behind his desk and rushed me. I launched myself into Ted, shoving him at Pit Face. Their legs tangled, and they fell.

A woman behind the desk shrieked. When the other one snatched up the phone, I lunged behind the desk, kicked her hard in the shins, then jerked the phone line from the wall. Turning to Ned, I pointed at the open room, where the girl lay on the bed.

"Don't you get it? That girl's a slave! The cops are on their way. Do you want to be a hero or a villain when they arrive?"

Ned took a moment to process, then looked at Pit Face who had rolled to a sitting position and was pulling something from his suit. Ned erupted forward and kicked Pit Face in the head. He did it once more after the man went down.

Gasping, Ned leaned over and grabbed Ted's arm. "Come on, man, let's get out of here!"

They ran down the hall to the stairwell with the woman who'd shrieked hard on their heels. Just as the three of them reached the end of the corridor the landing guard burst through the doorway. One of my iron pumpers shoved the guy and he disappeared backwards with a shout and a crash.

Doors began opening along the hallway, and men peered out, straightening clothes and zipping zippers, before fleeing for the stairs. Some of them carried their shoes. I ran for the room I hoped held Lena, and shoved the door open.

A tall, fat man in a gold necklace and nothing else lay on a bed, snoring. The girl with hair the color of raw sugar huddled in a chair in the corner. She'd wrapped a sheer, spangled sheet around her body.

"Lena?" I asked, closing the door behind me.

Her head turned slowly. Her eyes had trouble focusing.

"I want to help. Is your name Lena?"

"Yes."

I leaned over a pile of clothes and picked up a large Hawaiian print shirt. "Here, put this on." I handed it to her, but she was slow, unable to concentrate. "I'll do it," I said.

Slowly, I pulled the sheer cloth away from one side of her. Bite marks and bruises covered her breast. Like an evil presence, a sea horse tattoo stared at me from the underside of her forearm.

Get a grip, Nikki.

I slid Lena's right arm into the sleeve of the shirt. She seemed more aware now, pushing away the rest of the sequined cloth, sliding her left arm into the shirt's other sleeve. I buttoned her up. When she stood, the shirt hung almost to her knees. "Let's get you out of here," I said.

A loud snore from the bed startled us. Lena's eyes widened in fear, but when the guy didn't wake up, she whispered, "Pig!"

We crept to the door, Lena hanging behind me. I eased it open a crack and peered out.

Chakri and the man with a pony tail stood sideways near the desk. A tattoo on the arm of the pony tail guy stopped me cold. Horses galloping from the sea. Driven by a man with a pitchfork. I had to be looking at Gonzales.

In the hall, the woman I'd kicked in the shin sat in a desk chair rubbing her leg as she spoke to the men. "No, I don't know who she was."

Chakri murmured words I couldn't make out. Behind me Lena moved closer, saw the men, whimpered, and stumbled back. The woman in the chair looked up.

She pointed at me. "That's her!"

I slammed the door shut, then pulled Lena to the wall by the door's hinges. Throwing it open again, I pushed it back until it hid Lena from sight. Plunging out, I smashed Chakri with my shoulder and kept going. But Gonzales was too fast.

He grabbed my arm and had it twisted up behind my back before I could kick or claw. My shoulder felt like it was being ripped off. I kicked at his leg but he lifted me up by my twisted arm until I screamed.

I heard shouts and the thud of heavy shoes speeding up the stairs. A man in a blue windbreaker burst through the door and pointed a gun at us.

"Fort Lauderdale Police!" he shouted.

Another cop came in fast and aimed his gun. "Drop the girl. Get down! On the floor. Now!

Gonzales threw me toward them. I landed on my hands and knees, groaning as the hard jolt hit my shoulder. Gonzales turned and ran. Disbelief filled Chakri's eyes. He swivelled his gaze from me to the cops. Gonzales bolted into a room at the end of the corridor.

Chakri ran after him. I pushed myself up with my good arm, sprinted forward, then dove at Chakri. My tinted glasses sailed through the air as I crashed into him. We tumbled to the floor. I could hear a cop yelling.

"On the floor, face down! Do it!"

I did, and the cops were all over us. The last thing I needed was my hands shoved behind my back and my wrists bound with plastic cuffs. But it was good to watch Chakri get trussed up like a chicken, until a cop pushed me face-first back on the floor. Raising my head a fraction, I saw Rick Harman and a blond female cop enter the hall. I remembered her – Officer Hayes, from that first night on Hallandale Boulevard. The nice cop. Before the bitch Bailey had arrived.

"Rick!" I called. I dropped my head and felt the carpet pile burn my cheek.

"Nikki? What the hell?"

I heard him rushing toward me. "This one's all right. Get those cuffs off."

Someone did, and Rick helped me into a sitting position.

"Where's Carla?" Fear rattled his voice. "Is she all right?"

"Yeah, she's outside in her rental."

Rick's cell vibrated and he turned to answer it. I

glanced at Chakri. His eyes were so malevolent, I wanted to scoot backwards. Instead, I held his gaze. Why hadn't I noticed before? His face was immobile because it was stretched tight from plastic surgery. I smiled.

"They're going to have fun when they run your fingerprints, aren't they?"

If he hadn't been cuffed, he would have hit me. My smile grew wider.

Two cops came out of the room where Gonzales had fled.

"You won't believe this shit," one said. "That room connects to the building next door. The guy is long gone."

"Fucking Gonzales!" his buddy said. "These rooms are loaded with underage girls."

I could see police leading young women from some of the rooms. I rubbed my shoulder. Then Rick's call ended, and he turned back to me.

"Are you okay?" he asked carefully.

"I think so."

"Damn it! I told you two to stay out of this. You're lucky you're not dead! What the fuck did you think you were doing?"

I shook my head, clearing fog from the pain in my shoulder. "I was looking for . . . Lena!" I jumped up and dashed to her room. The fat guy on the bed still snored. Behind the door, Lena crouched where I'd left her.

"The police are here," I said. " You're safe now."

She gave me a pitying look. "You don't know anything. No one is ever safe."

In spite of what she said, her eyes still held a glimmer of hope, a wistful expression like that on the carving of the mermaid. Still, I didn't know how to answer her, and didn't because Rick and Officer Hayes stepped into the room.

"Is this Lena?" he asked.

"Yes," I said.

"We'll take care of her. Officer Hayes, why don't you

put Lena with the other girls?"

"Where is she going? What about *Jade*? " I asked Rick. "Where are you taking them?"

"Nikki, we're looking for Jade," Rick said.

Office Hayes gave me the sympathetic smile I remembered from the murder scene. "The girls are downstairs. We're sorting it out with Fort Lauderdale PD."

Rick turned and spoke to two uniformed officers. "Get this guy," he said, pointing to Chakri, "out of here. And somebody wake up sleeping beauty here." He waved toward the fat man still snoring on the bed.

Hayes led Lena away, and while Rick and the two officers were occupied, I eased into the hall and hurried toward the room where Gonzales had escaped. Empty. Turning, I went toward the stairs, checking every room along the way. No sign of Jade. The cops had cleared most of the girls out, and the male rats had long since fled the sinking ship.

I raced down the stairs into the event room and stared. The place was a zoo. I saw Pit Face in handcuffs, some of the johns still holding their shoes, cops everywhere, attendees herded into one corner, and the girls.

Someone had given them blankets to put on. Officer Hayes and several female cops were with them. I drifted closer. Not one of the girls had a seahorse tattoo. Why?

I stared at the pretty, young faces. Eyes unfocused, expressions strained, they were barely more than children. I kept searching.

Jade wasn't there.

Chapter 39

The night In Fort Lauderdale seemed to go on forever. After the cops finally rounded everyone up, they took Carla and me to the Lauderdale police station on Broward Boulevard to give our statements.

Though I didn't see Lena again, I passed Chakri sitting in the vice department hallway. He wore handcuffs and sat with his smarmy looking, slick-haired man who wore a large diamond pinky ring. Probably his lawyer. A large and manly woman officer with cold eyes stood over them. I couldn't resist a little finger wave.

By the time Carla dropped me off at the Sand Castle, I barely had time for a shower before heading to the track. The night left me exhausted, but underneath it was a strange energy, possibly fueled by the powerful rage I'd experienced at Worldwide.

At the barn, I got a good gallop into La Bruja first, then left her in Orlando's good hands while I took Diablo out. In my head, tapes from the previous night played repeatedly, making it hard to stay in the present until Diablo snaked his head toward another horse that galloped past, and tried to savage it with his teeth.

I snatched Diablo's head back with the reins, pulling him away.

"Hey, watch it!" the rider yelled at me.

"Sorry," I called to the guy's retreating back.

When we got around the track and back to the barn in one piece, Orlando took Diablo from me and started to lead him away.

"Hey," I said. "You hear any more from Inspector Stonehouse?"

"No, just what he say before. 'Stay out of trouble.'"

"Good." I replied. Our stable needed Orlando more than ever, but right then he needed to keep Diablo moving, so I walked with them for a ways.

"When we race La Bruja tomorrow," I said, "we'll need help. You used to work for Tom Smith didn't you?" I'd only met Smith briefly. Training in the next barn over, he had a big operation with two licensed assistants.

"Sí." Orlando replied.

With Jim absent, I had to find a licensed trainer to saddle La Bruja in the paddock before her race. I couldn't do it. I'd be busy in the role of jockey.

"Do you think someone over there could saddle La Bruja tomorrow?"

"I will ask. Should be no problem. I let you know."

I smiled. "Thank you, Orlando." He was a gift, and reminded me a little of our Maryland groom, Mello. He had Mello's uncanny ability to find what you needed, sometimes almost before you asked.

With Ambivalent gone, Orlando and I got the morning finished up fairly quick, but I was dragging. As soon as I got into my car, I turned my phone off, drove to my room, and after a hot shower, crashed into oblivion.

#

I've heard people can process events and make decisions while sleeping, and it's probably true. When I woke up, something inside me had changed, and the energy I'd felt that morning had returned and intensified.

I lay still a moment and thought about my past, about my mom dying and leaving me with Stanley. The bastard had left me feeling guilty and unclean for years. But had I been any more responsible for ending up with him than those girls at Worldwide were responsible for being made into prostitutes? *No.* The realization hit me hard, snapping a mental chain.

It wasn't my fault. I didn't do anything wrong.

Suddenly wracked by an explosion of sobs, I grabbed my pillow and clutched it like a life raft. I let the storm rage and when it was over, I felt cleansed, healed.

I lay still a while, then got up. Several tissues and a face wash later, I checked phone messages. Nothing important and no message from Will.

But I'd wanted a message from him, so I called him. When he answered, I said, "I'd like to see you."

"Sure," he said, and I could almost hear his slow smile. "How about an early dinner? Billy's Stone Crab. My treat."

He wasn't shy about spending the money he'd won in a recent race. Wild horses couldn't keep me from an offer like that.

#

At the restaurant on Ocean Boulevard, guests can either ride an elevator to the second floor's swanky restaurant or sit on the veranda in one of six booths next to the Intracoastal waterway. A no brainer for me.

"The veranda," I told Will.

He smiled.

I climbed into the wood slat and green upholstered booth, surprised when my movement caused the bench to swing back and forth.

A waiter hovered by us holding menus.

"I'll sit next to her," Will told him. Then he stepped on the booth's bottom rail, plopped down next to me, and grinned as the bench slid back. "Dine and glide."

The waiter handed us menus.

"Do you have Four Roses single barrel?" Will asked.

"Yes sir."

"That's great. Bring two, on the rocks," he said glancing at me.

Across the ribbon of Intracoastal, a heron stood still as a yard ornament, his long legs on the muddy bank, his feathers silhouetted by the sun that lay on the western horizon. The water smelled faintly of shellfish and gasoline, and in the distance I could hear the engine of a boat chugging toward us.

Our waiter brought the bourbon, and I took a sip.

"Firewater," I said to Will.

"You don't like it?"

"I love it!"

I sipped more and told him about the previous night in Fort Lauderdale. He listened intently.

"So what do you think?" I asked.

"I think you didn't pay close attention when I told you to keep your distance from these people."

"Oh for God's sake," I said. "You sound like Rick."

"Too bad," he said. "I'm halfway in love with you."

I grew still as the heron.

Will held his hand up, palm out. "Hold your hand against mine."

I did. Hadn't realized his hand was that big and his fingers long enough to fold over the first two joints of mine. Maybe size matters, but the electric jolt I got from his hand impressed me way more. Felt like a herd of wild stallions were running free in my veins.

"Did I ever tell you that I know how to weld?" he asked.

We weren't going to have a guy conversation *now* were we? "Uh, no."

"You hold a rod," he said, "and it's on fire with positive electricity running through it. You clip a negative charge to a piece of metal and touch the rod to it. The heat is searing. It melts them together."

His eyes were so intense.

"But," he said, "if you stare at the brilliant welding light, you could go blind."

I pulled my hand back from his and touched his lower

lip. Full, sexy.

He moved in fast with a slow kiss. We were both trembling when he pulled back. "Whoa," he said. "Can we take this out of here?"

I couldn't speak, but managed to nod.

He flagged the waiter. "We need a check, please."

"We can't go to your place," he said. "It's like Grand Central. And I've got roommates at my house."

I'd driven up and down Ocean Boulevard so many times, I'd memorized half of it.

"There's a little motel about a block from here," I said. "We could walk there."

#

By the time we got into that room, I was liquid with desire. We entered a maiden sprint race, breaking hard and driving to the finish. The sensations were new to me, yet a million years old.

At first, it hurt, but in a exquisite way. Then it just felt so good. I must have moaned the latter part out loud because I remember Will saying, "Oh, yeah. It truly does."

When we'd gone the distance, we lay panting on the bed, where I eventually surfaced from a haze and glanced around.

"Look," I said. "We never even pulled the covers back."

"Who had time for *that*?"

Suddenly conscious of my nudity, I burrowed under the sheets. Will followed me right in. We lay next to each other, basking in a kind of afterglow, until he guided my hand with his.

Who knew jockeys were so big? Or that Will's skin could be so hard, smooth, and hot all at the same time?

"*Again?*" I asked. "Is this usual?"

"It will be with you. I want to take it long and slow. You ready?"

#

Later, he went out to get us coffee, and I lay in a dreamy languor thinking about the exquisite things he'd done to me. No wonder sex was such a driving force in people's lives. I'd never thought I could feel like that. Finally, I forced myself from the warm bed, using the time to wash up and get dressed. A flushed young woman who looked incredibly happy stared back at me from the bathroom mirror. I gave her a little salute, then turned my phone on, startled a second later when it rang in my hand.

"Nikki," Carla said. "You need to check your messages more often."

"I thought you were with Rick."

"I was, but the department called him in. I just talked to Klaire. She's been trying to reach you, too."

Couldn't I just bask for a while?

"What's up?" I asked.

"I don't know. Klaire sounded *weird*. She wouldn't explain. Says she has to talk to you. Call her, please. Find out what's going on and call me right back. Okay?"

"Sure. I'll do it now."

After disconnecting from Carla, I reached Klaire, who sounded tight as a wire. "Nikki," she said. "There's a rumor about Gonzales. He may have a new girl for sale. I couldn't ask too much, but –"

"No way. What do you mean, for *sale?*" Is Gonzales crazy? He just escaped the police! Wouldn't he keep a low profile, disappear or –"

"Nikki, let me finish. It's happening Monday night. The girl's going to be auctioned, and it sounds like Jade."

"Holy shit," I said. "No wonder you didn't explain it to Carla!"

"My contact heard the girl is blond, unusually beautiful, and still a virgin. Gonzales has a couple of other girls, too, but this one is the prize. People are coming from overseas to bid on her."

I felt sick. "We have to call the police!"

"No! You can't risk it, Nikki."

"But Rick warned us there might be a leak. We can tell *him*."

"You want to bet the girl's life on Rick?" she asked.

Now that she'd put it that way, I didn't know what to do. "Do you have a sense about Rick or anything like that?"

"No. I think I only get messages from those with a strong telepathic ability. Besides, I don't trust cops. Especially ones that arrested me in the past." She grew silent.

I moved toward the rumpled bed and sank onto the edge. My free hand slid toward the center of the sheets, where I could still feel the warmth of being with Will. Damn everything.

"So what do we do, Klaire?"

"The auction is very private, but it will be fronted by a party. They will have live music, dancers, and a fortune teller. But I've arranged for the woman they've hired to tell fortunes to become ill. She will send me in her place."

"What?" I asked. "Are you crazy?"

"Let me finish," she said, impatience hardening her tone. "You will come with me as my assistant. We will find a way to disrupt the sale."

I closed my eyes. The woman was nuts.

"No. We have to call the police or the FBI. *Somebody.*"

"If we do that, the auction will disappear. Jade will vanish. I *know* this. You *have* to come with me."

Chapter 40

When Will returned, we plumped the pillows and sat against the headboard, recharging ourselves with hot, sweet caffeine. I loved lying next to him, shoulder to shoulder, hip to hip, breathing in his scent, reveling in the memory of his lips, his tongue and his hands. Not to mention his magic fingers.

But Klaire's words kept drowning out those hot memories, pulling my thoughts into a cold stream of apprehension.

As I stared at the cup in my hands, I could feel his gaze on me.

"What happened since I left?" he asked.

"Klaire called." I said, and told him.

"You can't go to that auction."

"That's my decision, Will."

"No." He shifted and turned toward me, placing a hand on my thigh. "You don't understand."

"I understand that if I can help save Carla's daughter, I will."

He sighed. "I should probably tell you something."

I didn't like the sound of this, afraid a gulf was about to open between us.

"Go ahead," I said.

"You know what the TRPB is right?"

"Sure, the Thoroughbred Racing Protection Bureau." As far as I knew, it was the *investigative* arm of the Thoroughbred Racing Associations of North America, with a mission to keep racing clean and maintain public confidence in the sport. Something sorely needed, but where was Will going with this?

"What about it?" I asked. Then it hit me like a bucket of

ice water. "You *work* for them!"

"Only occasionally. On a part time, contract basis."

"How nice," I said, pulling away from him, feeling betrayed. "So what are you investigating now, me?"

"Whoa, no." Then he swallowed. "Currito Maldonista."

"*Currito?* You son of a bitch! You know all this and don't tell me until after you *sleep* with me?" How could he care about me and not say anything? I fought the sting of tears. I wasn't going to let him see me cry.

"I'm telling you now. He's a Colombian drug lord, Nikki. The DEA is involved."

I closed my eyes. This was surreal. But was I really shocked about Currito? No. But Will's admission knocked me way off balance.

"But, if Currito's what you say he is, why the hell did the state of Florida give him an owners license?"

"The DEA wanted him here."

I stared at him, feeling a bitterness grow inside me. I'd been feeding this guy information for days. He'd sucked me in and hung me out.

"Look," he said, "I don't want you going to that auction with Klaire. There's a lot of scary stuff going on in South Florida right now. You said yourself there's a leak in the police department. I don't want you getting hurt."

"So now that I've slept with you, you can tell me what to do? Let me ask you something, Will. Were all your romantic moves about helping your investigation?"

"No, not true, Nikki." He reached out to touch me.

"Forget it. I'm out of here!" I grabbed my tote and ran from the room. I tore down the block, grabbed a taxi at Billy's Stone Crab, and ignored Will's repeated calls on my cell. At least he'd had better sense than to chase me down the street.

Once I was locked in my room at the Sand Castle, I called Carla.

"It wasn't anything that important," I lied. "Klaire wanted to make sure I was all right after all the stuff that happened at Worldwide. I think she had a dream about it or something. You know how she is."

"Yeah, but she sounded so weird. Like she'd found out something awful."

"No. Listen, my neighbor's knocking on the door." I was such a liar. "I gotta go."

When we disconnected, I threw myself on the bed. Damn Will. Damn everything. I had to get some sleep. La Bruja was running tomorrow. The day after that was Monday and the *auction*. Should I go? I padded into the tiny kitchen and got my bottle of Wild Turkey out of the cabinet. I poured two fingers into a glass and took it with me to bed.

#

By one o'clock the next afternoon, I sat at the lunch counter in the jockeys' room moving a spoon around in a carton of blueberry yogurt without eating much. My race on La Bruja ran at two p.m. Glancing at the video monitor behind me, I saw the entrants for the first race circling the paddock.

I turned back to fiddling with my yogurt. The first thing I'd done when I arrived in the jock's room was scour the day's program to see if Will had a race. Fortunately, he only had two rides at the end of the day. I intended to clear out before then. I didn't want to see him.

Someone tapped me lightly on the shoulder and I almost jumped off my stool. The assistant clerk of the scales. I'd been so lost in thought I hadn't seen him coming.

"There's a Carla Ruben waiting outside. Do you want to see her?"

"Yes," I said. "Tell her to come in."

She did, and sat with me at the counter where she ordered a diet Coke. She wore a tawny animal print dress and a brown-and-gold necklace. The outfit matched perfectly with the gold flecks in her brown eyes.

"Nikki," she said, staring at me. "I came to wish you

luck, but what's up? You look like hell."

"You mean aside from my recent fight with a slave trader and being up with you all night at the police station?"

"Yeah, aside from that. You look different."

I wouldn't tell her about the auction and Jade. She'd freak. So I told her about Will, and even though I explained how Will had played me, she got a big smile on her face.

"Oh my God," she said. "You finally did the deed! Look at you! You're blushing. How was it?"

"*Carla*. Could you keep your voice down? Did you not hear me say he's been using me?"

She waved a hand in dismissal. "I don't believe that for a minute. Give the guy a break. He can do his job and fall in love with you. I bet he can do all kind's of things at once. Did he?"

I caved. "Oh my God, Carla. You should have seen his eyes. They were . . . on fire. He was so amazing. I had no idea a man could make me feel like that. He was . . ."

"The perfect fit?" She really had an evil grin.

"I gotta get ready for this race." I pushed back from the counter as if mildly offended, amazed that the memory was powerful enough to put a smile back on my face.

#

After what I'd heard about Currito the night before, seeing him in the paddock rattled me. A drug lord? I struggled for a pleasant expression and hoped it didn't look as phony as it felt.

He studied my face a moment, making me worry I'd given myself away. But he didn't know that I knew. I was being paranoid. But who could blame me?

He had a man with him – maybe late twenties. His long black hair was loose and fell almost to his shoulders. He had a three-day beard, was tall and had a runny nose. The guy needed a tissue.

Currito shook my hand. *"Buena suerte*, Nikki." Wishing me good luck. "This is Victor."

When I shook Victor's hand, he left something wet on my palm. I tried to be sneaky about rubbing my hand dry against my riding pants, holding his gaze so he wouldn't notice. Victor looked vaguely familiar. Could he be the stranger I'd seen on our shedrow the day Diablo ran?

"Nice to meet you," I said. "Are you in business with Currito?"

Currito's bad eye started ticking. "No," Currito replied quickly. "He is a relative. What is your plan for La Bruja."

Though La Bruja's past performances defined her as a horse without a late speed kick, she had plenty of stamina.

"I hope she breaks well and stays fairly close behind the front runners. I'll ask her to run at the end." Pretty much a standard plan for a distance race.

"Very good," Currito said. "Victor, let us find our seats."

He seemed anxious to leave. He hadn't even waited for the call of "riders up." But as soon as he and Victor disappeared, the call came, and in moments I was on the track and heading for the gate on a nervous La Bruja.

#

Orlando had arranged for a friend of his, a pony boy at Gulfstream, to take us through our warmup and to the gate. The man rode a large, pinto gelding and handled La Bruja well, doing what he could to keep her calm, letting her stretch her legs in a rhythmic slow gallop on the backstretch.

When we arrived at the gate, he handed the lead strap to an assistant starter, who loaded us into post position two. The rest of the field of twelve loaded calmly into the metal contraption, and I heard Larry Collmus announce, "They're all in line!"

With a clang and a crash the gates sprang open. La

Bruja rocked forward one step, stumbled badly, and threw me onto her neck. I watched the ground rush toward me and locked my arms straight, my hands on her neck, trying to push back. Her nose hit the dirt, but she threw her other leg out, caught herself, rose up, and steadied.

Her recovery threw me back into the saddle, where I was able to regain the stirrup I'd lost and regather the reins. But the field was so far ahead. Clearly the stumble had cost us the race. *Damn it.*

La Bruja was a nice filly and I wasn't going to use her up trying to catch the field. She could run another day. I let her settle and sat quietly in the saddle, keeping a long hold on the reins, not urging her to run hard. She closed some of the distance, and at the far turn, I pretended to whip and drive a bit so I wouldn't get in trouble with the stewards. They tended to hand out fines when they decided a jockey hadn't tried or had "stopped riding."

By the time we got to the stretch, La Bruja passed two exhausted horses and actually caught two that were still running. At the wire, we flew past the eye of the digital camera and finished ninth.

I galloped La Bruja out with the rest of the field, pleased by her determination to pass as many horses as she could before I slowed her down and turned her back toward the paddock. This filly could run all day! A mile and a quarter might suit her well next time she ran.

But judging from the dark look on Currito's face where he stood with Orlando waiting for us to come in, there might not be a next time. As I headed toward them, I noticed Victor was not with Currito or on the apron among the crowd that stood there. As La Bruja jogged me closer, Currito turned abruptly and walked off the track.

"*Señor* Maldonista, he not happy with you," Orlando said as he grabbed La Bruja's bridle.

I slid from the filly, my polished boots landing with a thump in Gulfstream's sandy soil. "So what did he want me to do? Beat her to death down the stretch?"

Orlando heard the anger in my voice and wisely responded with a classic Latin shrug. Those shrugs are hard to yell at.

When I removed the saddle, and Orlando started to lead the filly away, he made his last comment over his shoulder. "*Señor* Maldonista say he see you back at the barn."

"Great!" I shot back, then walked toward the jocks' room to weigh myself in on the scales. In spite of my efforts not to, I visually searched for Will, hoping I would, or maybe would not, see him. He wasn't around, so after changing, I headed back to the barn where Currito waited for me, arms crossed, expression still dark.

"You did not ride La Bruja down the stretch. After the bonus you received from me, I should think you'd have better sense than to quit before the finish line on one of my horses!"

The way his bad eye ticked, he must be really upset. He was too good a horseman to react this way. I wanted to ask what was really bothering him, but didn't want to fuel his bad mood.

I took a breath and spoke calmly. "She didn't have a shot, Currito. Not after she stumbled at the break. I didn't want to abuse her."

He said something sharp and fast in Spanish that I couldn't follow, then threw his hands in the air, a frustrated gesture not typical of him.

"*Victor*," he called out.

At the same moment Orlando appeared at the top of our shedrow, leading La Bruja for another turn around the shedrow. When Currito received no response from the missing Victor, his eyes drifted to Orlando.

"Where is Victor?"

"*No se, Señor*," Orlando replied. He dropped his gaze and kept going with the filly.

"Excuse me," I said and walked away from Currito, down the shedrow to La Bruja's empty stall.

Except it wasn't empty. Victor stood in the shadows, turned so his side faced me. I stared as he snorted the contents of a rolled bill up his nose. *Jesus Christ, no wonder Currito was upset.* Who wouldn't be with an idiot "relative" like this snorting what must be cocaine? Anyone on the backstretch could have peered into the stall and seen him.

Victor still didn't notice me as he wiped two fingers under his nose and let the hundred-dollar bill unroll in his other hand. I could see the white powder from the stall entrance where I stood. I remembered what Jim had said about substance transfer. Had it been Victor that day? Had he rubbed his hand on Diablo? Touching Diablo would have been enough to transfer the drug into the colt's system.

"Listen, you idiot!" I said. "Get that crap out of my barn. Now!"

The guy turned his head toward me slowly, not in the least alarmed. "Or what? You'll tell Currito? He is my uncle. He will do nothing." His lips spread in a slow, arrogant smile.

"*Victor!*" Currito had moved silently to stand behind me. "You dishonor your family! I have warned you about this before. I will not tolerate your disrespect."

"You think you are the great man," Victor hissed. "I could tell her things about you. I could tell her –"

Currito rushed past me. "Enough!" he yelled, then slapped Victor's face, the sound ringing in the narrow confines of the stall. "You want to end up like your father?"

Victor's eyes smoldered with a low burning hate, but he followed his uncle from the stall. I seemed unable to breathe until the two of them disappeared from the barn moments later.

My head spun with questions like a slot machine until it settled on a triple jackpot. Was Victor the son of Currito's dead brother?

Chapter 41

By the time Orlando and I fed our four horses, finished cleaning the shedrow, and hung up our freshly washed bandages and saddle towels to dry, the sun had moved well toward the western horizon. To the east, between two tall condos, I glimpsed a sickle moon rising over the ocean.

Stretching, I savored the mingled scents of fresh laundry, liniment, and molasses. Watching Diablo snatching wisps of hay from his net was both familiar and comforting.

Orlando leaned his wheelbarrow against the shedrow wall and hung his rake upside down on a nail driven into the wood siding.

"So, Nikki, you work things out with Señor Maldonista?"

"He wasn't really mad about the race," I replied. "I think it was something else."

"Si," Orlando said, "he not happy with the guy he bring with him. I think this man is the one we see here before Diablo's race."

No flies on Orlando.

"You could be right," I said, watching him, curious about his thoughts.

"This *sobrino*. How you say, nephew?"

I nodded. "Yes."

"This nephew he very angry with Señor *Maldonista*. I think he rub cocaine on Diablo to hurt *su tio.*"

To hurt his uncle. It made sense. People could be vindictive. And maybe in this case it was warranted. Except Victor had taken it out on the horse, too.

"So what do you think, Orlando?" I asked.

"Me?" He flipped his hair back on one side, then

shrugged. "I think we no get involved. We do nothing wrong. The *policia* have no case against us."

I couldn't blame him for his response. His green card was not the same thing as citizenship, and he didn't want to be shipped back to Mexico.

"Okay," I said. "Let's forget about it for now."

"*Bueno*," he said.

My cell began vibrating. Glancing at the ID, I took the call from Carla.

"Hey," she said. "I hear it will be warm this evening. "We should try Azure here at the Diplomat. You want to come down for dinner?"

Azure. The outdoor bar and restaurant I'd glimpsed through the glass wall of the Diplomat lobby. It wasn't like I was having dinner with Will or anything. He hadn't called again, and I was damned if I was going to call him.

"Sure," I replied. "Let me finish some paperwork and clean up. Meet you in an hour?"

#

I walked through Diplomat's lobby and stepped onto the rear terrace. The light had begun to fade, but when I paused at the top of a tiled staircase, I could still see the ocean washing the shore farther down. Though the raw scent of saltwater and sand hung in the air, the hotel had tamed the beach with terraces, dining areas, swimming pools and white concrete planters overflowing with tropical flowers. For all these efforts, the ocean crashing against the shoreline below remained wild and unruly.

One terrace down, I spotted Carla in a plunge-neck white dress. She sat on one of the wicker chairs around a low table where candle light reflected off the glass of two cocktails. No surprise to see Rick.

Carla and Rick belonged on a nineteen forties movie set. Approaching them, I wondered how he paid for his wardrobe on a vice cop's salary. His tropical-blue tee shirt looked like silk and so did his white jacket and pants. Pants didn't flow and drape like that if they weren't expensive.

After our greetings, I sat, and Rick ordered me a drink.

Turning to him, I said, "I was wondering what happened to Lena. Is she okay?"

His jaw tensed slightly. "She's fine."

"Can I see her?" My question popped out, surprising me as much as it seemed to startle Rick.

"No." His voice held more patience than annoyance. "I can't really talk about her. Immigration is involved now. Suffice it to say the girl is foreign and will be going home."

"Really?" Carla asked. "Don't you need her to testify at a trial or something?

His smiled. "You two are relentless. Let it go, okay?"

"Okay," she said, "but you better be more forthcoming about my daughter then you are about Lena."

"You know I will," he said, leaning toward her, his hand closing over hers. "I already promised you."

The waiter broke the silence by appearing with my drink. Carla watched me take my first sip, and I could see her little mental cat feet changing direction. She was about to pounce.

"Nikki, have you seen Will?"

"No."

Carla waved an impatient hand at Rick and me. "I could grow old and die before I ever dragged information from you two. What is up with Will, anyway?"

"Nothing," I answered and switched to one of Carla's favorite subjects – clothes.
"Rick, that is one nice suit you are wearing."

"Isn't it gorgeous!" Carla said. "Can you believe it used to belong to a drug dealer?"

I stared at Rick. "You got that out of a drug bust?"

He grinned. "Well . . . it might have originally belonged to a wealthy Cuban currently enjoying the hospitality of the

US federal prison system."

Apparently closed cases made safe subjects, and he warmed right to it, leaning back in his chair. If he'd had a cigar, he would have struck a match and fired it up.

"You wouldn't believe how cheap we can get confiscated items."

"And first pick, too," Carla said.

"Anyway," he continued, "these crooks are not exactly rocket scientists. "I'm working a case with the DEA, right? We bust this character, Larigo. He's got a ton of cash in his suitcase and enough cocaine to elevate half of Fort Lauderdale."

Rick was having a good time, and Carla's eyes glowed as she listened to him.

"So, Larigo, he starts yelling, 'I've *never* seen this money before. I don't know how it got in my suitcase.' But he wants a receipt when we confiscate the cash, right? So I write him one for a hundred and fifty grand, and he looks at it and freaks. Starts yelling, 'This is wrong! There was two hundred and fifty-seven thousand, five hundred dollars in that suitcase!'"

Carla burst out laughing, and I may have snickered. He continued telling war stories, a nice enhancement to the dinner that followed. I enjoyed myself and relaxed. When we finished our plates, Rick excused himself to make a phone call.

Carla stretched in her chair, causing the tops of her breasts to round and gleam in the light from the candles. "I really like Rick."

"You should," I said "He's funny as hell. Cute, too."

She grew quiet for a moment. "So tell me about Will."

I pushed my empty plate away. "How would you like it if you'd been going out with Rick, thinking the whole time he was in the hotel business only to find out he's an undercover cop? That he lied to you?"

"I see your point," she said. "But, Nikki, I think you have a lot of trouble trusting men in the first place."

I couldn't argue with that and shrugged.

"After the way you ran out of that motel room, he might be afraid to call you right away. I'm telling you, this guy is crazy about you, Nikki. *Call* him."

"I'll think about it," I said.

Rick's cop tales were more fun than Carla's questions. I was afraid the subject of Jade would come up again, too. Carla might read me and know I was holding out on her. I didn't want to lie to her again, but how could I tell her where I was going with Klaire in about twenty-four hours?

Damn. Apparently I *was* going to the auction.

"Carla," I said, placing two twenties on the table. I didn't want her paying for my dinner on top of everything else. "I'm really tired. Would you say goodnight to Rick for me? I've got a big day ahead of me tomorrow."

"Sure."

When I hurried up the steps, I could feel her watching me walk away. I retrieved my Toyota from the parking lot. Driving along South Ocean, I flipped on the radio. Some guys who sounded like they'd been on three-day bender were singing a mournful song about a "memory motel."

I hit the steering wheel with the side of my fist. *Damn Will Marshall, anyway.*

Chapter 42

I tried not to squirm as I sat at Klaire's vanity table. Her bedroom was another surprise in her outwardly dilapidated and seedy home. At the back of the house, invisible from the street, the room rose to a cathedral ceiling with skylights. Klaire's cottage took "shabby chic" to new extremes. Through the room's tall French windows, in the dusk outside, I could see thick hedges and palms shielding this part of her house from her neighbors' eyes and the street.

Klaire stood next to me attaching another auburn-and-copper streaked extension to my hair she'd rinsed earlier with copper color.

She wore a head cloth and peasant outfit in dusky purple-and-black. She had a can of mace on the table and had armed herself with a full set of astrological rings and necklaces. A large, leather bag lay on the floor next to her. I didn't want to know what was in there.

"You make a pretty gypsy woman," she said, studying me in the vanity's mirror. The men will flock to get their palms read."

"But I don't know anything about reading palms." In vain I tried to scratch the back of my head. Klaire had sprayed, ratted, and pinned the hair back there to death.

"It's very simple. Let me explain it to you again," she said patiently. "Read their dominant palm."

"I know, I know. Ask them if they are left handed or right handed." I was going to be so busted when I tried to do this.

"Exactly. Tell them lines are not written into the human hand without reason. Get them in the mood." She grasped my left hand, pointed at the marks she'd inked into place earlier.

"Life, head, and heart," she murmured.

The astrological symbols she'd drawn on the "mounts" of my palms looked like art from a medieval scroll. I especially liked the little quarter moon she'd inked onto my "luna" mount, the area near my wrist below my little finger.

"Wont they think I'm using a cheat sheet?" I asked.

"No. They'll love it. It validates you in their minds. Gives them something to focus on, encourages them to reveal themselves to you.

Nikki Latrelle, con artist.

#

By the time Klaire finished with me, coppery hair cascaded down my shoulders over my low-cut peasant top. I wore a turquoise plastic wrist band that identified me as a party employee, a long blue skirt, moccasin-boots, and a heavy necklace made of astrological symbols. Beneath the skirt, I wore nylon cargo shorts. Side slits hidden in the folds of the skirt allowed access to the pockets of the pants.

Klaire had spread grease paint the color of cafe latte over the white skin of my face, neck and chest and smoked my eyes with dark blue shadow, heavy black liner, and mascara. I looked pretty cool, but was too nervous to enjoy it.

It hadn't helped when Klaire told me she'd been receiving dark messages from the other side. She'd refused to tell me what they were, other than we had to be very careful. Hadn't helped when she'd given me a small dagger, a tiny vial of knock out drops, and a little can of pepper spray for one of the pockets of my cargo pants. The other was loaded with a handful of three-quarter-inch cherry bombs.

What was her plan? Knock everyone out and blow the place up?

As she finished her own makeup at her bedroom vanity table, I pulled the two-inch dropper bottle from my cargo pocket and held it up. "Will this stuff really knock someone out?"

"Cold enough to take their money or anything else you want. One drop will do it. "

"What happens if I spill it? Will it absorb through my skin?"

"Better you don't find out," Klaire said.

Chapter 43

It was almost dark when Klaire and I walked between the huge stone columns supporting the portico of a mansion. Modeled in the classic style of the Romans, the structure stood by a lagoon of the Atlantic Ocean. The double entry doors stood wide open. We passed through into a broad hallway of green-and-black marble where our footsteps echoed off the cold, polished floor. Reaching the hall's end, we entered an enormous ballroom with a domed ceiling featuring a fresco of lecherous gold satyrs and shy nymphs.

To the immediate right of the entrance, a magnificent stone staircase with a carved marble balustrade climbed to a gallery that ran at right angles along the adjacent wall. A single arched door led off this gallery, and two men dressed in white robes peered down at us from the doorway above.

I stared back at them, then whispered to Klaire, "What is this? A toga party?"

She gave me a warning glance and nodded in the direction of a gauzy, white, tent, that looked like it had been stolen from a Cleopatra set.

"That's where we set up," she said.

As we moved toward the back of the room, Klaire had told me the party's cover was to celebrate the fiftieth birthday of a local billionaire also connected to the flesh trade. Apparently, most of the attendees didn't even know about the auction.

Our twenty-foot-wide tent stretched between two green-and-black marble columns, a number of which formed a ring inside the square room. Looking up, I saw the pillars supported the massive dome. I got dizzy staring at one of the satyrs who leered down at me from the ceiling so far above.

I took a steadying breath and followed Klaire into the tent. Two small tables inlaid with zodiac signs stood before a curtain.

"Do we sit at the tables?" I asked.

"No, you sit at one, and the man who handles my visitors sits at the other."

"Who is he?" I asked.

"A friend. He'll be here shortly."

I'd lay odds the gold curtain behind the tables was there to separate Klaire's section from us underlings.

Noise from the ballroom made me glance back. Workmen rolled boxes of liquor and setups to a bar on the left side of the room. Caterers worked at large tables decorated with glittering candelabra and arrangements of red roses. They placed trays, bowls, chafing dishes, and plates laden with food among the flowers and candles.

To the right beneath the gallery, a stage held a piano, speakers, numerous microphones, and a drum set emblazoned with the name "Dagger." I hadn't known the rap artist from the night of Jade's disappearance would be the evening's talent. No way this was a coincidence.

A roadie on the stage tested a microphone. His electrified voice echoed eerily from the domed ceiling and floated over the marble floor.

Behind me, Klaire was leaning a placard against one of our zodiac tables. The sign read, "Zayna, Palmist *Extraordinaire*."

"Cool," I said. "How much do I cost?"

"You don't," she said. "You're the free come on. I'm the main event."

She parted the gold curtain, revealing a long gilded table with curlicues carved into the front edge and legs. Her crystal ball sat dead center. A throne-like chair stood behind the table facing one of her sphinx-head client seats.

"When did you bring this stuff in?" I asked.

"Earlier. The man who will sit next to you brought it

in."

"So, does this guy have a name?"

"Today his name is Ajeet."

#

A while later, Ajeet -- a slender Indian, or maybe Pakistani, of indeterminate age -- swayed near the top of a stepladder that wobbled in front of Klaire's curtain. He wore a turban and robe and carefully hung a gold-and-black sign advertising, "Klaire Voyante, Renowned Mystic, Channeler, and Psychic."

Since no one was looking, I allowed myself an eye roll. Then Ajeet climbed down from the ladder which he folded and carried away.

I stared at my inked hand for the hundredth time, muttering, "The lines on the hand are not written without reason." I examined the markings nature had drawn on my left palm. Did the X on my heart line represent Will? And what about the crooked, deep cross on my lifeline that seemed to coincide with the present time? Did it suggest serious trouble?

Ajeet returned and saw my face. "It will all work out."

"Sure," I said.

When he lit several sticks of incense in a ceramic burner on his table, I waved away the smoke. The gold curtain behind us parted, and Klaire stepped out just as a pungent whiff of spices drifted to me from the food tables. It mingled with the heady scent of roses, freshly sliced bar citrus, and Ajeet's choking incense.

"It is almost nine o'clock," Klaire said. "The party will start momentarily. You will play your role until Dagger comes on about ten. Then you must do what we talked about."

#

My first customer, a stout, blue-eyed man of about thirty-five, stared at me across the table while I examined his palm. He wore expensive shoes, a silk Hawaiian shirt, and a small bandage on the inside of his elbow. Maybe he'd had blood drawn earlier that day.

"You have a nice touch," he said. "I could last all night with your touch. I mean *all* night."

Okay, so he liked women, fine. But his budding enthusiasm might need a little nip.

"You have health issues," I said. Who *didn't* have health issues? "I see a change here on your lifeline." I pointed to an almost indecipherable mark. "You are seeing a doctor."

The blood left his face. "Wow. How did you know?"

Mimicking Klaire's breathless soothsayer voice, I said, "It is written."

In my peripheral vision, I could see Ajeet glance at me from his station. Score one for Nikki.

"There is a woman in your life." I said, and felt his hand twitch slightly. "She is very important to you."

"Yes, but I haven't seen her in a while."

Klaire had told me to give them what they want. I tried to look mysterious and pointed at a mark on his heart line.

"But you will see her again. Soon!" I paused, "Your body may suffer, but your spirit soars and will bring her back to you!" *What a load of crap.*

"Yes!" he said. "I've always known she will come back to me."

I almost felt guilty, except this guy might be attending the auction. The hell with him.

"But here," I said pointing to a spot where three lines converged and crossed his life line, "I see trouble. A tumultuous event that will put you in grave danger." *Like cherry bombs and a police raid.*

"What is it?" Worry darkened his eyes.

This was the cue I'd been waiting for. "You must consult Ms. Voyante. She is all seeing. She will know."

The guy twisted in his chair and spoke to Ajeet. "Put me on that list you got, okay?"

Ajeet bowed his head and said, "Your wish is my command. It so happens Ms. Voyante can see you now."

What a surprise.

I released the man's hand, and he stood and hurried to Ajeet's table, where he was ushered into the inner sanctum.

Dealing with the next client, I began to feel like a frantic horse in the starting gate. I wanted to bust out and race for Jade. Instead, I got to kick a drunk man's leg beneath the table after he slid his hand up my skirt. Since it wasn't time to disrupt the evening, I restrained myself from putting a lighted cherry bomb down his pants.

"You know," I said to him, grasping his hand and glancing at his palm, "your future doesn't look so good."

"Yeah, well screw you, too!"

After I sent him to Klaire, a man with a lei, a big belly, and a grass skirt settled himself across from me. I could see telltale marks on his knuckles where he'd had crude prison tattoos removed. I might have glanced at his hairy belly before mentioning heart disease. He became annoyed.

"Listen, you little witch, I'm right as rain, enjoying the good life, soaking up the sun." He smiled. "You're the liar for hire."

I smiled right back and touched a mark on his palm. "Oh, look at this. This isn't good. You are about to lose your freedom! This is the mark of *confinement!*"

He snatched his hand away. "What the hell are you talking about? I'm not going back in!"

I gave my best imitation of Orlando's Latin shrug. "It is already written."

He left in a huff, then one of the party goers I suspected was a hooker stopped by. She was as easy to read as the track's overnight sheet, and I felt sorry for her.

"Your life line shows you've traveled a difficult road," I said, studying her palm which smelled like booze. "Your childhood was . . . painful."

"You're pretty good," she said. "Do you know that? Or are you guessing?"

" I *know* it," I said, meeting her gaze. "I'd bet my life on it."

She grew quiet after that, and by the time she left, I was thinking about a second career in palm reading.

#

And so it went with a full gaggle of eager victims until the lights flickered just before ten. I finished my last pre-break palm reading with a man in a Star Trek tee shirt. Ajeet ended the session with his dramatic announcement that the "road to the truth" would continue after Dagger played.

When Klaire's final patron and my Trekkie guy left, Ajeet dimmed the lights inside our tent. I stood, stretched, and rubbed my neck. Who knew palm reading was so exhausting?

A man drifted by our tent. The one with head and shoulders resembling those of a vulture. I hadn't seen him since he'd been in the limo outside the entrance to Gulfstream. The son-of-a-bitch was probably there to bid on Jade. Too bad he hadn't been thrown in jail with Chakri. I looked around for Klaire. She must still be behind her curtain, so I parted it slightly and found her sitting behind her table.

"Klaire," I whispered. "I think one of the buyers just walked by! Should I head upstairs now?"

"Wait until Dagger starts. People will be less likely to notice you."

"Isn't he supposed to be on stage by now?"

As if on cue, an insanely loud electronic beat began thumping. It reminded me of the SUV with the thugs who'd gunned down the girl.

Klaire mouthed the words, "Be careful."

I couldn't hear her voice over the noise, but nodded, turned, and walked back to the front of our tent.

The ballroom lights were turned down and I could see strobe-lit figures on the stage. Above it, a Jumbotron showed a close up of the guy before the microphone. He wore a tiny gold loincloth. Gold jewelry weighted his neck, wrists and ankles. A knife tattoo dripped red drops beneath one of his eyes. Classy guy.

He started rapping in time to the beat. His shouted, rhythmic lyrics were violent as he described a woman's ass and other assets I really didn't want to hear about. People on the floor danced, most of them with fists held high as they gyrated back and forth. They wore everything – togas, bikinis, miniskirts, suits, and Speedos.

I searched the crowd for the Vulture and spotted him heading toward the staircase leading to the gallery. My exact destination. I touched my hair extensions, then slid my hands into my pockets. Everything seemed to be in place.

Skirting the dancers, I moved across the ballroom past kiosks selling Dagger CDs and tee shirts. In the gallery above me, The Vulture disappeared through the arched door where I'd seen the two white-robed men upon my arrival. I flew up the stone staircase to the gallery where people leaned on the balustrade watching Dagger and the dancers below. The women among them looked like hookers. When I walked past, no one gave me a second glance. I might appear exotic, but I was still the hired help.

I reached the arched door and stepping through, I found myself in a large foyer. Two sets of double doors faced me from across the room. To my left, yet another white-robed man stood with his back to me by an unmarked door. These men must be guards, and this one leaned over his cell phone, with a finger in his ear, trying to hear over the music.

"What?" he yelled. "No I can't hear you!"

I slipped behind him, straight to double doors. I tried the first one. It was locked. The second one opened and I entered a small amphitheater. I stared past rows of padded seats to the stage's painted backdrop. The artist had a thing about well-endowed satyrs . . . doing peculiar things to naked women. *Yuck.*

Since it was still a couple of hours before the auction, no one else was around. Where was the Vulture? I zeroed in on steps leading to a door on one side of the stage. I raced down the aisle toward it with Dagger's nasty lyrics chasing right behind.

Up the steps. Grab the door knob. *Locked.* But I could hear voices on the other side. Damn, there had to be another way in. The unmarked door by the white-robed guard? I darted back through the amphitheater, slowing my pace when I reached the foyer outside.

The guard was facing me now, his phone no longer in sight, but he still blocked the unmarked door. Thickset with a three day beard, he looked like a bit actor for a mob movie.

I gave him my hopeful look. "Someone told me there was a ladies room up here."

"They told you wrong," he said, but his voice was pleasant enough. "You have to use the main one downstairs."

"There's a line, and I'm on duty."

He pressed his lips together. "Let me see your wrist band."

I stepped closer and he inspected the turquoise band. It had little black daggers on it.

"You're the fortune teller. With Voyante, right?

"Yeah, and I really have to use a powder room!"

"Okay," he said. "Right this way."

Always good to be in with the right crowd.

He pulled a key card from his robe and slid it into a lock mechanism. A moment later, the door opened onto a service hall.

He pointed to the right. "It's on your left, about halfway down."

"Thanks."

"Listen," he said, as I scurried past him. "If you have time later, maybe you could read my fortune."

"Absolutely." I couldn't think of anything I'd rather do.

He was watching me, so I found the necessary room and scooted inside. I used the facilities, hoping the noise of the flushing toilet and running faucets would reassure the man. I waited a few more moments then eased the door open a crack and peered through. He was gone.

I took off in the other direction, slowing when the hall branched right and left. I went right, hoping it would put me behind the auditorium. I passed an alcove holding a satellite kitchen, with a sink, commercial refrigerator and cabinets. A table held a plastic tray and cocktail napkins. I opened the refrigerator and found cans of soda. I pulled out half a dozen cans, placed them on the tray and hurried down the hall.

Spotting steps and a door like the ones in the amphitheater, I rushed forward with my tray. Two heartbeats later, I reached the door and pulled it open.

Chapter 44

A lovely, painfully young woman stared at me with drugged eyes. She sat on a metal chair. Luminous blond hair flowed to her shoulders. The diaphanous white robe she wore did little to hide her budding curves. A steel bracelet circled one delicate ankle. Heavy metal links welded to the bracelet chained her leg to a thick ring bolted in the floor.

I stepped closer, then froze. Carla's huge brown eyes stared back at me. The perfect nose, the high cheekbones, the sensual mouth. *Jade.*

I'd also found the Vulture, who fortunately had his back to me. He leaned over another girl seated a ways behind Jade. A chain bound her leg as well.

The same two robed guards I'd seen on the gallery stood in the back of the room watching the Vulture, no doubt making sure he didn't handle the merchandise.

Three other young women, all bound and appearing drugged, huddled in chairs closer to the guards. Someone must have sprayed them with perfume because a musky, sensual odor weighed heavily in the air.

One of the guards turned to stare at me.

I gave him a bright smile. "They told me to bring some sodas."

He nodded, appearing unconcerned. My wrist band worked way better than management intended.

"I'll have one of those," he said.

I set my tray on an empty chair, popped a can, and handed it to him. The Vulture ignored me, still busy studying the goods.

"Anyone else? How about you?" I asked Jade. She was too out of it to respond. I walked toward her with a can, glad she'd been placed apart from the other girls. "Jade?" I called softly.

She heard me and slowly turned. The drugs had dimmed the lights in her eyes. I moved close enough to whisper without being overheard by the others.

"I'm here to help you."

She blinked once and her eyes filled with confusion. At least it was a step up from vacant.

"Who *are* you?" she whispered.

I didn't want her agitated, and kept my voice calm. "I'm Nikki." My heart beat so hard, I was surprised I could hear my words. "I'm going to get you out."

"It's too late." she whispered. "I'm being sold at midnight."

Behind her, the Vulture shuffled to the next girl, but made the mistake of touching her.

"Watch that!" A guard moved quickly to run interference. "You know the rules!"

Using this distraction, I moved even closer to Jade. "I have to leave. But I *promise* I'll get you out before midnight."

She made a funny little noise, and tears welled in her eyes. Her shoulders started to shake, and one of the guards glanced at us.

I returned to my tray, smiling at him. "Shall I leave these cans here for you guys?"

"Sure," he said.

Turning, I walked quickly from the room.

#

On the gallery, I tried to ignore the man wearing a laurel wreathe and a loose toga pressed against the back of a woman leaning over the balustrade. Their carnal, vulgar thrusts kept time to Dagger's beat.

I rushed past them and fled downstairs. I didn't examine the dancers on the floor too closely, either. When I reached our tent, it felt like an oasis.

I slipped through Klaire's gold curtain. She was at her table touching up her makeup.

"I *found* her!" I forced myself to lower my voice. "She's upstairs, just like you thought."

"And is she chained?"

"Yes. And there are four other girls, two guards in robes, and that guy that looks like a vulture."

"The girls' preview was supposed to be over by nine," she said. "Our vulture friend must have special privileges."

Or special money.

I glanced at my watch. Almost eleven. Dagger's sexual frenzy would take a break soon. The evening's schedule had Klaire and I back to fortune telling for about forty-five minutes. But we planned to leave with Jade before that. And get the other girls out. If we could. At this point, everyone was so drunk or high, they probably wouldn't know if we were there or not.

"I think one of these hair things is loose," I said.

"Let me see it."

I sat in the sphinx chair, grabbing the opportunity to eat a power bar and guzzle some soda while she secured the loose extension and touched up my eyeliner.

"Tell Ajeet to be ready to move," she said.

I stepped through the gold curtain, reaching my chair just as Dagger's pounding beat crescendoed then ceased. Ajeet had left the lights dimmed, but one of the party animals stumbled into the tent anyway.

I glanced at his face, saw the hideous scar. Trembling, I sank to my chair. Why was he *here*?

Unsteady with drink, drugs, or maybe both, Currito pulled out the chair across my table with a jerk before slamming into it.

"Pretty gypsy lady." He leered at my low cut peasant blouse. "You must tell me my fortune."

Chapter 45

I threw a panicked glance at Ajeet, than turned back to Currito. I didn't know what to say. In my peripheral vision, I saw Ajeet stand and slip through the gold curtain.

Currito laughed and reached a hand to touch the long hair near my breast. I grabbed his wrist and stopped him. He seemed to find this amusing. His laugh became uncontrollable. Beads of sweat covered his forehead, and his jagged scar grew scarlet.

As I watched, his tightly woven, formal facade continued to unravel. I stopped breathing a few beats, watching a deeper personality emerge, something so ugly it made his scar seem a thing of beauty.

"I *like you*," he said, his laughter subsiding to a giggle as he snatched his hand from my grasp. "So bold." He squinted and leaned forward. "You are familiar to me. Do I know you?"

He didn't *recognize* me. I released my breath. Ajeet would warn Klaire, and for the moment, her disguise was working. I adopted the breathy, low soothsayer voice.

"Perhaps we met in a dream, but I don't know you. I have never read your palm. May I see it?"

He put his left hand, palm up, on the table.

"Ah," I said. "But this is not your dominant hand. May I see the other."

He giggled again. "Pretty palmist, I'm not impressed. A good guess. But most use their right hands."

I examined his damp, right palm. A scar sliced across it, severing his life line in half. His brother's mark? Probably better to ignore it.

"You are far from home, but you have family nearby."

He snorted. "Another easy guess. But you are wrong. I brought my home with me. Now give me something profound, pretty gypsy."

I was drawing blanks, rattled by Currito's presence, the words not coming like they had earlier. What had he meant about bringing his home with him? *Think.*

"But you *do* have a family member close by." I paused and touched his lifeline with a fingertip. "I sense a strained relationship."

"You disappoint me. What man does not endure a troubled family connection?"

His superior attitude irritated me. I let my gaze take in both scars. "But most don't have a tragic mark from family relations gone bad."

Currito stiffened, and I felt like kicking myself for saying too much. But he chose to laugh.

"Bravo, *bonita* lady. I have a horse who is like you. He, too, is very bold. And," he paused a moment, "I have a beautiful home on the sea. I want to take you there."

He leaned forward and stroked my hand with his. I pulled mine away but forced a smile. I'd wondered where Currito stayed. He'd never disclosed a location to me or Jim, always making the contact himself.

"You have a home in Miami?" I asked.

His chest expanded with pride. "Much better. I have a yacht."

Bingo! Currito's image blurred as Klaire's words played back in my head. Her vision of Jade on the water. *Surrounded by the sea.*

I realized my lips were parted and closed my mouth. I fought to produce a poker face. Currito traded more than cocaine. He had abducted Jade. A *slave* trader, Like Chakri. But high end. He loved the finer things. Pedigree and beauty meant a lot to him.

Suddenly his puffed up arrogance shifted to another direction. Whatever substance he was on, it seemed to rise and fall in waves of intensity. His eyes became greedy.

"I want you on my yacht. *La Sirena* is beautiful, like you. You will love her. She has her own helicopter. A swimming pool. She was built for me by Blohm and Vosshis!"

I had no idea who Blohm and whatsis were, but I didn't like the direction our conversation was heading.

"We should finish your reading."

"No. That is not important to me." He listed to one side of his chair, then giggled. "You could do a reading for my onboard guests! I am famous for my entertaining."

I didn't doubt it. "Let me see your palm again," I said, hoping to end his fortune and get him to leave.

"No!" He rose unsteadily from his chair, then half fell, half lunged across the table. He grabbed at my breast with one hand and caught hold of several hair extensions with the other. I jerked back, feeling a sharp pain as two hair pieces ripped free, probably taking strands of my hair with them. He stared at the long locks in his hand, then my head. I could see the realization hit him.

"Nikki? What are you doing here?"

"Uh, I . . ."

"What game do you mean to play?" Anger narrowed eyes. His darker self took over. "Perhaps you are a whore like the others?"

He put a knee on the table, then scrambled across. I stood up fast, knocking my chair over. Turning to run, I saw Klaire come through the gold curtain. She pointed something at Currito. He cried out and dropped off the table like a cockroach. Twitching violently, he lay on the floor. *Stun gun.* Klaire threw several objects into the crowded ballroom. My God, she'd brought smoke bombs.

"Nikki, this way!" She dashed back through the gold curtain. Smoke billowed at me from the ballroom. My eyes stung, my nostrils burned. I ran after her. Ajeet parted the fabric of the final white curtain, exposing an exit door in the ballroom wall. The three of us fled through it into a service hall. When the door slammed behind us, we paused, dragging in breaths of smoke free air.

I dug into my pockets, performing a mental inventory. Cherry bombs had to be lit. Knock out drops had to be administered. I pulled out the can of pepper spray and held it by my side.

"Ajeet," Klaire said, "I told you where Nikki found the girls. You know this place. Take us there. Now!"

We flew down the concrete service corridor paralleling the back wall. We turned right and continued running until Ajeet pushed through a fire door and we rushed up a staircase. We must be shadowing the route of the stone staircase. Slamming through another fire door, Ajeet led us to the same branch in the service hall where I'd decided to go right earlier.

I broke into a dead run, passing Ajeet, then the beverage kitchen, and flew up the steps. I yanked open the door to the room that held Jade. It was empty.

"No," I cried, turning to Ajeet and Klaire as they burst into the room. "They were here, chained to those bolts." I pointed at the metal rings. "I *promised* her. How could Currito's people have gotten her out so fast?"

"Now that I know who he is," Klaire said, "I can assure you he has people everywhere. They saw what was happening downstairs and got the girls out. But we have delayed the auction."

"I know where they're going," I said, and explained about *La Sirena*.

"Of course," she said. "It means 'the Mermaid.'" Then she passed a hand over her eyes as if she didn't like the picture my words painted.

"Klaire!" Ajeet hissed. "There's no time for this. We have to get out!"

We fled from the room, back into the corridor, retracing our steps to the first floor, running down a length of hall before easing into a large service kitchen filled with anxious caterers. The smell of smoke was strong.

"What is it?" a woman yelled at us. "A bomb?"

"I think so," I said. Might as well add to the general pandemonium.

"This way," Ajeet called.

The three of us burst through a door to a wide paved driveway filled with catering trucks. The back wall of the mansion rose above our heads and frightened workers flowed out the service door. Ajeet ran straight into the gardens, racing down steps and a stone path that lead to a wide lagoon. I could see the ocean in the distance, feel a damp breeze stir against my face.

When we reached the lagoon, two armed guards appeared out of nowhere and trained their weapons on us.

"*Bomb!*" I shouted.

Ajeet placed his hands on either side of his head as if terrified of a pending explosion. "Run for your life!"

The guards paused, exchanged questioning glances before they lowered their guns and ran toward the house. We kept going toward the ocean.

Chapter 46

After dropping Ajeet off, Klair sped us toward her home on Blue Water Way. I decided not to call Carla. She might confide in Rick and word could reach the wrong person. What *could* I do? Did immigration handle people smuggled out of the country, or only those coming in?

"Can't we call the Coast Guard?" I asked. "They wouldn't have to wait for the local police to get involved, would they?"

"I doubt it. Let me think."

Klaire stopped the Jag on the street two houses down from her bungalow, but left the car idling. Overhead, the streetlights cast a dim glow, and a sharp breeze swayed the palms, making the small branches of nearby tropical plants rise and fall as if a spirit moved among them.

"Someone is in my house!" she said. "I didn't think they'd be here this fast."

"I don't see anything. Who is it?"

"Bad people."

Currito? Though the Jag windows were closed, I felt a chill, as if the breeze had slipped inside and found me.

"You have your car keys?" she asked.

I pulled them from my tote and let the metal wink back at her in the dash lights.

She eased the Jag forward, pulling up next to my car near the end of the block. Fortunately, when I'd parked the Toyota hours earlier, I'd been unable to find a space in front of her house.

"We must separate, then flee!" she said, looking anxiously back toward her house. "Do not call me on my cell. I will get in touch with you."

"But –"

"Just get out and get in your car!"

I did, running from her car to mine, slamming into the driver's seat, cranking the engine. Klaire screeched the Jag forward, turning into a driveway. I followed in a squeal of rubber. The driveway was more like an alley and cut through to the next street over.

Moments later we were gone.

#

I circled around the Sand Castle parking lot, all my nerves on full radar. I had the windows down so I could listen. The breeze off the ocean had sharpened, making the palm fronds overhead rattle and drop debris onto the pavement. Did the coconuts up there ever drop on pedestrians' heads?

I needed a shot of bourbon, hair extension removal, and a double-lather shampoo. I'd had too many adrenalin rushes that evening and wanted to lie down. More than anything, I wanted to do something about Jade. Who could I call?

I parked the Toyota close to the exit, face out. Leaving the car, I headed for my room, avoiding the streetlights as much as possible.

A figure separated itself from the shadow of the motel's wall and hurried toward me. I froze, then heard a familiar voice.

"Nikki?"

"Stella?" Why was she whispering and wandering about after midnight?

"Don't go to your room," she said. "That schmuck with the tattoos has been hanging around your door for the last hour. I think he's lying in wait."

"His name's Gonzales." I was too tired for this. *Shit.*

"Whatever, he's a putz," Stella said.

"Exactly. Thank's for the warning, Stella. I gotta

disappear. Don't talk to him, he's dangerous. And for God's sake, don't tell him you saw me!"

"My lips is zipped. You can count on me. Listen, that nice guy Will came by earlier looking for you. Brought Lou and me a six pack."

Will! I could be so obtuse. That's who I would call.

"Yeah," I said. "He is a nice guy." *When he's not lying.*

"You be careful," Stella said.

I gave her a little salute and hurried back to my car. After pulling from the lot, I drove down several side streets, keeping an eye on my rearview. No cars in sight. I wasn't being followed. Stopping the Toyota, I eased it backward into a driveway, cut the lights, but left the engine running. Then I called Will.

He answered on the first ring. "Nikki, Where *are* you?"

"It's a long story."

"Tell me."

I did, and he listened without interruption until I finished.

"So," I said. "I guess you were right about watching Currito. I just wish you'd *told* me."

"We can worry about that later. Right now, you can't go back to your motel. And you need to ditch your phone."

"I can't ditch my phone –"

"You're not thinking, Nikki. They'll use it to track you."

"I'll just turn it off."

"That won't work, Nikki. You have a brand new phone. They make 'em so they track on or off."

I didn't respond. The world was too complicated

"Nikki, please make sure you're not being followed, check into a motel under a false name – you got cash?"

"Yeah, but –"

"Listen to me. Get to a safe place."

I felt like I things were slipping more and more out of my control. "Do you want to know where I go?"

"No," he said softly. "You don't trust me, remember?"

"That was low, Will."

I need to make calls to the right people," he continued as if he hadn't heard me. "If we're lucky, we can stop the *Sirena* before she takes Jade into international waters."

"But how will you find the yacht?"

"My contact in the DEA can alert the Coast Guard. You've done enough. Stay out of it!"

"Okay, okay," I said, feeling a deep exhaustion hit me. It was time to
drop the reins.

"You'd better get going," he said and disconnected.

I threw the phone onto the seat in frustration. Will got to me in more ways than one. I focused on the phone instead, giving it a hard look.

"You cheap little spy." I got out of the car, lay the phone on the pavement before the front tire, and drove over it. I could feel the back tire hit the thing, too. *Nikki takes charge.*

#

I didn't want to go to a motel. Instead, I did what I've always done when things are at their worst and I need to be comforted and have a safe place to sleep. I went to the barn.

Sleeping in stalls was nothing new to me and I'd learned from long experience that horses are careful not to step on you and will usually stand over you while you sleep. If they know you and like you, if they consider you part of the "herd," their instinct is to guard you.

An added benefit is no one ever expects to find you asleep under a horse.

It was almost 1:30 a.m. when I drove past the stable gate and into the relative safety of the backstretch. The stables were quiet, the hour too early for anyone to be around. I parked the car out of sight behind a dumpster and went right into the stall of my old friend Imposter and buried my face in his neck, drinking in his horsey smell.

"I'll be right back," I said. I removed the gypsy skirt and blouse, then went to the wash stall hoping the bottle of Mane-and-Tail shampoo I'd there seen earlier was still lying about. It was, and after a few curses and bobby pin gouges, I removed the extensions and threw them in the trash barrel with the gypsy clothes.

Turning on the water, I waited for a warm flow, then doused my head and slathered on shampoo. I scrubbed away the hair color and grease paint, being mindful to keep my cargo shorts dry. After a rinsing, I shook my head like a dog. Short hair has its advantages.

Rubbing my head with a towel and pulling on one of the extra tees I keep in the tack room, I returned to Imposter. He'd always been neat about pooping in one area of his stall, and I curled up in a clean corner on a mattress of fresh alfalfa, silently blessing Orlando for being a conscientious groom.

Imposter's warm breath tickled my head as his curious lips nuzzled my damp hair I put a hand up and patted his soft nose, before settling myself deeper into the hay.

#

Imposter's restless pacing and inquisitive whinny startled me awake. A low vibration shimmered through the barn. A truck engine. Imposter nudged me with his nose then moved to the stall gate, his ears and eyes forward, intent on whatever was out there.

I scrambled to my feet and peered outside. A two-horse trailer pulled by a Dodge pickup with a loud diesel engine idled outside. Parked right beside *our* shedrow. What the hell?

I dove away from the see-through wire gate as lights flicked on in the stall next door. Diablo's stall. Whoever it was had gone in there before I'd had a chance to see them. I moved to the side of the stall and peeked through a tiny gap in the boards.

A wizened man quietly threaded a chain through the rings in Diablo's halter, getting ready to slide the metal links over the horse's gum. The colt seemed to know him, and wasn't putting up a fight. An old groom from South America? Someone was helping him, but the view was so narrow I couldn't see who. I moved further along the slat, peeked again. If not for the wooden stall partition, I could have touched the Poseidon tattoo. Stifling a cry, I stepped back. *Gonzales.*

They were here to take Diablo to *La Sirena*! The horse was so valuable and dear to Currito, he couldn't bear to leave the colt behind. Diablo would lead me right to Jade, I *knew* it.

Chapter 47

Peering cautiously from the depths of Imposter's stall, I watched the men try to load Diablo. As soon as he realized their plan, Diablo went ballistic. How dare they try to separate him from his fillies and his buddy, Imposter? The groom got him as far as the trailer ramp, where Diablo refused to place a hoof on its rubber matting.

The groom stood by Diablo's head, coaxing, his Spanish words soft and gentle. Gonzales stood behind waving a whip at the horse's hindquarters. Diablo threw a vicious kick at Gonzales, but missed. *Rats.*

The two men appeared to be at odds, the groom wanting to handle the horse with kindness, Gonzales preferring to whip the horse into obedience. He proved this assessment by cracking the whip hard on the horse's flesh. Diablo responded with an angry scream, backing up so fast he dragged the groom off the trailer ramp. The colt continued his backward charge then shot a hind leg at Gonzales. The connection sounded like a home run hit. I had to restrain myself from cheering.

Gonzales doubled over, his hand clutching one thigh. The tone of his curses made me glad my Spanish wasn't so good. The man's leg held, apparently not broken. Furious, he limped to the cab of the truck and removed a nasty looking cattle prod. He spewed some words at the groom, his gestures indicating the man was to move the colt back to the edge of the ramp.

"*No es necessario!*" The groom's voice shook as he eyed the prod. But apparently he decided Gonzales was more lethal than Diablo and worked to coax the colt back to the trailer ramp.

I was on my hands and knees staring through Imposter's front legs as the nervous gelding watched the battle outside. Did Gonzales have the papers to get the horse off the track? If I'd had my phone, I would have called the security guard at the stable gate. But he'd probably been bribed, anyway. These people had too much money and power, and I had to stay out of sight. No one knew where I was and I needed to keep it that way.

The groom tried to quiet Diablo with soft words while rubbing his head. Gonzales hissed some words, and the groom again urged Diablo to step on the ramp. Gonzales leapt forward and snapped the horse with the electric prod. Diablo screamed and burst up the ramp. He dragged the groom who clung to the lead shank with him. The groom stumbled and fell forward into the trailer. Diablo trampled him as he exploded inside. Gonzales sprinted forward, yanked the ramp up, and fastened the security bars in place. He worked furiously to lock the upper Dutch doors, then ran to his Dodge pickup.

The trailer rocked wildly and I could hear the screams of the groom beneath Diablo's hooves. The other horses neighed frantically. I could hear one of my fillies whirling in her stall. Anxious whinnying sounded from neighboring barns.

Why didn't someone come? Probably because the fight with Diablo had only lasted moments. I glanced at my watch, almost three a.m., at least an hour before anyone showed up.

Gonzales didn't waste any time firing his engine and driving away. I didn't waste any time going after him.

#

As soon as the trailer rolled out of sight, I ran to my Toyota and followed. Damn Will for telling me to lose the phone! But if he was right and I called for help, Currito's people could intercept my call and know exactly where I was and what I was doing.

When Gonzales neared the stable gate, I feinted right as if going toward the track kitchen. This way, he wouldn't see me in his side-view mirror when he stopped for the guard. But he didn't stop. The security bar rose and the rig sailed through. Had he bribed the guard?

I pulled back onto the drive and slowed at the gate. Since my license hung from my rearview, the guard waved me through. If *I'd* had a trailer behind me, he would have forced me to stop, demanded papers, and checked them against my cargo.

Ahead of me, Gonzales' big Dodge rumbled out of Gulfstream and headed north on Route 1. At three in the morning, the usually heavy congestion was still locked away in parking lots and garages. It was easy to to let a few cars to slip between me and the trailer while I followed its red running lights from a safe distance.

We zipped along Route 1, drove through the Hollywood traffic circle, and continued north. Gonzales must be headed for one of the ports of Fort Lauderdale. Reaching the southern outskirts of the city, he ignored the expressway leading to Port Everglades. Apparently Currito's yacht wasn't so big it moored alongside the gigantic container ships and cargo vessels that used the major port. Then again, were we really headed for Currito's yacht? And what about the groom? I didn't like to think about him lying on the trailer floor.

A few minutes past the Port exit, Gonzales made a right on Seventeenth Street which led to the docks of Fort Lauderdale. After crossing the Intracoastal bridge, he exited onto Access Road. I followed, trying to concentrate on his truck and trailer instead of the extraordinary luxury crafts looming into view around me.

I gave up worrying about being seen. Even thought it was well before dawn, there was more traffic here – delivery trucks refurbishing supplies, and an eighteen wheeler loaded with diesel for the underground tanks that fueled water craft.

My generic blue Toyota shouldn't be that noticeable, and fortunately, the trailer blocked the view usually provided by the rear mirror.

Gonzales pulled into the wide gravel lot of the "Seaside Marina," where night lights revealed a concrete wharf built alongside the Intracoastal. Shaped like a T, the long section of the platform ran parallel to the parking area. A freighter towered above the far side and two large yachts snuggled against the lot side, the water lapping at their hulls.

When I saw "La Sirena" painted on the bow of the closest yacht, I rolled to a stop. Dock lamps and the craft's running lights revealed a sleek, modern outline. The yacht was so long! Had to be at least a sixteenth of a mile. Maybe more like 350 feet. Her immense size dwarfed the helicopter perched on the top of her three decks.

Currito's wealth staggered me. Drug money. Human flesh money. Who needed so much money?

I cut my lights and slid the Toyota's transmission into reverse, backing quietly out of the lot, finding a spot behind a parked delivery truck on Access Road. A stiff salt breeze stung my cheeks when I left the Toyota and raced toward the yacht.

Chapter 48

Crouching against the first parked car I reached, I watched Gonzales shut down his engine and climb from the cab of the Dodge. The trailer's narrow human door opened, and the groom crawled into the shadow where the rig blocked the streetlight. I couldn't see how badly he was hurt. At least he was moving.

Two live oaks grew on a stretch of grass separating the parking area from the dock. Their leaves cast comforting, dark shadows over the picnic tables scattered beneath. Gonzales reached the groom, leaving his back to me as he bent over the injured man.

I made a beeline for the trees and crawled under the picnic table closest to *La Sirena*, maybe fifteen yards away. The odor of varnish, garbage and dead fish rode the night air.

Midway down the side of *La Sirena*, a gangplank stretched from the lower deck to the dock. Currito emerged from and opening and walked onto the plank. His nephew Victor appeared behind him. With his long, dark hair pulled into a pony tail, Victor reminded me of someone else. Maybe Gonzales?

Currito called to Gonzales, then motioned toward the back of his yacht, where a wider ramp with high sides joined the stern to the concrete platform. When Gonzales nodded, the groom struggled to his feet and went back inside the trailer. I was glad the guy could still walk. I wished Gonzales couldn't.

Gonzales opened the trailer's rear and dropped the ramp. With a crash of hooves, Diablo backed off the trailer. For a moment he stood like a statue, then emitted a whinny more like a challenging scream, an unanswered call to his own kind. I slipped out from under the table and flattened my body against the trunk of an oak.

I heard tires crunching on gravel and peered around the trunk of the tree. A car rolled past the horse ramp, heading toward Currito. It stopped beneath the pier's dim lights and the engine cut off. The driver door opened and Rick climbed out, pausing a moment.

A weird falling sensation rocked through me as the overhead lamp silhouetted his profile, triggering a memory and terrible recognition. I'd seen his profile before – at the same distance, at the same time of night. The cop who'd made jokes at the crime scene where those men killed the girl. He had been at the murder scene.

Everything I knew shifted. Rick was the leak! I stared at Victor and his pony tail. I'd bet my life he'd been in the SUV on Hallendale Beach Boulevard. And I'd bet he was the one who'd pulled the trigger.

The loud ringing of hooves made me glance toward the stern. Diablo was loading agreeably. Must he cooperate *now*? Men were closed the horse ramp, and Gonzales walked toward Currito who was still on the gangplank. Victor had disappeared.

Rick hurried around the hood of his car, opened the passenger door and dragged someone out. *Oh God, not Carla.* Dark streaks and lumps on her face. Her clothing torn. The son of a bitch had beaten her.

As Rick jerked her toward the gangplank, I ran closer and sank into the long shadow of a palm.

"You bastard," I heard her mumble, through swollen lips. "You lied to me." Tears streamed down her face.

"Yeah, I guess I did." He grinned. "But you had a good ride, right?"

I was close enough I could see his betrayal in her eyes, could almost smell his evil. How had he hidden it so well?

"Is Jade even here?" Carla asked.

"Oh yeah, she's here."

"How could you *sell* her? Her voice rose, like she'd reached a new breaking point.   "Shut up, Carla. Just shut up!" Rick grabbed her arm and yanked her roughly onto the gangplank.

"You *traitor!*" She jerked away from his grip, then slapped his face.

He came right back with a fist to her jaw. With a groan, she collapsed onto the walkway.

He stood over her. "I told you to stay out of it. But you had to know everything, didn't you? But you still don't get it. You think I'd work *my* life away for a cop's salary and a fucking pension? I don't care about these stupid girls. And if people want to use cocaine, let 'em."

I reached for the pocket with the can of pepper spray.

"Rick, don't do this," she cried, suddenly placating and needy. "I *love* you!"

She rose from the gangplank, leaned into him, and jerked his gun from his shoulder holster. He tried to knock the gun away. Carla shot him in the chest.

"You piece of shit!" she said. Then she shot him again.

I watched blood spurt down his chest. Mesmerized, Carla stared as he slumped to the ramp. Gonzales was heading toward her. I started to shout a warning.

A hand clamped over my mouth, an arm locked around my neck. *Victor.* I whipped out the spray, twisted, and shot him in the face. He screamed, letting me go as his fingers clawed his eyes.

On the ramp, Rick's eyes stared, empty and unseeing. I screamed Carla's name, racing toward her. Gonzales ran past Currito, still heading for Carla. He held a gun. With a silencer.

"No!" I screamed. *This couldn't be happening again.*

Gonzales shot Carla. She sagged onto the ramp. Gonzales walked calmly toward her and shot her in the head. Making sure.

Screaming, I rushed him. Something zinged past my head. *Jesus Christ*

Currito yelled, "Stop! She'll bring money."

An angry roar behind me. Someone smashed into me, slamming me down. *Victor.* Then Gonzales and Currito were on me, knocking my pepper spray onto the plank. A foot kicked it over the side. Plastic cuffs circled my wrists, then my ankles. Currito stuffed a piece of cloth in my mouth.

They trussed me up like a pig. Currito grasping me beneath my shoulders and Gonzales holding my legs. As they carried me on board, the yacht's diesel engines roared to life. I felt its vibration through their hands.

From one eye, I could see crew members dragging the two bodies on board, pulling in the gangplank. Victor following us, his reddened eyes streaming. The sharp metallic odor of blood reached my nostrils. Then I was inside the ship.

Outside, the crewmen called in loud, urgent tones, readying *La Sirena* for the sea.

Chapter 49

They carried me into a lounge almost as wide across as the ship. By twisting my head, I cloud see the outline of the neighboring freighter through the far glass wall. It's twinkling lights receded as *La Sirena* steamed forward, bring a familiar sinking sensation – like the night I'd looked up and down Hallandale Boulevard for help and no one was there.

"It will be awkward carrying her down the stairs." Currito's voice. "Put her down. Gently. I don't want her bruised."

Acid burned my stomach. Why had I believed innate goodness existed in humans?

They placed me on the floor. Gonzales removed the plastic cuffs from my ankles and pulled me to my feet.

"Stand up, bitch."

I could see the whole room now and stared in horror at Carla's body dumped on the floor next to Rick's. Now was not the time to cry. If I lived through this, I would find a way to recognize evil before it engulfed me – or anyone that I loved.

Gonzales half jerked, half led me down a spiral metal staircase to the deck below. He paused at the base of the stairs.

At the rear of the ship, the passage opened onto the rear deck. The injured groom hobbled toward us, staring at me with concern, but not surprise. He may have been kind to Diablo, but he worked for Currito, and was no friend of mine. I turned my head from him. Currito's harsh voice broke the silence.

"Pedro, get back to your work! This is not your business."

"Si," the wizened groom said quickly, before turning and heading for the deck. Gonzales steered me left into a long passage. Dim service lights glowed overhead, and closed doors lined the corridor. Cabins?

Gonzales hustled me froward quickly. I half jogged to keep from falling. He reached a door, turned the handle, and pushed me inside so hard I fell on the floor. The door closed and locked behind me.

As I lifted my head, my fingers pushed against a thick pile of carpet. A gleaming base of polished wood lay a few feet from me. A bed. Lush rose-and-green fabric encased the mattress like a slipcover. Drawers in the base. A matching chest to the side.

I struggled into a sitting position and realized I had company. Jade gazed at me from where she lay on the bed, propped on one elbow. She wore a pink tee shirt and matching boxer shorts.

The cabin, the girl – it all looked so pretty and normal. I shook my head, sat up straighter.

Jade frowned. "You're kind of late."

Great, a smart ass. But bold. *Like Carla.*

I breathed in. "Things . . . fell apart before. I'm sorry. We tried to get you away from these people."

"But who *are* you."

"My name is Nikki. Your mother, Carla, was my friend."

Jade's eyes narrowed. "*Was*? What happened to her?" Her gaze fell. As if suddenly interested in the rose-and-green fabric, she traced the pattern with one finger. When she looked up fear had replaced the boldness. "I heard two gunshots . . ."

I let my breath out. "I'm sorry, Jade, she was trying to save you. Your mother . . . she didn't make it.

"Which mother? My *real* mother, or this Carla person?"

God, I hadn't even thought about the mother who'd raised Jade. Had she been killed in front of Jade? I started to speak.

"No! I don't want to talk about them." Stony faced, she

turned away from me, her finger tracing the pattern again. A sheet of luminous hair fell forward and hid her face.

"Okay," I said, giving her time.

I stood, walked to the door and tested the handle. Locked. I turned back, moving past a glass-topped table to the cabin window where I pulled the curtain aside. Below, the water streamed smoothly past. The big diesel engines vibrated gently beneath my feet, powering *La Sirena* past million dollar homes, swimming pools, and private docks lining the Intracoastal. I leaned forward, trying to see where we were headed. Moored cruise ships and steamers came into view, but *La Sirena* swung left. As we turned, I could see the harbor entrance and the open sea.

Think Nikki. I slipped my hand into one pocket. Morons! They had left me with the firecrackers and knockout drops. My pepper spray was probably floating somewhere in the harbor, but the small, sharp dagger pricked my finger at the bottom of the second pocket.

"Why are you smiling," Jade asked sharply.

"We might have a weapon," I said, holding up the knockout drops.

"Whatever." She said it like I planned to shoot a rhinoceros with a squirt gun.

"Who comes in here?" I asked.

"Currito, comes sometimes," she waved a hand at the glass-topped table and chairs between the bed and the cabin window. He likes to bring sandwiches in here and drink wine. He just stares at me."

I glanced at the table. A pitcher of water, glasses and an opened bottle of wine lined a large tray on the table.

"But," Jade continued, "mostly Victor comes in. I hate him. The way he looks at me . . ." She started shaking.

I didn't want her spiraling into the horror of her situation. "That ass," I said. "I shot his face with pepper spray a few minutes ago."

She brightened. "You did? Cool!"

Definitely Carla's daughter.

"Carla shot one of the bad guys," I said, unable to control a desire to make Jade like her mother. "Carla was totally cool."

"If you say so." But her eyes had gone empty. Thirteen years of neglect couldn't be fixed with two bullets.

A metallic, scraping sound. Someone inserting a key in the lock. We stared at the door. The handle turned and Currito and Victor stepped inside.

Currito smiled at us then closed the door. The skin around his eyes was darker than usual. Must be stressed out. *What a shame.*

"Nikki," he said, "must you always disappoint me? You get away from me only to let yourself be caught again?"

I didn't answer him. The small vial of knockout drops burned inside my curled fingers.

"Do not think you will be rescued," Currito said. "Your dear friend Rick told no one. He made certain news of our departure would not leak. Your little friend Mr. Marshall? Rick intercepted his messages to the DEA."

"You see, Victor? An example of the importance of friends in the *right* places."

Victor nodded, then glanced at me. "She's a whore. I would like to kill her."

"No, no, Victor. She's young and pretty. You know the rule with the women. Take the money. Let someone else have the flesh.

I turned away, unable to look at the man. "I need to sit down," I said, moving unsteadily to the table before sinking into a chair.

"May I?" I asked, stretching across the table to grasp the handle of the water pitcher.

"Of course," Currito said. He smiled.

I poured water into a glass and drank most of it. "Jade?"

"No thanks," she said, wrapping her arms tightly

around her knees. She looked so small on the big bed.

"Pour me some wine, bitch." Victor said. His eyes were still badly swollen and red, yet he turned to look at Jade's long smooth legs on the bed.

"Sure," I said. I stood and pulled the whole tray closer and managed to knock two wine glasses over. One rolled toward me and I grabbed for it, only succeeding in knocking it to the carpet.

"Who would buy this stupid woman?" Victor said, contempt in his voice. "She is a cow."

"Do your *eyes* hurt, Victor?" I asked, then ducked my head and shoulders under the table to retrieve the wine glass. As I felt around for it, I worked the stopper off the vial with my thumb. I tipped a few drops from the vial into the glass, letting the vial drop to the floor. I straightened quickly, poured wine into the glass, and held it out to Victor.
"To your health." I'd made him *so* mad! I controlled an insane desire to laugh.

"We will sell you," he said. "And when the buyer is finished with you, I will find you."
He smiled. "Then you will become a street whore."

Jade's face drained to white. I stopped breathing. Victor grabbed the glass from me and downed the contents in one greedy swig. I exhaled.

Chapter 50

Klaire's potion worked immediately. Victor's eyes widened, he made a choking noise, then sagged forward onto the glass table, knocking the wine bottle over. It rolled across the table, slopping red wine that spread and dripped onto the carpet below.

"Victor!" Currito cried, rushing forward, grabbing his nephew's shoulders.

I hardened my heart as I slid my fingers around the dagger. *God help me.*

I lunged across the table and drove the knife up into Currito's good eye. He shrieked horribly, screaming as he pulled the knife out. I snatched up the wine bottle and hit his head as hard as I could. When he dropped the knife, I snatched it up. His blood smeared onto my fingers. I pushed back from the table, jumped from the chair, and grabbed Jade's arm.

"We're getting off this ship!"

She stared at me, her confused gaze shifting to the two men slumped over the table. She seemed numb. I jerked her arm.

"We have to *go!*"

"But we're locked in."

"Maybe not," I said.

At last she moved, scrambling off the bed, following me to the door. The handle turned. I pulled the door open. Then we were in the passage outside. I pushed the lock button and yanked the door closed behind us. I looked right and left.

Where was Gonzales? Most likely closer to the bow. Maybe up top with the captain. But we heard voices toward the rear and fled down the hall in the opposite direction, stopping at the spiral stair case. From the lower floor, the sound of the engine vibrated upward. We peered down. Two men in a short sleeved shirts with epaulets walked in the passage below. Crewmen.

Looking up the stair shaft, I got an impression of quiet emptiness. We scooted up, finding ourselves in the lounge I'd been dragged through before. No one there. Not even the bodies of Carla and Rick. What had they done with them. I shuddered and forced myself to look around.

Soft recessed lighting glowed overhead. Couches upholstered in silver and white leather. A black marble bar I hadn't seen before across the room. I motioned Jade to follow, and ran to the bar. Opening its narrow side door, we slipped inside, and dropped to the floor.

"What are we doing?" Jade asked.

"Hiding. Then I'm going to find us a lifeboat."

"Your not leaving me in here," she said. "You did that before. Please, don't do it again."

"All right," I said, easing up for a look over the bar counter. Nothing. I strained my ears for voices or sounds. Quiet. On the back wall a long couch faced a coffee table and a huge flat-screen for videos and satellite TV. I didn't see a phone. But I did see a silver lighter lying next to an ashtray.

Windows filled the wall across the room. I could see the railing outside, lit by the lights on the yacht.

"Come on," I said.

We crept from the bar. I made a "wait here" motion and jogged to the coffee table, where I slid the silver lighter into my pocket. I gestured at the sliding door in the wall of glass windows, so close to where Carla and Rick had been lying on the floor. A long damp spot marked the carpet, and the chemical smell of rug cleaner hung in the air. I didn't look too closely.

I slid the glass door open and eased my head out. I jerked back. Too late. *Gonzales.* He shouted and ran at me.

I flicked the silver lighter, grabbed a cherry bomb from

my pocket, and lit the short fuse.

"Run!" I shouted to Jade.

I tossed the bomb into the doorway. We tore across the lounge and plunged down the spiral staircase. I heard loud popping noises and a shriek from Gonzales above us. We kept going. At the bottom, I lit a second firecracker and threw it down the passage toward the front of *La Sirena*. We ran in the opposite direction, Gonzales's feet pounding down the stairs. I opened a cabin door, and we slipped inside. I left the door open a crack and watched the hall. Bang! The little bomb exploded and Gonzales raced in that direction, probably thinking he was hot on our trail.

We bailed out of the cabin through the acrid smoke filling the passageway. We ran toward the back of the yacht, passing the room we'd escaped from earlier – still closed up, locked, and silent.

We paused when we reached the wide opening to the rear deck. The crew probably used it to bring in supplies. A pleasant odor reached me from an open door. The galley. I was so hungry. I could swear I smelled bread baking.

I suspected the huge dumbwaiter outside the galley serviced the ship with goodies from the yacht's kitchen. I imagined a dozen cocktails with little umbrellas and sandwiches rising from the galley to the sun deck.

Time to get with it. How long did I think it would be before Gonzales sent some crewmen after us? Before he saw what I'd done to Currito and Victor?

I shifted my attention to what lay beyond the opening.

"Let's see what's out there," I said.

Chapter 51

Slowly, we stepped onto the rear deck of *La Sirena*. The area stretched before us, appearing deserted. Where did they keep the life boats? I didn't see any. In unspoken agreement, we moved to the side railing and stared out. We were in the open sea, plowing straight out, slicing through those twelve miles to international waters.

The dim outline of a steamer moved silently away from us at right angles. Screaming for help across a dark ocean didn't seem an option. Beyond *La Sirena's* wake, a web of night lights shimmered and winked from an increasingly shrinking coastline.

A loud splash from below. We peered over the rail. Jade's breath sucked in. I followed her gaze. Pale skin and hair floating on the surface. My horror quickly dissolved. Not a body, only a fish, maybe a porpoise or dolphin. He must have flashed his white underside. What looked like hair had to be seaweed. With a loud splash, a glistening tail surfaced. Whatever it was, it dove deep into the sea.

I turned from the railing. Did I smell horse? Jade followed me toward a large dark area in the center of the deck. As we drew closer, the image solidified. A swimming pool. A temporary railing enclosed it. No reflection from water. A dry material must fill the bottom. A cleated, aluminum ramp lay on the deck behind the pool.

"There's something in there." Jade's voice quivered.

I stared into the dark pit. Diablo's eyes gleamed back through the rails. He lifted his head into the ambient light. His ears pricked forward, his nostrils working to place my scent. He whinnied.

I called softly, "Good boy."

He shook his head up and down and nickered.

"¡Hala! He *know* you," a male voice said.

Whipping my head toward the sound, I saw the injured groom, Pedro, sitting on one of the chaise lounges by the pool. His expression wasn't threatening, more curious. Still, he worked for Currito.

"How you get away?" he asked.

"We haven't yet," I said.

"*Estos hombres* son muy malas!"

I didn't need to be told the men were very bad. "We need a lifeboat. Will you help us, Pedro?"

He stared at me a moment. "Si. I will help you."

Shouting erupted overhead. Gonzales at the railing of the deck above. He pointed at Jade and me. Two men were with him. *Shit.*

"Pedro," I whispered. "Can you get Diablo out of there?"

At first, he looked at me like I was crazy. Then understanding, he nodded. "What you do," he said, "is better than to stay with these men."

"Are there life jackets?" I asked.

He pointed to a supply cabinet near the rear entrance.

"Jade, grab two life jackets out of there!"

"But what are we *doing*?"

"Just get the fucking vests!"

She ran for them, and when I turned back, Pedro had already opened part of Diablo's railing. He grabbed the aluminum ramp and slid one end into the pool.

Diablo stomped one hoof onto the ramp and snorted. He shook his head up and down, eyeing the cleats with alarm. He tested it, placing another hoof on the board.

With soft words, Pedro encouraged the horse to come up. The groom turned to me.

"The thing you need," he said, pointing "*está allí.*"

I ran to the temporary supply cabinet by the pool and ripped the door open. I pulled out two lead shanks, grabbed a tiny exercise saddle, and the neck strap of a martingale. I started to turn, then plucked a coiled lunge line off a hook.

Diablo snorted and blew, as his hooves crashed up the metal ramp. I ran back to him just in time to grab his halter and snap the leads to the rings on either side of his nose.

Pedro took the saddle from me, threw it onto the colt's back, then pulled the martingale strap over Diablo's head. It settled around the colt's neck. God, or Diablo, or somebody liked us, because the colt stood there like a rock.

Pedro got the girth fastened. Jade handed me a life jacket, hers was already on. I set mine down and snapped the clip on the end of the lunge line to a ring on Jade's life vest.

"Keep the line coiled up and hold it tight," I said.

"What the hell are we *doing*?"

"You don't want to stay here, do you?"

"No!"

"Then jump!"

She froze. No time for that. I was older, fitter, and probably twice as strong as Jade. I grabbed her, pushed her to the railing, and threw her overboard.

When I turned back, Pedro's eyes were as big and round as Diablo's hooves. "*Madre de dios!*"

But he gave me a leg up to the saddle. I picked up the lead lines, then hooked two fingers in the neck strap. I turned Diablo's head toward the railing.

"*Buena suerte,*" Pedro whispered, then disappeared down the ramp into the depths of the pool.

Crap. I'd left my life jacket on the deck. A bullet whined past my head. Men ran toward me.

"Come on, Diablo, move it!"

He snorted, eying the rail with doubt. I locked my fingers into his thick mane and the martingale strap. He whirled toward the men running at us. He must have picked up Gonzales's scent. With a half rear, he bolted toward them with me hanging on for dear life.

Gonzales's two men shrieked as Diablo bore down on

them. They scattered like rats, diving to either side. Standing steady, Gonzales aimed his gun at Diablo. But he underestimated Diablo's rocket speed. The horse knocked Gonzales down as he pulled the trigger. The shot tore past my head, the gun skittered across the deck.

I clung to the strap, my knees in a death grip on the colt's shoulders. How far behind the yacht had Jade drifted? On the ground, Gonzales crawled for his gun.

I turned Diablo toward the rail. "Yah! I yelled, slapping his neck with a lead line.

He started forward then balked, his metal hooves striking sparks on the deck as he propped and stopped.

"Come on you son of a bitch!" I screamed, and slapped his shoulder as hard as I could with the palm of my hand.

He snaked his head back and forth angrily. I could *hear* his thoughts.

You want me to jump? Watch this.

He pinned his hears, then charged the rail, gaining speed, gathering himself. He sailed into the air, and everything shifted to slow motion. The rail passed lazily beneath us, the sea foamed far below. Plenty of time to lean back in the saddle, slide my legs forward, and brace my feet against the stirrups for the inevitable downward plunge. We continued floating straight out, I saw Jade bobbing in the water below, and then we began our descent.

The water rushed toward us, I took a deep breath, and we plunged into the sea.

Chapter 52

Diablo dove down, descending deeper and deeper. The ambient light from the surface receded to black and still we went down. A strong current had us in its hold.

Beneath me, Diablo jerked, raising his forelegs, dropping his hindquarters. I lost my grasp and floated away from him as he began his ascent to the surface.

The water closed in around me, ripping me away. I couldn't see Diablo, no longer knew which way was up. No air. I had to breath. Couldn't I take one breath?

I saw tangled, wet hair. A sudden, familiar face. The wistful eyes of the mermaid from the sea horse box. Was I *dead*?

Something bright and glistening pushed against me. It drove me rapidly, faster and faster. I broke the surface, gasping for air. Choking. *What* had happened?

I saw Diablo close by. Paddling easily, he watched me swim to him and let me slide onto his back. I grabbed the strap. I choked up salt water, coughing and gasping as I drank in the air. Why was I alive? Where was Jade?

Something small bobbed in the distance. Beyond it, I saw a glow. The sunrise, or the shoreline? Reaching into the water, I found Diablo's lead lines and turned his head toward the floating object.

"Jade!"

I heard her faint, strangled cry and urged Diablo toward her. His strong hindquarters drove like pistons, churning us forward. It was like riding a horse on a merry-go-round. He surged up and down, his hair sleek as a seal. I could never have stayed on without the saddle and the strap. Not with the whitecaps that washed over us every few moments.

Diablo swam closer to Jade, and something brushed against my leg. A nylon line. Jade's line! I grabbed it.

"I got you, Jade! I got you!"

She moaned, and I looped the end of the line around Diablo's neck strap and tied it in a knot.

Where was the yacht? I searched the endless horizon on four sides. I spotted *La Sirena* in the distance behind us. She rolled through the swells toward a now recognizable glow of the coming dawn. I turned my head to the glimmer on the opposite horizon. Had to be the lights from the shoreline! Diablo could probably smell the land.

He power stroked past Jade and the line tightened as we towed her behind us. She was fighting to keep her head above the swells, but making a pretty good job of it. I was afraid to pull her to the horse. She could be struck by Diablo's legs. I could fall off – without a life jacket. I decided to leave well enough alone.

The sea fought us with swells and white caps, some washing over Diablo's head. He continually snorted and blew to clean his nostrils, and I found a sort of rhythm, grabbing a breath when I could, closing my eyes repeatedly so I wouldn't be blinded by the salt water.

Diablo, all heart, swam determinedly toward shore, towing Jade in his wake. Riding my sea horse, I watched the lights of the shoreline grow brighter. Soon, I could make out the shapes of buildings and I knew where I was. I spotted a familiar water tower rising above the sand.

Spotlights and the steadily rising sun behind us illuminated the bulbous form and the painted words, "Welcome to Hallandale Beach."

Chapter 53

I sat on a hay bale with Will outside Diablo's stall. Leaning against the shedrow wall with my eyes half closed, I listened to the comforting sound of his quiet voice.

"So," he said, "the whole lot of them are going to the state pen. For a really long time."

"It won't bring Carla back," I said. The satisfaction of knowing Currito, Victor, and Gonzales had been rounded up by the Coast Guard didn't do much agains the horror of Carla's death.

"I guess the funeral was pretty tough," Will said.

"Very." I said. "I still can't believe Carla and Rick's bodies had washed ashore *together*."

The family had flown Carla's body to Baltimore and I'd attended her funeral with Jade. I had strong feelings for the girl. Probably identifying with her sense of abandonment, with how much she looked and even acted like Carla.

"An adopted aunt in Boca has agreed to take Jade in," I said. I planned plan to spend time with Jade. No matter what.

Will placed a hand lightly on my arm. "So, are we okay?"

"Yes. Just don't say something dumb like, 'a man's gotta do what a man's gotta do.'"

"Wouldn't think of it." He grinned. "So what are you doing tonight?"

"You're getting a little ahead of me," I said. "I've got something I have to do this afternoon."

He held his palms out. "Okay."

"I'd like it if you came with me."

#

The cemetery wasn't far from Hollywood beach. The two of us stood over a small memorial stone marking the spot where the girl's ashes had been buried.

"Her name was Dana," I said. "She had a family. She was abducted, like Jade. They held the girls together. Then took Dana away. That night, she died on the street.

Will put an arm around my shoulders. "I'm so sorry."

"I'm okay," I said. "At least I finally know her name." I knelt on the soil, took a garden trowel from my tote bag, and dug a hole about eight inches deep. I pulled the sea horse box from my bag and removed the little mermaid carving. I put her in the ground next to Dana.

Then I took Will's hand, and without speaking, we left the cemetery. It was time to get back to the horses.

Acknowledgements

A huge thanks to the individuals who took their time to answer endless questions regarding law enforcement procedure: Detective Travis Mandell, Media Relations Coordinator, Fort Lauderdale Police Department, Anthony Maniglia, Community Service Aide, Hallandale Beach Police Department, J. Todd Scott, Special Agent DEA

96952649R00154

Made in the USA
Columbia, SC
09 June 2018